Heir
PRESUMPTIVE
HENRY WADE

Heir

PRESUMPTIVE

HENRY WADE

PERENNIAL LIBRARY
Harper & Row, Publishers
New York, Cambridge, Philadelphia, San Francisco
London, Mexico City, São Paulo, Singapore, Sydney

A hardcover edition of this book was originally published in England in 1935 by Constable & Co Limited and in the United States in 1953 by Macmillan Publishing Co., Inc., and is fully protected by copyright under the terms of the International Copyright Union. It is reprinted by arrangement with The Estate of the Late Henry Aubrey-Fletcher.

First PERENNIAL LIBRARY edition published 1984.

Library of Congress Cataloging in Publication Data

Wade, Henry, 1887-1969.
  Heir presumptive.

  I. Title.
PR6001.U3H4 1984   823′.912   83-48965
ISBN 0-06-080708-3 (pbk.)

84 85 86 87 88 10 9 8 7 6 5 4 3 2 1

CONTENTS

CONTENTS

Heir
PRESUMPTIVE

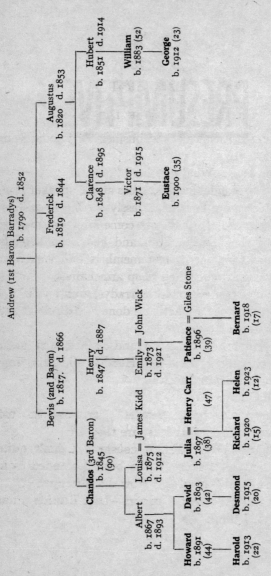

Andrew (1st Baron Barradys)
b. 1790 d. 1852

Frederick
b. 1819 d. 1844

Augustus
b. 1820 d. 1853

Clarence
b. 1848 d. 1895

Hubert
b. 1851 d. 1914

Victor
b. 1871 d. 1915

William
b. 1883 (52)

Eustace
b. 1900 (35)

George
b. 1912 (23)

Bevis (2nd Baron)
b. 1817. d. 1866

Henry
b. 1847 d. 1887

Chandos (3rd Baron)
b. 1845
(90)

Louisa = James Kidd
b. 1875
d. 1912

Emily = John Wick
b. 1873
d. 1921

Albert
b. 1867
d. 1893

Julia = Henry Carr
b. 1897
(38)   (47)

Patience = Giles Stone
b. 1896
(39)

Howard
b. 1891
(44)

David
b. 1893
(42)

Richard
b. 1920
(15)

Helen
b. 1923
(12)

Bernard
b. 1918
(17)

Harold
b. 1913
(22)

Desmond
b. 1915
(20)

Members of the family alive in 1935 are shown in **thick type,** their age at that time being given in brackets.

THE HENDEL FAMILY

CHAPTER I

" HULLO, Eustace ; bad business this about your cousins."

" Cousins ?   What cousins ? "

Eustace Hendel looked across at the speaker from the table where he was listlessly sorting over illustrated papers. He had just come into the smoking room of the Jermyn Club and had been vaguely conscious that one or two members had looked at him curiously from their deep armchairs.

" You're related to old Barradys, aren't you ? "

" Yes. Why ? What's he done ? You don't say he's passed out at last ? "

" No, not he, but his grandson has, and great grandson, too. Howard Hendel and his son. Drowned down in Cornwall."

" Good Lord ! "

" Sorry about it, Hendel ", grunted an old member. " Near relatives, are they ? "

" Oh, no, pretty distant cousins ; I don't quite know how we stand. We're both descended from the first Lord Barradys. How did it happen ? "

" It's in the evening papers—Late Edition ; not the 6.30, I think."

Eustace Hendel picked up a couple of evening papers and retired to a corner where he could read them without interruption, though his fellow-members did not usually take so much notice of him even as they had tonight. He found what he was looking for on the front page of the *Evening Planet*.

SHOCKING BATHING FATALITY

FATHER AND SON DROWNED

" A tragic accident occurred at Coombe Cove on the south coast of Cornwall at an early hour this morning, when Mr. Howard Hendel, grandson and heir of Lord Barradys, and his only son Harold were drowned while bathing before breakfast. Details of the accident have not been received but it is understood that Mr. Howard Hendel's body has been recovered, but not that of his son. An inquest will be held tomorrow and it is believed that the funeral will be at Coombe on Thursday or Friday.

" Mr. Howard Hendel was managing director of the great north-country engineering firm of Hendel Brothers, of which Lord Barradys is chairman. Lord Barradys, who was ninety this year, is the third baron, being the grandson of Andrew Hendel, the founder of the firm, who was raised to the peerage by Queen Victoria in 1852, the year of his death. Lord Barradys's only son,

the Honble. Albert Hendel, died in 1893 and the
late Mr. Howard Hendel then became heir to the
barony. The new heir is Captain David Hendel,
who served in the Coldstream Guards from 1913
to 1921, and who now lives at Clarge Hall, Market
Harborough. He married in 1914, Beryl, only
daughter of Sir John Fastings, of Coote, Denbigh-
shire, and has one son, Desmond, who was born in
1915."

Eustace Hendel put down the paper and started
thinking. He was not conscious of any great
feeling of grief. He had seen very little of his cousin
Howard and could only remember his boy as a brat
in a sailor suit—he must be nearly grown up now,
though. He had always regarded that branch of
the family—the elder sons' branch—as prigs, and
he was aware that they regarded him as something
equally unpleasant in the other direction. Still, it
was a bit of a shock, and he felt genuinely sorry for
Blanche, Howard Hendel's wife ; she was a fine-
looking woman and had always been decent to him—
the only one of ' that branch ' who had.

The Hendels had always followed a strict family
tradition in their treatment of elder and younger
sons. Old Andrew Hendel, who, from a humble
beginning as a fitter's mate, had founded the great
Hendel business and with it the family fortunes,
had been proud of his title and had laid down a

principle that the barony was to be maintained and
developed in a proper degree of grandeur, but as a
man—and a working man at that—he had firmly
believed in boys having to make their own way in
the world ; all the money, therefore, had gone with
the title, generation after generation, while the
younger sons were given a good education and a
modest nest egg, and told to make their own way
in the world.

* In this way, of old Andrew's sons, Bevis, the
elder, had succeeded to the title and a modest fortune ; Frederick had been killed in a pit explosion
at the age of twenty-five, as a mining engineer,
learning one stage of one branch of the family
business ; Augustus, Eustace's great-grandfather,
had been a doctor and had built up a modestly
successful practice in Newcastle-on-Tyne. In Bevis's,
the ' Baron's branch ', title and money had gone to
Chandos, the present Lord Barradys, while Henry,
the younger, had become a solicitor only slightly
above the ' pettifogging ' grade. Of Augustus's two
sons, to whom in any case there was no title and only
very modest moneys to descend, Clarence, the elder,
had burnt his small patrimony and left nothing to
his son, Victor, who had left but little more to
Eustace ; Hubert, the younger, had done rather
better and his son William was now a fairly prosperous wine-merchant in London.

* See genealogical table, facing p. 1.

Eustace, therefore, had started life with little more than his good looks and by no means negligible brains ; he had elected to follow in the footsteps of great-grandfather Augustus, and his father's legacy— Victor had been killed at Suvla in 1915—had just sufficed to carry him through his medical training and buy him a small share in a country-town practice. Here his brains and ability would probably have kept him in reasonable comfort and an obscurely safe existence, but his other inheritance—his good looks—had intervened ; by good luck, or ill, he had attracted the attention of a rich widow, who had made a pet of him, showed unmistakable signs of adopting him as a husband, and then conveniently died, leaving him the staggering sum of twenty odd thousand pounds.

That was the end of Eustace's ' safe and obscure existence '. He had given up his practice, sold his books and instruments, come to London, and taken a flat in St. James's, from which he began the inevitable and rapid rake's progress which, eight years later, had landed him at the modest age of thirty-five in the hole in which he found himself to-day.

Sitting in the deep leather armchair at the Jermyn, Eustace's thoughts had not followed the whole course of family history recounted above, but they had brought him to the same finish. He stirred restlessly and pushed the evening paper on to the floor.

How, he wondered, would this news affect him ? Would it affect him at all ? Certainly Howard Hendel would have left him nothing ; Howard had never made any attempt to conceal his opinion of Eustace. The death did mean that there were two male Hendels less in the world, and that might mean more for the survivors when old Barradys died. Unfortunately there was no reason to suppose that the head of the family had any better opinion of Eustace than had his grandsons ; generations of north-country non-conformity were in his blood and he was probably a bigger prig even than Howard. In any case the old man must be pretty well ' ga-ga ' by now and that probably meant that no new will would be valid.

If only the whole lot of them had been drowned at the same time ! Not only Howard and his son, but David and *his* son too—and the old man ! Then everything would have come to him, Eustace. At least he believed it would. He had never been very knowledgeable about that sort of thing ; with all those male descendants in the direct line there hadn't seemed the smallest chance of his succeeding and he hadn't bothered to work it out. But he did know that he was descended from old Andrew, the first peer ; from Andrew's third son, Augustus. The second son, Frederick, had died unmarried, so if the first son, Bevis's, line died out, surely he, Eustace, would succeed ?

Stop a minute, though ; old Chandos had had a brother, Herbert or Henry or something with an H. He was dead now, but his descendants might succeed before the descendants of old Augustus. Eustace had never heard of any descendants of Henry—or was it Herbert ?—but admittedly there might be some without his knowing it. Probably he would find out at the funeral. He would have to go to the funeral, hellish nuisance though it was. It might be a chance to get back into the family graces, and that was more worth bothering about now. He must get back to his rooms and see what he'd got in the way of mourning garments. Nearly time to dress anyhow.

Eustace Hendel heaved himself out of his armchair and made for the door. The old member who had condoled with him on the loss of 'near relatives' gave him a friendly nod ; decent of the old boy ; he had never taken any notice of Eustace before.

Out in the hall, Eustace made for the racks on which hung hats and coats, mostly of sombre blue or black. His own grey herring-bone looked uncomfortably shabby in the hard electric-light. A hand seized his elbow.

" Hullo, old man ; going off to celebrate ? "

Eustace looked round. It was young Priestley, who had first told him the news. One of the few members who was friendly nowadays, but—perhaps

7

for that reason—Eustace did not value the friendship very highly.

" Celebrate what ? " he asked shortly.

Priestley chuckled.

" Don't be a hypocrite, old man," he said. " Two steps nearer the throne, aren't you ? "

Eustace felt his heart give a little throb. Was there something in it, then ?

" What . . . what do you mean ? " he asked.

" Well, that only leaves David and Desmond. Desmond's as good as dead and David isn't likely to marry again. And then you'll be Lord Barradys, what ? "

" I didn't know you knew my family so intimately ", said Eustace, wondering why he should feel irritated.

" Oh, I was in the Coldstream in the war—strictly ' duration ' of course, not my line in peace-time. I was in David's company for a bit."

" Were you really ? " Eustace felt his irritation die down. This might be useful. " I shouldn't have thought you were old enough to have served."

The two men were out of the club by now, walking up towards Piccadilly.

" Well, I didn't actually get to France ", said Priestley. " I joined the Household Brigade Cadet Battalion at Bushey. David Hendel was home wounded and commanding one of the companies till he was fit. Dashed bad luck that the war ended, before I could get out. What about you ? We must be much of an age."

" I missed it too," said Eustace drily. " I was trying to become a doctor and that takes time, even if there is a war on. I'm getting on this bus ; see you at dinner, perhaps."

He jumped on to a No. 25 and was borne away, leaving Priestley—' young ' only among the rather hoary veterans of the Jermyn—standing on the pavement, looking rather surprised.

Again Eustace wondered why he should feel so annoyed. Priestley meant well enough, was really quite a good fellow. But it was obvious that his claim of friendship with ' David ' was pure eyewash ; hundred to one that David had never realised his existence, and an eighteen-year-old cadet didn't mean much to a war-worn Regular captain. For a moment Eustace had thought that Priestley might be useful to him—in some way yet unrecognized ; the fact that he obviously wouldn't be was no doubt the cause of his annoyance.

The No. 25 bus took him to Holborn, and from there he walked to his rooms in Bloomsbury—not the part of Bloomsbury that was fashionable even to-day, but uncomfortably near the edge of Finsbury. These rooms marked a definite step in Eustace's downward career, but for all that they were the fruit of necessity they had been chosen with great care, after profound deliberation. As his income diminished, Eustace had surrendered one luxury after another ; his two horses at Bicester had gone first—hunting was not in his blood and he was even secretly glad to see the last of a horse's ears ; then had followed his gun in a Hampshire syndicate—a wrench, but not shattering ; then, in quick succession, two expensive 'friends'—though here the 'giving up' had not initiated from him ; the sacrifice of his Bentley had been a real blow—the sense of power and speed was like fire in his veins ; to lose that leaping, vital car—far more a living entity to him than any horse—had been the bitterest blow of all to Eustace.

Then had come the question of his rooms ; the rent of a good St. James's flat is a formidable item in a dwindling budget ; a bad one is not worth having. As his income diminished Eustace had begun to augment it by 'his wits', which meant impressing rich young men and quietly—and quite legally—relieving them of some of their surplus wealth. For that game one must inspire confidence, and nothing does this more assuredly than a good address—a solid, permanent-looking anchorage. Expensive hotels are no use for this purpose ; the greenest youth knows that they are no criterion of respectability ; but a sedate, 'established' flat in the Albany or in one of the quiet streets of St. James's, with a well-trained man-servant to add the finishing touch, would inspire confidence in the most suspicious pigeon.

Eustace's quiet games of bridge and poker in that flat had become well-known, perhaps too well-known for his liking, but there were always ' suckers ' to be found. To give that up meant a definite loss of income, but it had to go—the whole establishment, well-trained man-servant and all. Wages can remain in arrears for a time, though not indefinitely ; rent of an expensive flat cannot. At a month's notice—and he was lucky to get that grace—Eustace had had to look about for something else.

He had thought over the problem carefully and decided that if he must give up living in St. James' he would move to Bloomsbury but keep his St. James's club, the Jermyn. He had hunted the neighbourhood of Russell Square and at last, a good deal nearer Gray's Inn Road than he liked, had found two rooms kept by a couple of whom the wife was a fair cook and the husband a really clever and reliable valet. The last was an important consideration ; to be well turned out was no less vital to a man of Eustace's profession—his new profession ; it had never occurred to him to return to the hard struggle of medical practice—than to have a good address. To be reasonably well-fed by Mrs. Drage was fortunate ; to have his clothes properly brushed and pressed and cared for by her husband was nothing less than a godsend.

His decision to remain a member of the Jermyn was a matter of policy, but it had very nearly been an academic one. Rumours of Eustace Hendel's little poker parties had got about, had eventually reached the ears of the Committee of the Jermyn. That body had discussed the question of asking for resignation, but—being reasonable men—had come to the conclusion that it was unjust to judge a man on rumour alone and decided to take no action ; the fact that a judge and jury had recently awarded substantial damages in a somewhat similar case may or may not have had something to do with that decision. But if the Committee had to consult discretion, the members were under no such obligation. Most of them had always wondered how that fellow Hendel had ' got in ', and had been no more than blankly polite ; now they found it unnecessary to go so far. George Priestley and a few of the younger members had remained friendly, and as Eustace only used the club for writing letters and an occasional dinner, a certain chilliness in the atmosphere had not seriously worried him. ' Jermyn Club ' on the note-paper was what he wanted, and it was worth fifteen guineas a year to him.

CHAPTER II

EUSTACE HENDEL set out for Paddington at a distressingly early hour on Friday morning in anything but a cheerful frame of mind ; he was, in fact, both angry and frightened. On Wednesday evening he had dropped seventy odd pounds over a little game at a friend's house, and most of the seventy had gone to a young man whom he had thought he had in his pocket. An occasional loss was good for business, of course—it established confidence ; but seventy was definitely too much in the present state of his finances. That had been irritating enough, but Thursday had been worse. The morning post had brought him an ugly letter from a ' private banker ', demanding immediate payment of interest on a loan or an interview within twenty-four hours. Eustace had not got the money ; he had expected to provide himself with it the previous night, and instead of that had lost all that he had been scraping together over nearly three months. He had nothing to talk about, no suggestion to make, so he had ignored the request for an interview.

Instead, he had gone round to seek comfort and consolation from his girl and had received instead

something very like a blow on the other cheek.
Jill Paris was fond of him—so she had frankly
assured him—but she could not live on air. If
Eustace could not do something more regular and
substantial about an income, she would have to
return to work. Jill's profession was the stage, but
by preference she ' rested ', under suitable protec-
tion. She was an attractive girl, though not so
young as her slim figure, blue eyes and cindered hair
made her look. As an actress she had front row legs
and ability ; as a *protégée* she had a temper, genuine
affection, and a fair appreciation of the ethics of the
game. Eustace liked her a great deal better than
the much more expensive and less intelligent Sylvia
Vaughan and Denise Herron who had preceded her ;
the idea of losing her—and return to work meant
inevitably a change of friend—was almost more
than he could bear.

Finally, as he swallowed a boiled egg and scalding
coffee at little after seven that morning, Eustace
had inadvertently opened another letter from his
' private banker ' and received a shock from which,
as he paid off his taxi at Paddington, he was still
struggling to recover.

Coombe, on the south coast of Cornwall, is nearly
three hundred miles from Paddington, and in order
to get there even by mid-afternoon it was necessary
to catch a very early train—very early, that is, for
a man of Eustace Hendel's manner of life. The

8.30 a.m. would reach the junction fifteen miles from Coombe at 2.30 p.m. and from the junction a service of cars had been arranged, the funeral being timed for 3.30. Naturally, it would not be possible to get back that night, so Eustace was taking a suit case, with sleeping things of necessity, and with evening clothes in case by any chance someone asked him to stay with them—though he hardly thought that likely. On the platform there was a fair sprinkling of people in black clothes, and among them Eustace noticed two or three unmistakable Hendel noses—the hooked, rather predatory nose that looked so much more aristocratic than the family history warranted.

Getting into a first-class carriage was an obvious member of the ' Baron's branch '—the fair-haired line. This particular one, wearing a brushed-up moustache which suggested a Guardsman, was probably David, the brother of Howard and the new heir to the title. Eustace wondered that he had not gone down sooner. He had not seen David for a number of years, and but for the nose might not have recognized him. With him was a woman of about forty and a boy of, probably, seventeen. Eustace did not know who these were. David's wife had died two or three years ago and his son was certainly older than this boy and was in any case a chronic invalid. Unwilling to court a snub in his present temper, Eustace passed the carriage without further notice and climbed into a neighbouring ' first-smoker ' which was occupied by an elderly dried-up man of professional aspect.

Nobody else entered the carriage, and as soon as the train had shaken itself free of the gloom of Paddington Station the elderly man laid down his *Times* and looked across at Eustace.

" I feel sure that you must be a Hendel ", he said, " and by your dark colouring, one of the younger branch. If I may hazard a guess, you are Eustace, son of Victor, grandson of Clarence, great-grandson of Augustus—and so back to Andrew, the first peer."

Eustace laughed.

" You know more about us than I do myself ", he said. " I *am* Eustace, and definitely one of the younger branch."

" And I am William Christendome, senior partner of Christendome and Booth, solicitors. My firm has been in charge of the affairs of the senior branch of your family since the days of Bevis, the second baron."

Eustace pricked up his ears. Here was the very man to give him the information he wanted. But he would have to go tactfully ; family solicitors did not, he believed, like to be pumped.

" Glad to meet you, Mr. Christendome ", he said. " Bad business, this. D'you know at all how it happened ? "

"A bad business indeed, Mr. Eustace. A more tragic blow to the elder branch of a distinguished family it would be difficult to imagine."

Mr. Christendome wiped his gold-rimmed glasses carefully.

"Yes", he went on, "I think I may say that I know as much of what happened as anybody knows, or indeed is likely to know. Mr. Carr telegraphed for me at once and I got down on Tuesday evening. He . . ."

"Carr?" queried Eustace.

Mr. Christendome looked at him in some surprise.

"Henry Carr", he said; "husband of Julia, Howard's first cousin. Your—let me think—Julia would be your third cousin. She is the great-grand-daughter of Bevis, as you are the great-grandson of his brother Augustus. Her mother, of course, was Louisa, who married James Kidd."

Eustace's brain reeled before this whirlwind of relationship.

"Oh yes, yes, of course", he muttered.

"Howard and his son were staying with the Carrs", continued the solicitor, leaning back and fixing his gaze upon the ventilator. "They—the Carrs, that is—had taken a house at Coombe for their summer holidays and Howard and the boy had come down to stay with them for a week. Cornwall would be a great change for them, for Howard at any rate, from the industrial north.

Harold, of course, has only come down from Cambridge a year, but it has been a hard year in the shops and he, too, would welcome the change."

" The shops ? "

" Yes, Harold was to learn the engineering business from A to Z, going through the shops—that is to say, the works—the drawing office, and so on. Sound, very sound. Poor boy."

Again Mr. Christendome shook his head.

" Was it a boating accident ? " asked Eustace.

" No. They were bathing. I attended the inquest on Wednesday, of course. On Mr. Howard's body, it was ; Harold's had not been recovered. I had to return the same evening to collect various papers and attend to some other business. A long journey ; a very long journey."

" You must be pretty sick of it."

" It's all part of my business, Mr. Eustace. As I was saying, I attended the inquest and it appeared that Mr. Carr and his two guests had bathed before breakfast each morning, in Coombe Cove, which is perfectly safe and indeed, as Mr. Carr put it, rather uninteresting. On Tuesday morning, the fifth of their visit, Mr. Carr did not go with them, as he had a slight chill. It seems that the two Hendels, father and son, elected to go further afield that morning, and made their way to another cove, some way beyond, a rocky, dangerous place locally known as Davy's Cut—possibly some reference to ' Davy

Jones '. A notoriously dangerous place, with a heavy drag at high tide. As ill-luck would have it, these two went there at the beginning of the ebb—the most dangerous time, it seems, of all. A shepherd on the hills actually saw them enter the water. He shouted and waved to them, but could not catch their attention. He saw that they were in difficulties at once and ran down as quickly as he could, but when he got to the shore they were gone. Strong, experienced swimmers, too, both of them. Howard's body, terribly injured by the rocks, was washed up in Coombe Cove on the flood-tide, but Harold's has not yet been seen ; possibly the fact that he was lighter may be the explanation of that."

" Good Lord ; what a grim business. And Howard's wife ? Was she down there with them ? "

" Yes, poor lady. She has been wonderfully brave—astonishingly so, it seems to an old-fashioned man like myself. Naturally the whole business has been a terrible shock to her, but I saw no sign of a break-down, such as I would have expected."

" Good sort, Blanche ", muttered Eustace. " Was that David I saw getting into the train ? "

" Yes, Captain Hendel was on his way to Norway and has only just returned. He is with Mrs. Stone and her son Bernard. You know her ? "

" Not from Adam. . . . Eve, I should say. Who is she ? "

" She was Patience Wick ; her mother Emily was

the daughter of Henry Hendel, brother of the present Lord Barradys."

Eustace pricked up his ears. Henry; that was the man he had been wondering about—him and his descendants.

" I don't think I ever met any of that branch ", he said. " How many children did Henry have ? "

" Only one daughter, Emily ", said Mr. Christendome, quite unaware of the thrill of excitement which this answer evoked in Eustace. " Emily, as I said, was the mother of Mrs. Stone, again an only child, who has the one son Bernard, whom you saw with Captain David."

So Henry had had no son, and the title, of course, could not descend through his daughter ; that had been the point about which Eustace had been doubtful. Then, after David and his invalid son, came he, Eustace ! What a thought ! Eustace, Lord Barradys ! How fine it sounded. And all the money that went with the title. The great engineering business, coal-mines, cash—without a doubt the old man had got a fortune in gilt-edged securities alone. Eustace's heart pounded. If something happened to David and his son, as it had happened to Howard and his, all that would come to him !

Glorious thoughts flashed through his brain. Back to his old flat, his shooting syndicate, his Bentley—perhaps two Bentleys, a ' sports ' and a limousine. Horses—no, perhaps give them a miss ;

he hadn't really enjoyed hunting; shooting and motoring were more his line. A yacht, perhaps—a steam one, of course, that you could cruise round the world in—the Mediterranean and lovely women in pyjamas. Jill! It meant Jill his own for a certainty. He could get Sylvia or Denise back if he wanted them, or even some real tip-topper, like Catherine Dawne, or Cantolina. But he loved Jill. She wasn't in Sylvia's class, but she was worth six of her, for all that. He might even marry her, though that was hardly necessary.

Eustace's thoughts came back to earth with a bump. What was the use of talking like that? David would inherit the title and the money and everything else. His son, Desmond, was a wash-out, of course; it wasn't likely he would ever succeed and he certainly couldn't get a son. But David was still a young man, and handsome in his stupid, Guardsman way. Now that he was heir to the estate he would be certain to marry again, and there would be no shortage of candidates.

From boiling point, Eustace's spirits dropped to zero. That was always the way with him; he got worked up into a great state of excitement and enthusiasm and then something went wrong and he flopped straight into black depression. His thoughts flew back now to all the troubles that surrounded him: that damned letter from Isaacson; how the devil was he going to find the money to pay his arrears of interest, let alone redeem the capital ? How was he going to go on living even in his present wretched way ? His capital had dwindled to a few thousand pounds ; it brought him in a hundred or so a year—just enough to keep him in clothes and tobacco. All the rest had to come from what he could pick up with his wits—cards and so on. And the supply of suckers was running low ; what's more, they didn't seem to be such fools as they used to be ; one of them had actually taken a cool seventy off him only two nights ago. Off him, Eustace Hendel !

Then there was Jill ; she had as good as chucked him. Jill ! Eustace felt a pricking at the back of his eyes as he thought of losing Jill. Damn it, he couldn't ; he loved her !

Mr. Christendome, noticing that his companion's attention had begun to wander from his dissertation upon the Hendel family tree, had dropped the subject and buried himself in the *Times*, blissfully ignorant of the ugly thoughts that had begun to form in Eustace Hendel's brain. The train rushed on through the gleaming countryside and in this first-class carriage two men sat immersed in their several problems ; Mr. Christendome sought for a word of six letters to fit the clue ' Dramatic in Mayfair ', unaware that the answer was to be found in his companion's heart.

CHAPTER III

THE party from London reached Coombe with fair time to take their places in the little church. A large crowd of sympathetic onlookers—natives and holiday visitors—watched the final scene in the churchyard, their interest centred on the beautiful woman who had suffered this terrible double loss and who now bore herself with such quiet dignity and self-control. As the little party of mourners moved from the grave to the lich-gate, hats were doffed and tears trickled down the cheeks of complete strangers who had been moved beyond their own control by this tragedy of the sea.

The cars which had brought the London party from the junction to Coombe now carried the women to Henry Carr's house, while most of the men walked the short distance up a country lane. On the way, Mr. Christendome introduced Eustace Hendel to a handsome, fresh-complexioned man, with a dust of grey on his black hair and clipped moustache.

Henry Carr was a solicitor, with a sound practice in a London residential suburb. He was still on the right side of fifty, but life had not been too rosy for him, and it was to his credit that only those grey hairs were the outward evidence of the trials and difficulties through which he had fought his way. Only two years after the war his firm, of which he was then the junior partner, had been broken up by a financial scandal which had ended in the suicide of one partner and the disappearance of another. Carr had struggled to clear up the mess, had sacrificed all his own savings in an attempt to recoup the clients who had suffered ; he had earned great respect for himself, but the firm's credit was ruined and he had had to start again on his own to build up a new business. After fourteen years he was, as he called it, ' on his legs again ', and few people realized now the bitterness of the struggle which he and his wife had faced, to keep up the appearance necessary for his business and to give their two children a good education and a fair chance in life.

" Mr. Hendel tells me that he has not had the pleasure of meeting you before ", was Mr. Christendome's tactful version of Eustace's declaration of ignorance.

Henry Carr smiled.

" That has been my misfortune and certainly not Eustace's fault ", he said. " You'll forgive my calling you by your Christian name ? " he continued ; " after all, my wife's your not very distant cousin."

Privately thinking it rather cool, Eustace agreed

that Christian names broke a lot of ice. At least this man didn't suffer from the damned stand-offish superiority of his wife's family.

" I wish we could put you up tonight ", went on the younger solicitor, " but the house isn't big and even with Dick and Helen on sofas we can only just squeeze in David and Patience . . . oh, and I believe her boy's in my dressing-room ", he added with a grimace.

" I am sure Mr. Hendel will be very comfortable with me at the *Boatswain's Mate*, where I slept on Tuesday night ", put in Mr. Christendome tactfully. " Ah, here we are at your house. Mrs. Howard has been very wonderful all through this time ; I hope that she will retire now and not consider it necessary to be present at the reading of the will."

Blanche Hendel, however, was of the generation of women that had learnt, in four terrible years, not to retire in the face of trouble. She met Eustace in the garden of the Carr's holiday house and thanked him for coming all that long way to her husband's funeral.

" I do think it's wonderful of you, Eustace ", she said. " We've seen so little of each other in all these years and I feel that it's been a good deal our fault. I always told Howard that the family hadn't got the clan spirit that one expects from north-countrymen."

Eustace was touched by this confession and felt a

25

good deal of his resentment melt away, but after all, he reflected, Blanche wasn't a Hendel ; she had always been pleasant to him ; it was her husband and his family who had been such insufferable prigs. He was confirmed in this view a few minutes later when his cousin David, answering to Blanche's call of " David, here's Eustace ", greeted him with a curt nod and " Yes, we travelled down together."

Blanche Hendel flushed and Eustace made an effort to relieve her obvious distress by enquiring after David's son.

" Desmond's an invalid ", replied David shortly. " Blanche, oughtn't you to go and rest ? "

" I'm perfectly all right, thank you, David ", replied Blanche, with a touch of anger in her voice. " Come and have tea ; Julia said it would be ready in a minute."

The two men, in silent antagonism, followed her into the house, where Eustace was introduced to yet another cousin, Julia Carr, and her two children, Richard, a sturdy boy of fifteen, and Helen, a hardly less sturdy girl of twelve. Julia Carr, though she possessed the Hendel nose, had none of the other family characteristics which Eustace so much disliked. Perhaps the troubles through which she had passed had rubbed off the sharp corners of pride and self-satisfaction so noticeable in David and his dead brother, Howard. Certainly her figure had no such angles ; she was rather short and definitely

26

plump, in keeping with a gentle and placid manner. Quite evidently she was a mother and a housewife before anything else ; Eustace quickly came to this conclusion as he noted the care with which she presided over her excellent Cornish tea and saw the affectionate glances which she exchanged with her husband and her two jolly children. A throw-back to the north-country working-class from which her family had sprung, thought Eustace with amused contempt.

As soon as tea had been cleared away, Henry Carr, after exchanging glances with David Hendel, courteously bowed Mr. Christendome into the arm-chair at the head of the table. The old lawyer extracted some papers from the attaché case which never left him, unfolded a thick bundle of parchment, cleared his throat and began :

" Mr. Howard Hendel, when he made this will in 1929, thereby cancelling his former will and codicils, expressed the wish that at his death it should be read aloud to those members of the family who attended his funeral. I agree with him in thinking that that is a very proper procedure, though I realize that it is rapidly falling into disuse. The will is not long ; the estate, as many of you are doubtless aware, was settled by the second Lord Barradys upon his son Chandos, the present Lord Barradys, for life, and thereafter upon the heirs of his body. Upon the death of Chandos's son, Albert, in 1893, his son, the late Mr. Howard Hendel, became tenant in tail. In the absence of any break in the entail, the estate would normally have passed in due course to Howard's son, Harold, but in the circumstances of this tragic occurrence, the settled estate now passes automatically to Mr. Albert Hendel's second son, Captain David Hendel."

Mr. Christendome paused to bow ceremoniously to David, who flushed uncomfortably.

" There are, of course ", continued the solicitor, "certain bequests of personal property, and these are embodied in the will which I shall now read to you."

Adjusting his glasses, Mr. Christendome plunged into the technical phraseology of ' the last will and testament ' of Howard Hendel. Of his considerable personalty, Howard had left a substantial sum to his wife, absolutely, but the bulk of it was to be held in trust to provide an annuity for her, reverting to the holder of the settled estate upon her death. To the Trustees of this fund, David Hendel and Richard Christendome (son and partner of Mr. William Christendome) were left sums of £500 each. A legacy of £2,000 went to Julia Carr ; £500 to Desmond Hendel (David's invalid son) ; £500 to Patience Stone (grand-daughter of Henry Hendel) ; £500 to his personal secretary, George Purdis ; £200 to Reginald Stotworthy, secretary of the firm of Hendel Brothers ; £50 to Eustace Hendel ; £50 to Albert William Tagg. . . .

Eustace heard no more of the recital. He was conscious of a rush of hot blood into his face, followed by a feeling that every drop of it had left his body, leaving him cold and stiff. Fifty pounds! Pushed in somewhere among a lot of clerks and servants! Fifty pounds! To him, Eustace Hendel, who had kept a flat in St. James', horses at Bicester, a thousand-guinea Bentley, Sylvia Vaughan and Denise Herron—and who now desperately needed £500 or £1,000 to keep Jill Paris and his own head above water. Fifty pounds! A bloody insult! Shoved in among a lot of Taggs and Stotworthys, quill-drivers and boot-polishers! Deliberate. A deliberate insult. Howard, blast him, knew perfectly well that things had been going badly with him and he had taken the opportunity to rub it in by a bit of cheap charity. Fifty pounds! . . .

There was a scraping of chairs on the wood floor, a clatter of tongues. The formal affair was over. Blanche Hendel, beginning at last to show signs of the strain which she had endured, was saying good-night.

"Do stay down here a few days, Eustace. It's such lovely air and I should like to see something of you after all this time. Julia's going to talk to you."

Sweet of her. No nonsense, no pose; she meant it. Again Eustace felt his anger cool down. He would have liked to stay, but he couldn't stick that damned fellow, David.

29

" Eustace, won't you come up here tomorrow for a day or two ? David's going by the early train, and Patience can't stay either. It would be so nice if you'd come and help me with the children ; there's golf, if you care for it, and bathing of course. Oh ! "

It was Julia speaking now. Silly woman, making a *faux pas* like that and then calling attention to it.

" Henry will have to be seeing to things ", went on Julia Carr hurriedly. " It would really be kind of you if you'd come. Dick and Helen are such a handful, and Blanche and I would love to have you."

There was no particular warmth in her voice. Blanche had put her up to it, of course. Still, it might be rather nice ; a change and all that. And Blanche was a topper—and very lovely.

" Awfully good of you ", muttered Eustace. " But . . . well, I've only got these clothes and some evening things. Not much use down here."

" Don't let that worry you."

Henry Carr put a friendly hand on his shoulder.

" I can fit you up with some slacks and a flannel shirt and a pull-over. Come along by all means ; I shall be glad of your company."

So it was settled. Eustace walked back to *The Boatswain's Mate* with Mr. Christendome. He paid little attention to the lawyer's tactful conversation. The old man had noticed the effect which the reading of the will had had on his companion ; he had, in fact, rather sympathized with his obvious feelings. He made no reference to the subject now, but talked of Blanche Hendel and of Julia Carr and her children. The two sturdy youngsters, awed by the solemnity of the occasion, but unable always to repress their natural high spirits and curiosity, had appealed to the old lawyer; he rambled on about the attraction of youth and health while Eustace chewed morosely the cud of his discontent.

The Boatswain's Mate proved to be comfortable enough, if rather overcrowded, and the food was excellent. After dinner the two men drank a bottle of vintage port in the little private sitting-room which Mr. Christendome had rather miraculously managed to reserve. Mellowed by the wine, Eustace forgot his grievance and tried to pump the solicitor about the family affairs, but Mr. Christendome, though he too was enjoying himself, was too well seasoned to allow his palate to influence his tongue. He disclosed an encyclopædic knowledge of family history, but evaded Eustace's not very subtle attempts to investigate the settlement of the Hendel estates. Eustace was disappointed, but not deterred; if this old stick wouldn't talk he had another string to his bow; Henry Carr was pretty sure to know all about it and it should be no difficult job to get it out of him while he was staying in his house.

CHAPTER IV

SETTLED ESTATE

THE following morning was clear and beautiful, with every promise of a hot noon. As he shaved, Eustace felt his spirits rise. The view from his window looked straight over the Channel, clear green and calm and dotted with craft of all descriptions. It was years since Eustace had been to the sea, apart from crossing it occasionally in a ship, and he was conscious now of a re-awakened thrill that he had not felt since his boyhood. A car came down the village street ; as it passed Eustace caught a glimpse of the handsome face of David Hendel, unsmiling and cold. In his own improved spirits he felt almost sorry for the fellow, stuck-up ass though he was ; there couldn't be much fun to be got out of life when one was as proud and disagreeable as all that.

After breakfast he made his way up to the Carrs' house and was fitted out in a pair of grey flannel trousers, a flannel shirt and some old sand-shoes. Henry Carr's figure was much the same as his own ; a year or two ago the trousers would not have met round his waist, but the reduction of his standard of living had been reflected in Eustace's figure.

After a wasted day, as they naturally regarded it, the Carr children were clamouring to get down to the sea. Julia, not unreasonably nervous after her cousin's accident, would not let them go without a grown-up and Henry Carr was busy clearing up arrears of business connected with the inquest, the funeral, and the continued search for Harold's body. Eustace found himself a popular arrival and was soon being hustled off by Dick and Helen, all three loaded with baskets and towels, with orders not to return before tea and to be very careful.

"Regular old fuss-pot Mum's getting", declared Dick as soon as they were out of earshot.

"Well, you can hardly blame her", said Eustace. "She naturally pictures you being drowned too, and I suppose you're of some value to her."

"We shouldn't be such fools as to bathe in Davy's Cut", replied Dick. "I can't think what induced cousin Howard to go there."

"That's a good word—' induced '; where did you get it from ? " asked Eustace, who had little experience of the modern child.

"Dick won a prize for long words at school", declared Helen admiringly.

"It wasn't for long words, fool ", retorted her brother with some heat. "It was the English Essay Prize. They teach English at Hailborough."

"Must be an odd place ", said Eustace.

"Oh no, quite decent." The boy was unconscious

of irony. " But I say, I wonder Dad didn't tell
them about the Cut. When they went without
him, I mean."

" It never crossed his mind ", declared Helen
solemnly.

" What d'you mean ? How d'you know ? "

" I listened."

Dick took his sister by the arm and shook her

" Explain properly, can't you ", he said. " Where
did you listen ? What to ? "

" Th'Inquest. It was at the School. I listened
outside the window. You were playing golf with
mummy."

This was too much for Dick. He was well aware
that his mother had taken him to play golf in order
to keep him away from the Inquest, which he had
passionately wanted to attend. Helen had com-
plained of feeling sick and had been allowed to stay
at home with a book. This was the result. Girls
had no sense of honour.

" You shouldn't have done that ", he said severely.
" You were on *parole*—practically."

" What's p'role ? "

" Never mind. What did you hear ? "

Righteous indignation had given way to curiosity.

" Oh, lots and lots . . . but I've forgotten it."

Irritating female.

" What did you mean about . . . about Dad not
telling cousin Howard about the Cut ? "

"Oh, I remember that now, 'cause you said about it. Someone asked: 'did you warn them not to bathe in the Cut?' and Daddy said: 'it never crossed my mind'."

"Your father had been bathing with them every morning before that, hadn't he?" asked Eustace.

"Yes. He just happened to be indisposed. . . ."

"He had a belly-ache", declared Helen, who preferred accuracy to purity of speech.

"Helen! That's vulgar."

"It's what Jones told Mr. Marsh."

"Jones is a vulgar man. It was indigestion."

"Same thing", declared Helen.

"What about yourselves?" asked Eustace. "Don't you bathe before breakfast?"

"Oh yes, of course, but we didn't get back from school till Tuesday night. Dad had to begin his holiday a week before us for some reason—something to do with the office, he said."

"I see; that was lucky."

"Oh no, I don't think so, cousin Eustace. If we'd been here it wouldn't have happened."

"No, I suppose not. You've been here before? You know the place?"

"Yes, twice before", said Helen. "It's lovely. I say, let's go down to the Cut and see if cousin Harold has been washed up."

This certainly was a tempting proposal. It was eventually decided to bathe first in the safe waters of Coombe Cove, lunch on the cliffs, and then explore the Cut while digesting before the afternoon bathe.

Eustace thoroughly enjoyed the hours that followed. The hot sunshine, splashing about with the children in the clear water, Julia Carr's delicious picnic lunch on the cliffs, and then the excitement of searching among the rocks of the Cut as the tide went down. It was a tempting spot for a bathe. Great rocks stood out in the deep water, offering magnificent opportunities for high diving ; the absence of other bathers contrasted very favourably with the overcrowded beach of the Cove ; the high cliffs, rising almost sheer from the sea on each side, gave an impression of majesty to the scene. Eustace could imagine that a keen swimmer who was unaware of the dangerous drag might well prefer this spot for his morning dip. It was easy to see how the accident had happened, but he wondered that there was no notice up to warn visitors. Anyhow, he wasn't going to shed crocodiles' tears over it ; he had disliked Howard and had hardly seen Harold. If only David and his son Desmond had been in the party too, what a clearance it would have made ! What a marvellous stroke of luck for him ! Or wouldn't it ? He must find out some more about that settled estate. He really didn't know who came next after Desmond. Not that Desmond counted ; he wasn't likely to have any children.

For the rest of the afternoon Eustace's thoughts were never far from the subject. Succession to the peerage and estates! How magnificent it sounded. It meant Jill and comfort and money to play with and position—the House of Lords! Good Lord, what a prospect! If only David . . . so his thoughts whirled round in a cycle.

The rather ghoulish efforts of the Carr children to find their cousin's body came to nothing and the party returned home in time for tea. Blanche Hendel was writing under a tree in the garden, looking, Eustace thought, a great deal more drawn and exhausted than she had on the previous day. She spoke cheerfully enough to him and the children, but he noticed her wince at the sight of their bathing things.

Eustace made no attempt to approach the subject of the Hendel succession that evening. He was going to be there two or three nights and he thought it wisest not to seem too eager. He found Henry Carr more agreeable than his first impression had led him to expect. He was friendly, interested in other people beside himself and his own family—a rare virtue, in Eustace's experience; he avoided talking about the elder branch of the family, probably guessing that it was a sore subject with his guest, but he drew Eustace out about his own life, his father, and his Uncle William and cousin George. Eustace had a good deal of respect for his uncle, the wine-merchant, who had always been kind to him and had not attempted to lecture him on his extravagance. In the days of that extravagance Eustace had bought his wine from his uncle and he still occasionally went into the office and had a glass of sherry or madeira with him. The son, George, had just joined the business after three years at Oxford and two in France and Spain. He was a pleasant enough youth but, being unsuitable for poker parties, Eustace had not cultivated his acquaintance. This latter point Eustace did not explain to his host.

On Sunday Eustace went to church for the first time for many years. The Carrs seemed to take it for granted that he would accompany them and one of Henry's suits was pressed into service. There was more bathing in the afternoon and evening, and after dinner that night Eustace felt justified in approaching the subject that was never far from his mind. Henry Carr had produced some good port, and after a second glass of it, Eustace launched his first *ballon d'essai*.

" That idea of entailing an estate that old Christendome told us about ", he said ; " how does that work ?   What's the point of it ? "

Henry Carr smiled.

" The point of it is to keep the estate in the family ", he said.   " It's fairly common in old families and with large estates.   Without an entail the owner, if he was an irresponsible fellow with no family pride, might leave a fine old family property to his cook, as the saying goes, or more probably to some attractive woman or some special crony. Where the estate is entailed, the tenant for life has only a life interest; it *must* pass to the tenant in tail. In this case, the second Lord Barradys settled the estate upon his son Chandos for life and upon the heirs of his body. That meant that Chandos, the present Lord Barradys, had only a life interest in the estate; it was bound to pass to his lineal descendants, just as his title was bound to pass to them. As it has turned out, Chandos's son Albert, who was the first tenant in tail, died before his father and his son Howard became tenant in tail; Howard has also died before his grandfather, and if he also died before his son, Harold became tenant in tail for the few minutes or seconds by which he survived his father. It's an academic point really, because as they both died the entail passes to David."

" And from him it must pass to Desmond ? "

" Yes—unless he bars the entail. A tenant in tail can break the entail with the consent of the tenant for life, but Lord Barradys would never give his consent, I'm sure. It's been a family rule ever since old Andrew's day and I can't see it being broken. As a matter of fact there are ways and means of breaking an entail without consent of the tenant for life, creating a base fee, and so on, but you won't want to bother with a lot of legal quirks. I take it you just want to know how the estate goes ? "

" Oh no, no." Eustace was not anxious to appear too curious. " I was just wondering how the thing worked. ' Tail male ', and all that. I've heard about it but never understood what it meant."

Henry Carr glanced at him keenly, opened his lips as if to speak, but closed them again. Eustace remained silent for a time, thinking over what had been told him. It seemed pretty clear. The estate went by lineal descent, just as the title did, Carr had said. If David and Desmond were to die the title must come to him because the elder line, Bevis's line, would be extinct, so far as male descendants were concerned ; Bernard Stone didn't count as he was descended through women and, thank goodness, the Salic law applied in England—so much he remembered from his schooldays. Frederick, Andrew's second son, had died childless, so the third son, Augustus's, line came into the succession, and of that line he was now the head.

Eustace had become so deeply absorbed in his thoughts that he did not realise how long the silence had lasted ; nor did he realise that his host was watching him with an amused smile on his lips. He started as Henry Carr pushed the decanter towards him.

" If I were Sherlock Holmes I should tell you

where your thoughts had got to now ", said the solicitor. " No, don't worry ; I won't. Have another glass ; it can't hurt you."

Eustace had not intended to drink any more, but, feeling slightly embarrassed by his host's remarks, he did as he was bid.

" It's interesting, all that ", he said. " Then Desmond is bound to succeed after David ? "

" To the title, yes, but not necessarily to the estate. As tenant in tail David can bar the entail, but, as I said, there's no likelihood of that happening." Henry Carr paused for a moment, watching the smoke of his cigar curl up in the candle light. " Unless he marries again ", he added.

Eustace felt his spirits drop sharply.

" You mean he might have more children."

Carr nodded.

" Desmond, poor fellow, isn't likely to live long. If David had a son by a second wife he might break the entail and re-settle on the younger son to avoid an extra set of death duties."

" I see."

Eustace finished his port in silence and declined a fourth glass. Henry Carr rose and pinched out the candles.

" Of course he may not marry again ", he said, " but there'll be a lot of women after him."

CHAPTER V

JILL PARIS

EUSTACE returned to London on Tuesday morning in a much more cheerful frame of mind than when he had left it on Friday. His new-found relations had been charming to him ; he had enjoyed the bathing and tennis, and he had learnt a good deal that might be useful and was certainly exciting. Only two lives stood between him and a fortune— not to mention a peerage ! One of those lives was practically negligible ; only David counted—unless he married again. It was enough to make a fellow think. He had been aware of some odd thoughts coming down in the train, when the position was much more uncertain in his mind than it was now. Insidious thoughts.

Henry and Julia drove him to the junction and saw him off. Blanche, of whom he had seen less than he had hoped, was very sweet to him as she said good-bye, insisting that he should come and see her as soon as she had settled down, whenever and wherever that might be. Eustace believed that she meant it and he certainly intended to keep his side of the promise. The children eagerly insisted that he should come and stay with them next holidays. Such friendliness was a new experience to Eustace Hendel; for an appreciable time he forgot his ugly thoughts.

As the Carrs walked back to their Vauxhall, Julia took her husband's arm.

" Poor fellow ", she said. " I don't suppose he's had much of a chance. His father was a pretty bad lot, and then coming into all that money from that awful woman."

Henry Carr laughed.

" It was a misfortune that most people would accept cheerfully enough ", he said. " What d'you think of him, really ? "

" Oh, I think he would be quite nice if he lived with decent people. All that living in a flat in London and having no work ! A wife's what he wants ; if we could find a nice girl. . . ."

" You old matchmaker ! "

Carr swung the Vauxhall out of the station yard and slipped into top.

" He's got some good stuff in him, I believe ", he said. " And some pretty rotten stuff too. A bit unbalanced, I should say. I wouldn't trust him far."

" Oh, Henry, that's hardly fair. You don't really know him. I like him, really. All the same, I hope he doesn't succeed."

Henry Carr looked quickly at his wife.

" Succeed ? Why should he ? Oh, the title, you mean ? "

" Yes, and all that. There's only David, really."
Carr smiled.

" I fancy he's got that idea in his head himself.
Apart from anything else, David's not dead yet . . .
and he may marry again."

Julia's face brightened.

" Oh, I hope he will ", she exclaimed. " There's
that Hope-Fording girl. He seemed rather attracted
by her, I thought, when we met them at the
Cannington's last summer."

" You thought so ? "

Carr took a case from his pocket and dexterously
extracted and lit a cigarette with his disengaged
hand.

" Well, of course we only saw them for a couple
of days, but I'm sure she was after him and he didn't
seem to dislike her as much as he does most women."

" Hardly sufficient evidence to support a breach
of promise case ", said the solicitor with a smile.

" No, but . . ."

" I know. Woman's intuition. Well, we'll see
what can be done about it. Wonderful how these
light sixes take the hills."

*   *   *   *   *

Eustace's return to his Bloomsbury lodgings were
an unpleasant anti-climax. Mrs. Drage came
straight up to his sitting-room and closed the door
firmly behind her. There was a grim expression on
her usually placid face.

" There was a man come here with a writ yesterday ", she said.

" A writ ? "

This was Eustace's first personal experience of that ominous word. It was an unpleasant shock.

" Isaacson, he said the name was."

The ' private banker ' ! So the fellow meant business. This was going to be serious.

" Silly ass ", he said, as casually as possible. " Just because I forgot to send him a cheque and have been away for a few days."

Mrs. Drage was not deceived.

" I don't want no brokers' men in this house ", she said crisply. " Gives it a bad name, it does. You've been prompt with your rent ; I'll say that, Mr. Hendel. And no trouble to speak of. But writs and brokers' men I won't have. That's plain."

" Of course not, of course not. I'll see about it at once. Don't you worry, Mrs. Drage."

The landlady sniffed, hesitated, and weakened.

" Oh well ; I'll say no more now ", she said. " You'd better let Drage have those clothes to press quick, Mr. Hendel. All crumpled they are. And your 'at."

Mrs. Drage was not only house-proud, but lodger-proud. It was one of her most valuable attributes.

But it was one thing to appease Mrs. Drage, another to pay Isaacson. He could, of course, sell some of his small remaining capital, but that meant loss of income and a further reduction in his standard of living. That would mean cheaper lodgings, with no valeting, which in its turn would result in loss of earning power; he must look tidy and well-dressed if he was to meet and play cards with rich young men. The 'vicious circle' of poverty and loss of earning capacity would turn very quickly against him if he descended any lower in his standard of living.

What was he to do, then? A successful flutter was what he needed. Poker was the most paying proposition; skill and experience counted for more there than in any other game, and it was easier to get out or to keep one's losses down if luck was against one. But to play high enough to win the substantial sum he needed he must at least be prepared to lose; he must have money; a stumer cheque would be absolutely fatal to him—to his reputation. And money, on an adequate scale, he had not got. He had often been in that position before and his way out had been to borrow from Isaacson and pay him back when he won. That was how the trouble had started; at first he had been able to pay back promptly, then luck had gone against him for a spell, rates of interest were high, and he had never been able to catch up—in fact he had been getting steadily further behind. Isaacson had soon realized what was happening, and that no doubt was the reason for this offensive line that the fellow was taking now.

There were other money-lenders, of course, but the blighters knew too much ; they seemed to have an information bureau, something like Scotland Yard. Possibly they pooled their information ; anyhow it was ten to one against his getting any sort of terms now that Isaacson had got his knife into him. He must find some means of squaring up with Isaacson and starting afresh. But how ? There he was back at the beginning again. Better go and talk it over with Jill ; she had brains and might be able to put him on to something. It wasn't at all the sort of thing that he wanted to talk to her about ; it would only start her off about her own position again and she had been bad enough about that last week. Still, she was fond of him and hadn't seen him for nearly a week and might be in a more reasonable and sympathetic frame of mind now. Better take her out to dinner ; some place she liked going to, a bit better than the ordinary. At least he had enough ready cash for that and if she produced an idea it would be worth the money.

After changing out of the funeral clothes in which he had had to travel back from Cornwall, Eustace walked round to Jill's rooms near Cambridge Circus. She called them ' her flat ', but that was a euphemism. She had no maid of her own but, with two other actresses who occupied the same house, was dependent on the attentions of a land-lady who lived in the basement. Eustace had been careful to keep on good terms with Mrs. Hollebone, had tipped her well and often and 'spoken her fair'; indeed, on any other terms his affair with Jill would have been impossible, because Mrs. Drage absolutely refused to have any good-looking young woman in her house; long experience had taught her that good-looking young women visiting a gentleman meant talk, and talk was bad for the reputation of her house. Fortunately it took all sorts of landladies to make a London world and Mrs. Hollebone ran her house on different lines; respect-able of course, nothing casual or promiscuous or rowdy, but no questions asked if all was nice and ladylike.

So tonight Mrs. Hollebone greeted Eustace with a smile but a shake of the head.

" She's out, I'm afraid, Mr. Hendel ", she said. " Been out a lot the last few days. 'T's my believe she's looking for a shop—round the agents, you know. I heard 'er talking to Miss Wilbraham—that's my second floor—last night ; talking about that new show of Lanberg's at the Cosmopolitan. Miss Wilbr'm was going to an audition this morning and it's my belief that Miss Paris was thinking of going along too. She's not been back since she left this morning."

This was bad news. It was only what might be

expected after the way she had talked last week,
but it was none the less of a blow for that. Eustace's
spirits sank lower than ever. What on earth was
he going to do now? If Jill was taken on by
Lanberg . . . quite apart from the fellow's own
reputation, the Cosmopolitan was London's favourite
trout-stream; every rotten fellow who wanted a
girl went fishing in it.

"Not but what Miss Paris couldn't do better
than the Cosmo", continued Mrs. Hollebone,
evidently reading Eustace's thoughts. "With her
figure and legs, and sings a bit too, and *personality*,
mind you; that's what gets across, as I tells 'er
myself. If she was me it'd be Cochrane and no one
less, so I . . . why there she is!"

There was a sound of voices outside and a girl
ran up the steps into the hall.

"H'llo, Big Boy; if it isn't you!"

An expression that Eustace particularly detested,
and only used by Jill in her more irritating moods.

"Hullo, Jill. I've just got back from Cornwall."

"Well, I didn't suppose you were still there.
Holly darling, I shall be out to supper. We're all
going to the *Réchauffée*."

"I came along to ask you to come out with me",
said Eustace doggedly.

"Bit late, aren't you? I must go and tidy
up."

49

She moved to the staircase and ran lightly up it. Eustace followed, but more slowly.

On the first floor, the door of a sitting-room was open. It was an untidy room, over-furnished and full of photographs of impossibly lovely girls and dark-eyed men with thin moustaches. Eustace took no notice of it ; the door of an inner room, evidently a bedroom, was open. He did not follow Jill in there ; he was no stranger to it, but in her present mood Jill would bite his head off. He waited gloomily, listening to the snatches of light-comedy song that came through the door. Presently the girl reappeared, passing a comb through her thick cindered-blonde hair. Eustace felt his heart turn over. Well as he knew her he was always liable to be overwhelmed by her beauty and grace. Jill Paris was well into the thirties, but she had taken care of her complexion, and her figure was perfect. Her blue eyes were conventional, but she had had the intelligence not to mess about with her eyebrows, with the result that she looked less like a chorus-girl than a general description would lead one to expect. She had a short nose, with finely cut nostrils. Her mouth was her weak point ; the most skilful use of a lipstick could not conceal the fact that it was thin.

" Jill, you're lovely."

" I know, dear ; so Lanberg told me this morning."

"Damn the fellow; you're not going to that dolls-house?"

"I might. I'm going out to dinner now."

"I wanted you to come to Valtano's."

The combing arm stopped. Jill looked at him quickly.

"Come into a fortune?"

"No, but I haven't seen you for a week and I want to talk to you."

The girl hesitated.

"Valtano talks to me", she said. "And none too often. Think I'll come. Mind if I bring Kitty Lovelace?"

"Of course I mind", said Eustace with a grin. It would be all right now. Jill was hooked; greedy little devil, she couldn't resist good food.

"Pig. Well, all right; I'll tell Kit I've had a telephone message from a Viscount; she can't resist them. She's waiting outside, or talking to Holly. Hold hard while I get rid of her."

It did not occur to Eustace, any more than it had to Jill Paris, to look at this arrangement from the point of view of the girl whose evening was being spoilt. They lived for themselves; not for other people. Eustace's spirits, always volatile, had jumped up again at the prospect of a dinner with Jill. His week's absence, coupled with the growing fear that he was going to lose her, had made him acutely conscious of what she meant to him. She was lovely, but he had known other lovely girls. She was sometimes rather common—he hated that ' Big Boy ' stuff—but she was Jill and he loved her. As Mrs. Hollebone had said : ' it's personality that gets across '.

Dinner at Valtano's was an unqualified success. The little Italian had the priceless gift of being able to make each customer feel that his or her presence in his restaurant gave him real personal pleasure. He advised them what to eat and what to drink with the delicious food he provided. Price was of no moment ; it did not come within his consideration, and, to do Eustace justice, when he was giving anyone a good time he did not pay undue attention to price either.

Jill was in her best form, ' bubbling '—as Jack Point so admirably expressed it—' with wit and good humour ', affectionate, eager to hear what Eustace had been doing, and looking more lovely, the poor fellow thought, than ever. The thought of losing her . . . no, put it aside ; sufficient unto the day should be the enjoyment thereof.

After dinner the couple returned to Jill's flat in Pearl Street. Eustace had told Jill a good deal of the story of his cousins' deaths, but he had had the sense not to talk about his ' dreams ' in a crowded restaurant. Back in the little untidy sitting-room, lounging on a sofa with his arm round Jill, he let himself go. Not bothering to explain all the intricacies of the family tree or of the entailed estate, he told her that practically only one life stood between him and a fortune, to say nothing of a title. He did not know how much the fortune was, but it must be substantial ; there were engineering works, coal mines, subsidiary companies, and without any doubt a large holding of gilt-edged stock ; trust the hard-headed old north-countryman to tie his money up safe. Eustace had little conception of the effect of these last years of world-wide trade slump upon such businesses as Hendel Brothers ; the Baron's branch had always been stinking of money and he did not doubt that that was still substantially their happy lot.

Jill listened to the story with close attention. If Eustace had been looking at her face while he talked he might not have found its expression quite so attractive as usual. It was not only for good food that Jill Paris was greedy. But Eustace was not looking at anything except the future. Good food and wine had warmed his blood and sent his spirits soaring. In his present mood the Hendel fortune and title were as good as his ; much wishing can obliterate almost any obstacle—in the wisher's mind.

Jill Paris was of a more practical temperament. As soon as Eustace's flood of optimistic narrative had subsided she wasted no time in counting unhatched chickens but came straight to the point.

" Who is this man that's in the way ? How old is he ? Is he married ? " she asked.

" David ? Oh, he's something over forty. He was a Guardsman but he retired after the war and doesn't do anything now except hunt and shoot and that sort of thing. Pretty well off already, I should imagine, but nothing to what he's going to be—if he succeeds."

" But is he married ? Why hasn't he got any children—a man like that ? "

" Oh, he has ; he's got a son—Desmond. He's . . ."

" Got a son ? ! Then how can there be only one man in the way ? "

Eustace felt the girl stiffen under his arm. He gave her a squeeze.

" Oh, you needn't worry about Desmond ", he chuckled. " He's as good as dead ; cancer of the spine, poor devil. He can't have children and he's not likely to live much longer. Rather a bore if he did succeed, of course, because it would mean another set of death duties, but it would be bound to come to me after him."

Eustace was already beginning to forget some of the less convenient qualifications of Henry Carr's explanation of the entail.

" But mightn't there be more sons ? Is his wife alive ? Is she too old ? "

" No, that's the snag. She's dead. David might

marry again. There'll be a lot of women after him, Henry Carr says."

" Who's Henry Carr ? "

Eustace explained. His spirits had sunk a little, or at least sobered, at this reminder of awkward realities. The girl was silent for a time, for so long a time that Eustace gradually became aware of her silence and was beginning to wonder what was wrong when she sat up abruptly.

" Eustace ", she said sharply, twisting round so that she could look at his face ; " d'you want to go on . . . with me, I mean ? "

" My God, you know I do, Jill."

His voice was thick ; there was no doubting the sincerity of that answer.

" Then you've got to do something about it."

" About what ? "

" This cousin of yours—David. If you're right about all this fortune, you'll be mad if you let him marry again . . . and have children who'll cut you out. You're nearly on the rocks now ; I know that as well as you do and I'm not going down with you. If you want me you've got to get this money."

Eustace stared at her. His dark, rather handsome face was spoilt by the occasional weakness of his mouth, especially when he was taken by surprise, as he was now.

" But how can I ? How can I stop him breeding ? I can't . . ."

" You can if you want to. Put something in his tea—or whatever he drinks."

Eustace's jaw dropped.

" You mean . . . kill him ? "

" Of course I do."

Eustace stared at her. It was only what he had thought himself, in the train and on the shore, but it sounded so much more terrible when spoken aloud, in this calm way—so much nearer to reality.

For a minute the two continued to look into each other's eyes. Then something, perhaps a realization of beauty—of the utter impossibility of losing it—seemed to break through Eustace's hesitation. With a gasp that was almost a cry he pulled Jill down to him and covered her face with hot, eager kisses. The girl responded, then pulled herself away ; her eyes were shining brilliantly, excitedly.

" What's the title ? " she asked.

" You little devil ", laughed Eustace, pulling her towards him again.

With a quick movement of her hand she tweaked the end of his bow tie.

" Celebrate ", she said.

CHAPTER VI

INVITATION

IT is one thing to come to an excited, hot-blooded decision ; quite another to set about cold-bloodedly planning to carry that decision into effect. So Eustace Hendel discovered in the weeks that followed. He was not handicapped by scruples ; his upbringing had provided him with no principles other than those of self-preservation and self-interest. He was not a coward ; he was quite prepared to face the risk of discovery and punishment which the decision involved. Although there were elements of weakness in his character, as was evinced by his volatile spirits and the ease with which he could be led by a stronger personality, there was a streak of obstinate determination in his make-up which would keep him to a disagreeable task once he had started on it. It was rather in the practical difficulties to be encountered that Eustace's troubles materialized.

He had one great asset. He was—or had been— a doctor, and he had a working knowledge of drugs, if not of the rarer homicidal poisons. He also knew the precise whereabouts of the vital spots of the human body. A lay murderer, however determined,

might have considerable difficulty in locating the
exact position of carotid artery, jugular vein, liver,
or even heart, as targets for his knife or bullet ; a
doctor would work under no such handicap. A
doctor possessed, too, ways and means of obtaining
poisons which were not available to the layman, at
any rate without great risk. There were books, too,
which most doctors possessed ; unfortunately
Eustace had sold his, with his instruments, when
he came into Mrs. Fotherwaite's money in 1926 ;
now he had perforce to hunt round second-hand
bookshops in order to find a Holt's *Medical Jurisprudence ;* it would have been easy to get a copy
from a medical bookseller, but it would also—
Eustace thought—be unwise ; avoiding them, he
had some difficulty in finding the book he wanted,
and at last did go to a second-hand shop near the
Euston Road which had been largely patronised by
medical students in his young days. Still, that was
twelve or fifteen years ago ; nobody would recognize
him now.

Having bought his copy, Eustace set himself to
run through the possibilities. Broadly, he thought,
they amounted to five : shooting, stabbing, ' the
blunt instrument ', strangulation, and poison. Each
had its advantages and very definite disadvantages.
Strangulation might be ruled out straight away ; it
was impossible to imagine any circumstances in
which an able-bodied man like David Hendel would

allow himself to be strangled or smothered, even in his sleep—unless, of course, he was first drugged, and in that case poison or stabbing would be much simpler.

Shooting was a fairly common form of homicide, but it was noisy and therefore dangerous. Eustace had no idea how to get hold of a silencer and even doubted whether such things existed outside the realms of crime fiction. He had not got a pistol, and that again was difficult to get in these days without running a risk of subsequent identification. He had a shot-gun. To stage a shooting accident seemed the only possible form of fire-arm homicide which was open to him—and what chance was there of his ever being in a shooting party with David Hendel?

Stabbing ; now, for a doctor, that had its attractions ; knowledge of anatomy gave him the vital spots of the body ; with that knowledge so little force was needed, without it a layman might hack and stab and do no fatal harm. Besides, what better weapon was there than a surgeon's knife ?

' The blunt instrument '—the battering in of a skull or more scientific fracturing of its base, had certain obvious advantages over its rivals. It was much commoner than either shooting or stabbing and so should be easier to stage in a way which might point to rough-house work, not to a planned murder. The weapon could be any heavy object found on the spot and so much less easily traced to an individual. It provided the best opportunity for surprise ; an attack—one blow—from behind. With his surgical knowledge the actual weight and direction of the blow presented no problems.

All these methods, however, postulated one condition : proximity to the object of attack. That clearly was going to be a fundamental difficulty. How was he going to get near enough to David to have any chance of making a personal attack upon him ? He was in the worst possible position to do so ; if he had known him intimately he might have stayed in the same house with him ; if he had been a stranger he could have got near him without attracting attention ; as it was he was neither one thing nor the other and any attempt to get near David, except for a momentary, casual meeting, would merely arouse suspicion.

There remained the method of poison. By that means alone was it possible to kill without approaching the victim. Difficult as it might appear, it was just possible to send poison by post, or at any rate to ' lay ' it in the absence of the taker. In some circumstances, of course, homicide by poison would be absurdly easy. Living continuously in the same house with a person, for instance, would give a man with knowledge every opportunity of putting him or her out without incurring any suspicion at all. Or if the victim were an invalid, or a hypochondriac, with a fixed habit of taking medicines or special foods, there would be ample scope for 'laying' poison without ever being in the presence of the taker. But was it likely that a healthy-looking devil like David took medicines or health-foods, other than occasionally? And what chance, again, was there of ever living in the same house with him? One chance perhaps; that Blanche might one day invite them both to stay with her in the new home which she was to make. And from that chance even Eustace turned.

So far, then, there had been nothing but a gradual elimination of impossibilities, with no compensating emergence of a feasible method—unless one counted poison by post, a thin chance. Dispirited, Eustace toyed with the idea of chucking the whole business, but here his streak of obstinacy came into play; he would not admit to Jill that he was beaten; at any rate not till he had made a really determined effort to carry out his declared intention.

Jill herself displayed characteristic self-control and detachment. She was quite prepared to give Eustace a fair chance to recover his position with her, but nothing less than success would do; she yielded to his wishes in so far as not joining Lanberg's 'Cosmopolitan' company was concerned, but she kept her name on the agent's books for a suitable engagement with a more reputable manager and even went so far as to accept a cabaret engagement for the autumn season. Eustace was angry and anxious but, being unable to repeat his Valtano treatment, he was helpless. For the time being . . . until he had got rid of David.

Of course David's death did not end the matter. Apart from the boy, there was still the old man, Lord Barradys, alive and kicking and only slightly eccentric at ninety. That type of man often lived to a great age, which might mean another ten years before the title and property came to him, Eustace. But once the succession was assured there would be no difficulty about raising the wind. Quite apart from money-lenders, the banks themselves would be ready to advance on such security. That swine Isaacson would be tumbling over himself with eagerness to arrange a new loan, and on very different terms to the present one. Damn the fellow, he could whistle for it. And that reminded Eustace that the money-lender had not repeated his attempt to serve a writ on him; surely that must mean that he had ' smelt the wind ', had realized the possibility of Eustace succeeding and was not anxious to antagonize a possibly valuable client.

Eustace's spirits bounded up as the idea developed. No doubt that was what it was; the fellow had regretted his dirty behaviour and was lying low, waiting to see how the wind really did blow. Surely this was the psychological moment to turn defence into attack, to go boldly and demand a fresh loan, on the strength of his prospects.

The idea had no sooner come into his head than he put it into effect. Putting on his tidiest suit of clothes, Eustace walked round to Jermyn Street and entered a door nearly opposite the Piccadilly Arcade. The house was an old one and there was no lift, but it was clean and well kept ; neat black and white plates indicated the occupants of the first two floors ; the tenants of the higher flights did not so advertise their location.

Walking up to the first floor, Eustace rang the bell of a door marked ' S. Isaacson, Private Banker '. It was opened by a neatly dressed girl who asked him to take a seat in the little waiting-room while she took his name. Eustace fully expected to be kept waiting, as a mark of disapproval ; he was agreeably surprised when he was shown into the principal's room at once. Isaacson rose and bowed him politely into a chair. The money-lender was unmistakably a Jew, but he was far removed from the popular caricature of his type. He was a small, clean-shaven man, with grey hair and gold eye-glasses. He allowed very little expression to appear upon his face, and when he talked his small, well-shaped hands remained quietly folded in front of him.

" I am glad to see you, Mr. Hendel ", he said. " I was hoping that you would call after my letter to you of July 24th."

" Couldn't manage it ", said Eustace casually.
" Had to go down to my cousin's funeral in Devonshire. I stayed there longer than I expected."

" Ah, yes. And you were perhaps too busy to
acknowledge the letter."

" Not too busy, no, but I had no immediate
suggestion to make, so there seemed no object in
writing."

" And you have now a suggestion ? "

Isaacson's tone remained quiet, almost un-
interested.

" Certainly I have. The whole position's altered."

Eustace tried to give an air of confidence to his
words.

" I am glad to hear it ", said the Jew quietly.

" I imagine that you saw about my cousin's
death ? "

" Mr. Howard Hendel's ? Yes ; a very tragic
affair."

" And his son too. That's altered things a lot."

" You have perhaps received a substantial legacy ?
May I congratulate you ? "

" Legacy ? No. A beggarly fifty quid. But of
course my expectations now are considerable. I
want a new loan on the strength of them."

Mr. Isaacson permitted himself a slight raising
of the eyebrows.

" A new loan ? On what security, Mr. Hendel ? "

" Why, dammit, man. I've a very good chance of

succeeding now. And what's more ", he added hotly, irritated by the other's quiet indifference, " what's more, you know it perfectly well. Why else did you withdraw your writ ? "

Isaacson gave his shoulders a faint shrug.

" I think it had its effect, Mr. Hendel ", he said. " I do not wish to carry things to extremes if they can be avoided, but you had ignored two letters from me and I gathered the impression that you did not think I was in earnest. It was necessary to show you that I was. As I say, I think you now realize that."

Eustace felt rather nonplussed. He had the sensation of striking with a club at a quick-footed man armed with a rapier.

" Well, anyway ; what about things now ? I could do with five hundred for a year, but not of course at anything like the rates you charge me on the present one."

" But I do not understand, Mr. Hendel. You speak of your prospects of succeeding ; succeeding to what ? The peerage ? "

" Yes, of course. David Hendel's only got one son and no wife. After them, I come."

" But a peerage is no security for a loan, Mr. Hendel, unless it is accompanied by estate, either real or personal. Unless you have some proof that you are likely to succeed in that respect, I fear that the position is hardly altered."

" But I know . . ."

Eustace stopped abruptly. It had suddenly flashed across him that he was doing an incredibly stupid and dangerous thing. If anything happened to David and he succeeded to the estate and suspicions arose, Isaacson might come forward and say that he, Eustace, had been expecting to succeed. Too late now to undo what he had done, but it would be wiser to say nothing about his knowledge of the entail.

" Well, I mean to say ", he went on lamely, " it must make some difference that there are now only two people between me and the peerage, instead of four. Halved the odds, hasn't it ? "

" Hardly that, Mr. Hendel ", said the money-lender quietly. " It makes a slight difference, yes, but not a substantial one. You forget, perhaps, the possibility of re-marriage on the part of Captain David Hendel, even though the life of his existing son may regrettably not be regarded as a good one." (' Damn these money-lenders ', thought Eustace, ' they know everything about everybody '.) " On the strength of this slight difference I am prepared to extend the existing loan for a further year on the same terms and I shall not press for an immediate payment of the outstanding instalment of interest, but beyond that I regret that I cannot go."

He rose to his feet, and Eustace instinctively followed suit, feeling that he was being dismissed.

The wind was out of his sails, however, and he walked out without further protest.

It was at least something to be relieved of the immediate pressure of the debt ; before the next instalment of interest fell due something might have turned up. Still, that was a very negative form of comfort ; the actual, concrete situation was just as serious as ever. He was living above his income, and even at that could not find enough money to keep Jill ; his earnings from play were falling off, undoubtedly because it was becoming more and more difficult to find pigeons and, without proper rooms, to tackle them under suitable conditions ; finally, he was in debt to a money-lender and could not even meet the interest on the loan.

Oppressed by gloomy thoughts, Eustace decided that a drink might cheer him up, especially if he could find some cheery soul to drink with him. As he was near Piccadilly Circus he turned into Julian's American Bar and looked about him. To his disappointment, there was no one whom he knew ; gloomily he wedged himself into a corner and ordered a double ' Julian's Dream '. This insidious cocktail comprises a variety of ingredients known only to Julian, but its basis, like that of nearly all other reputable cocktails, is gin, and, however you may conceal it with soft essences, a double gin is a notable corpse-reviver. By the time that he had drunk it and had a talk with ' Henri ' and exchanged

witticisms with a young lady on his left and ordered
another and drunk that, Eustace was seeing things
in a different light. His immediate troubles had
faded into the background, his future prospects
were golden, his courage and spirit were soaring ;
he would go straight back to his rooms, settle on a
plan of action for putting that . . . David out of
his way, and then take Jill out to dinner. A real
cracker ; Valtano's or anywhere else she liked.

Leaving the better part of a green note behind
him, Eustace emerged into daylight, felt momentarily
dazed by the roar of traffic, revived under the touch
of fresh air and set out for Bloomsbury. A slight
haze accompanied him, but he knew his way
sufficiently well not to be worried by that, and in
due course he arrived home. Going straight up to
his sitting-room, he pulled Holt's *Medical Jurisprudence* out of the drawer in which he had sufficient
discretion to keep it, and sat down in his armchair.
As he did so, he noticed a letter addressed to him,
propped against the clock on the mantel-piece. He
did not often get letters, but when he did, this was
where Mrs. Drage put them. It was a bore, and
rather an effort, having to get up again, but the
effect of Julian's Dream was still sufficiently
enlivening to make him curious.

The envelope was thick and prosperous-looking,
the handwriting, though unknown to him, was
obviously that of a man and not of clerical type.

Eustace tore it open, pulled out the large, four-folded sheet and began to read. As he did so, his jaw dropped and he stared in blank amazement at the paper in his hand. Pulling himself together with an effort of concentration, he read as follows :—

> Clarge Hall,
> > Market Harborough.
> > > 14 *Aug.* 35.

DEAR EUSTACE,

I am afraid that in my early start from Coombe I forgot to come and say good-bye to you and thank you for coming down to Howard's funeral. It is a long time since we met before that and it seems a pity that we shouldn't know each other better. I am wondering whether you would care to come up to me for a week's stalking next month ? I have got a small forest, Glenellich, on the west coast, north of Mallaig. The lodge is only a small one but you won't mind that ; it is fine country and first-class stalking. I suggest Sept. 2nd to 8th ; deer are well on and they will mostly be clean by then. There is plenty of high ground— it runs over 3000'—and of course they'll be on it then, so I hope you've got a good pair of lungs. I can lend you a rifle and a glass if you haven't got them. Of course, you may hate stalking ; I'm afraid there are no grouse, but there's a small river with sea trout and one or two lochs, so bring a rod if you like to.   Blanche is coming up then and probably one other woman.

I hope you'll be able to manage it.

Yours,
David Hendel.

CHAPTER VII

THE MOURNFUL CRY

FOR some time Eustace Hendel sat staring at the letter in his hand. He blinked his eyes and shook himself, almost ready to believe that he had drunk too much and was dreaming. The thing seemed quite incredible; for a week or more he had been racking his brains to discover how he could possibly get within striking distance of David Hendel, and here was the fellow, who had never before shown one glimmer of friendliness to him—had, on the contrary, been freezingly rude only a fortnight ago—here he was actually inviting him to come and stay !

Eustace dropped back into his chair with a loud bark of laughter. God, if the man only knew ! Talk about offering your cheek to the smiter ; this chap was holding out his throat to be cut !

Not for a moment did Eustace experience any compunction, any change of feeling towards his cousin as a result of this hospitable letter. He gave David no credit for it. It was perfectly clear what had happened ; the penultimate sentence showed that. Blanche, bless her heart, had been talking to David, had told him that he'd got to show a little

71

decent feeling towards his relations ; had probably
twisted his tail for his damn rudeness down at
Coombe. No doubt David thought a lot of Blanche,
everybody did ; no doubt he hadn't liked to oppose
her wishes so soon after . . . well, obviously he
would do anything within reason to please her.
Probably she was up at Clarge now ; it would be
the natural place for her to go to.

In a way Eustace regretted that Blanche would
be there when . . . he did what had got to be done.
It would be pretty unpleasant, of course, and a bad
shock for her, coming on top of her husband's death.
Still, it couldn't be helped. It was an opportunity
that simply couldn't be let slip. This wasn't any
change of heart on the part of David ; it was just
an act of more or less obligatory politeness ; once
his visit was over Eustace felt that it was any odds
against his being invited again ; he had no delusions
about that. All right, damn him ; there wouldn't
be any need for a second invitation. David had
made his false step ; he was for it.

Feeling truculent and excited, Eustace threw his
Holt on to the sideboard and, not stopping to change
into evening dress, took his hat and went round to
Pearl Street. Jill was in her sitting-room, curled up
on the sofa with an Edgar Wallace, the carpet
beside her littered with cigarette ash. She greeted
him with a lazy smile, which quickened to interest
as she saw the expression on his face.

"What's up, darling? You look pleased with yourself."

She made room for him on the sofa and after kissing her eagerly, he put David's letter into her hand with a triumphant: "What d'you think of that?" Jill read it quickly.

"Who's Blanche?" she asked, with the feminine knack of finding the point.

"Cousin. Wife of the man who was drowned the other day."

"What's she like?"

Eustace laughed.

"Lovely woman. Tall, fair, perfect figure, lots of money, 'and one that adores me'."

Eustace was no student of Shakespeare but he knew his 'Twelfth Night'.

"Damned liar", said Jill calmly. "How old is she?"

"About my age", replied Eustace untruthfully, "but what does it matter? The point is that now I can get at the chap."

Jill looked at him sharply.

"You really mean to?" she asked.

"Of course I do. I told you I was going to."

Jill looked at him steadily, taking a long pull at her cigarette.

"I didn't think you'd got the guts", she said calmly, watching the smoke trickle from her nose.

Eustace flushed angrily.

73

" I don't know why you should say that ", he declared. " I've been working out all possible ways of doing it, and I'm going to do it. The great difficulty was how to get near him ; now that's out of the way."

" How are you going to do it ? "

" I haven't settled yet ; it will depend on local circumstances ; probably a hypnotic or one of the Vegetables."

" Vegetables ? What *do* you mean ? "

" Vegetable poisons. But it will really depend on what I find out about him. If he's taking medicine of any kind of course it may be simpler to work on that ; a lot of people take hypnotics nowadays, though he's not the sort you'd expect to."

Jill Paris looked at her companion with a surprise that was tinged with admiration.

" But, darling, how do you *know* about all that ? "

" How do I know ? Why I . . ." Eustace checked himself abruptly. He had never told Jill that he had been a doctor ; never told any of his London friends. Some ridiculous idea that a purely idle life was more distinguished, more gentlemanly, may have been at the back of his mind. In any case it would be wiser now to keep quiet about it, even to Jill . . . unless he was forced to tell her.

" Oh, I've been reading a book about it ", he said casually. " Damned interesting."

" I daresay it is, but I don't believe you can learn

anything from books. Anyhow, how could you get hold of the stuff ? I should have thought an accident would be safer." Jill picked up David's letter and glanced at it. "What's this about a rifle ? What's that for ? "

"Stalking. Deer-stalking. Stags, you know."

"I thought you hunted them with dogs."

"So they do in some places—Devonshire, f'rinstance. But in Scotland you stalk them with a rifle."

"He doesn't say anything about Scotland."

"Yes, he does. Oh well, he says 'the west coast', that means Scotland. Anyhow, he says Mallaig."

"Never heard of it ", said Jill. "But look here, my lamb, if there's going to be shooting with rifles, isn't that the way to do it ? Couldn't you shoot him by mistake ? "

Eustace had never done any deer-stalking and knew remarkably little about it, but he had an idea that indiscriminate shooting, where one member of the party might get in the way of another's bullet, was hardly in the picture. It was not like ordinary shooting, where people were scattered about all over the place. At least, he imagined it wasn't. Still, it was worth thinking about. Presumably there were books about deer-stalking, just as there were about other sports . . . and other ways of killing people.

" Well, anyway, let's go and eat ", he said, pulling Jill on to her feet.

The girl stood for a minute, holding him by the lapels of his coat, looking up into his dark, handsome face as if trying to find something she had not previously known was there. Then with a quick tug she pulled his face down to hers, kissed him passionately on the lips, and with a little laugh ran into her bedroom, where he heard her singing cheerfully as she brushed her hair.

With unwonted restraint, Jill refused to allow Eustace to take her to an expensive restaurant. She pointed out that this trip to Scotland was going to cost money, that neither of them had any to spare, and that if it did all that was hoped of it then would be the time—and the means—for feeding gloriously whenever they wanted to. With some relief, Eustace agreed. They went to the Café Royal, had an excellent dinner, drank German beer, met several friends and finished the evening on the best of terms with themselves and the world at large.

On the following morning Eustace spent several more hours hunting round second-hand bookshops, with very little success. Books on deer-stalking were, he found, rather rare, while second-hand copies were, if anything, more expensive than new books. Eventually he took himself off to Hatchard's, where he found works both old and new on the subject, and finally bought a copy of Sir Hugh Fraser's *Amid the High Hills*. After luncheon he retired to his armchair and was soon deeply absorbed in what was evidently a fascinating subject. So enthralled did Eustace become that he found himself actually looking forward with keen anticipation to having a stalk himself, and he had almost forgotten his real object in buying the book when a chapter entitled ' A Stalker's Peril ' brought it back to him with a rush. As he read the account of the accident to the Fannich stalker, Duncan, Eustace felt excitement mount in him ; his heart beat fast, thumping against his side, and as he finished the chapter he threw the book down and, jumping to his feet, paced eagerly up and down the room.

As was usual with Eustace Hendel, his excitement carried him along in a burst of such unreasoning optimism that all difficulties melted away before his triumphant approach ; then, as he suddenly came up against the inevitable snag, his spirits suddenly dropped and his plan fell to pieces. So he went on for an hour or more, alternating between hope and despondency, but at the end of that time the faint structure of a workable plan had formed in his mind. It depended upon conditions which might never exist ; his ignorance of deer-stalking made it impossible for him to know whether they *could* ever exist, but if they did. . . .

At this point it occurred to Eustace that he had not yet answered his cousin's invitation, so he betook himself to his club, and on the Jermyn's distinguished note-paper, thanked David for his invitation, which he was delighted to accept, regretted his ignorance of the art of deer-stalking and his pleasure at the prospect of initiation, looked forward to meeting Blanche, and asked for instructions as to reaching Glenellich.

As he sealed up what he believed to be an excellent letter, friendly but not servile, Eustace congratulated himself upon his foresight in sticking to the Jermyn ; it would have been deuced awkward to have to write to a fellow like David on common note-paper with a written address—and such an address. That brought to his mind a question which had not previously occurred to him ; how had David known where to write to him ? Obviously that settled the point, if there had ever been any doubt about it, that it had been Blanche who was at the bottom of this invitation ; Eustace had given his address to Blanche and to no one else. No need for compunction, then ; no qualms about abusing a hospitality that was so obviously enforced.

During the next fortnight Eustace did what he could to perfect a plan that must to a great extent depend upon local circumstances beyond his control. So far as his own part in it was concerned he had no doubt of his ability, given the opportunity, to carry it into effect. A steady hand, the requisite knowledge and skill, and a certain cold-blooded determination in the face of very awkward circumstances—all these he had or could supply with such a reward in view. As to the risk, the very audacity of the plan should put it beyond suspicion.

Every day Eustace spent an hour in a first-class shooting gallery. A steady hand is the first requisite of good marksmanship, and though Eustace's hand was not now as steady as it had been when he was a practising surgeon it was good enough ; once he had mastered the art of squeezing, instead of pulling, the trigger, he advanced to a very tolerable degree of proficiency ; at least, he thought, he would not make a fool of himself in front of that superior cousin of his.

In the matter of clothes, he took counsel of an elderly member of the Jermyn Club, who overheard him discussing the subject with George Priestley. Fortunately he still possessed a couple of shooting suits, one of them of a sufficiently nondescript greeny-yellow to be suitable for the hill ; the other, definitely louder, would do for off days. He also had nailed shoes, and all he had to buy was a light mackintosh ; he had no intention of getting soaked to the skin and then lying for hours in a piercing wind on the tops—if he had got so to lie, he would lie dry. Other requisites, such as rifle and telescope, would have to come from David. He had no rod.

and as he had never been a fisherman he did not intend to bother about that part of the invitation.

The descriptions of climbing and crawling which he got from the books he read rather perturbed him. He was in no sort of condition and had never walked a yard if he could avoid it. He rather fancied that there was trouble ahead for him in that respect but it would have to be faced.

In due course arrived a second letter from David, written this time from Glenellich, giving him his itinerary and telling him that, though stags were still in velvet, heads appeared to be pretty good; interesting, no doubt, but Greek to Eustace.

On Sunday, 1st September, Eustace left King's Cross by the 7.30 p.m. express, seen off by Jill Paris and treating himself to a first-sleeper on her advice.

" You never know who mayn't be on the train ", she said. " You don't want to make a wrong impression for a start."

Nobody that Eustace knew was on the train, though several of the names on the typed lists displayed on windows of the first-class sleeping-cars were familiar to him from the pages of the sporting and society press; so, curiously enough, were some of those on the third-class lists, though these were of the type which appeared more often in the letter-press than on the picture pages. Too excited at first to sleep, Eustace wondered whether his extravagance was going to be worth the money, but he presently realized that the grey streak under his window blind was daylight and not moonshine, while on raising the blind he saw that the train was running through a country of grand heather-clad hills and tumbling streams. He wondered where they had got to; his watch showed a little after seven, and just as he was dropping off to sleep again the train pulled to a standstill and he heard the plaintive cry of a Highland porter: " Crrianlarrich. Crrianlarrich." Then, in a momentary silence, the echoing cry of a bird : " Curlew. Curlew."

With a sudden nervous shiver Eustace pulled the blankets round him and tried to sleep again. But sleep would not come. Something in that mournful cry had touched a nerve and a wave of depression flooded over him. In the cold light of morning there came to him the full realization of what he was going to do. Murder! Brutal, cold-blooded murder of a relation and a host. There was no blinking it. And under the eyes, almost, of a woman whom he cared for and who had just been through a terrible tragedy of her own. A horrible, cruel deed, if ever there was one.

With a shiver of repugnance Eustace buried his face in the pillow. He tried to recover the golden dreams of a rich, titled future that was to repay him for one horrible moment; to conjure up the clear, lovely face of Jill, who would be his for ever. They would not come; they were misty, unreal, meaningless. Only this horror that lay before him was real. He would have given, he felt, almost anything to be freed from this nightmare, this horrible alternative : on the one hand poverty, loss of Jill ; on the other, murder !

Across the dark flats of Rannoch, past the Black Corries of Glencoe, the train ran on.

CHAPTER VIII

G L E N E L L I C H

BREAKFAST and a burst of sunshine through the morning mist brought Eustace to a more normal frame of mind. He remained oppressed by the horrible cloud which hung over the immediate future, but he determined to go on at least until he had made a preliminary survey of what his plan entailed. Up to the very last moment it would not be too late to turn back—that was one of the beauties of the plan.

As the train ran westward from Fort William Eustace came more and more under the influence of the beauty which lay on each side of him. The serene waters of Loch Eil, the sloping hills which guarded Cona Glen, the sweeping corries which sheltered the Cameron deer, the thin silver streak of Loch Shiel, each more lovely than the last ; then, bursting suddenly on the view, the wide expanse of the sea, the great Atlantic Ocean itself, calm now but capable of lashing itself at short notice into a seething whirlpool of angry waves as it hurled itself past the isles and beat up the narrow Sound of Sleat ; calm now, cradling flat-topped Eigg, superbly profiled Rhum ; and last, as the train swung north towards Mallaig, there came to Eustace his first view of Skye, the grim pinnacles of the Black Cuillins, one of the glories of the world.

Sobered, almost cleansed, by this feast of beauty, Eustace Hendel sat still and silent even after the train had pulled up in the little terminus at Mallaig. He felt small and insignificant, his affairs unimportant, trivial. A porter opened the door of his carriage and he stumbled out, cramped after so much sitting. The platform was a bustle of activity, the centre of interest being a ' family coach ' which had been picked up at Crianlarich, bringing a party of tall men and fair women from Wales. The porter shambled off towards the van and a red-haired young giant in a blue jersey greeted Eustace.

" Will it be Misterr Hendel ? " he asked, his voice rising on the name.

" Yes. Are you . . . are you from . . . ? "

Eustace was relieved of his mackintosh and handbag.

" Jock will be bringing your trunk down to the launch. If Mr. Hendel will come this way."

Obediently Eustace followed his guide, feeling helpless in a strange, almost a foreign, land. The little port was seething with life, as it did only twice or thrice in a week ; the herring fleet was making ready for sea. At the end of the week it would return and the bustle be even greater ;

occasionally a storm would drive it to harbour in mid-week ; at all other times the little town slept, baked in rare sunshine, drenched in driving rain, or wrapt in thick swathes of mist. Now the sun shone, strong men rolled slowly to and fro in great thigh-boots, buxom girls carried gear and kit-bags, gulls wheeled screeching overhead. In the tiny harbour, tucked up against a flight of wooden steps, lay an open launch, about thirty feet long, white and graceful, a red ensign hanging limp from its staff in the stern.

Glenellich, on the mainland, is approachable only by sea ; so much David had told in his second letter. No road, no beaten path even, approaches it from inland and that, in these days of hikers and youth hostels, is one of the forest's greatest assets. There are moments when this isolation has its drawbacks, periods—sometimes weeks on end—when the raging seas make it impossible for any small boat to live in them, any larger boat to approach the shore. At those times the few, scattered habitations of Glenellich and kindred places are cut off from doctor, mail, and all but their own growing and stored necessities of life. Not that that worried the natives ; they had their ministers or priests, their local midwives ; their wants were simple, their hardihood inexhaustible. But to the visitors from England or America who occupied the shooting, fishing, or stalking lodges for a few weeks or months, such times might mean real discomfort and distress.

. But all this Eustace was not to know. The sea now was calm, the launch rode on it like a floating gull, the sun shone, the young boatman was strong and capable ; life, but for that dark cloud, would have appeared very easy and pleasant.

" Nice launch ", he said, uncertain of the degree of sociability expected under the circumstances.

" Aye, she is that ", replied the boatman, laying a hand affectionately on the engine-cover. " She'll take in a bit of water in a sea, though."

The porter appeared on the quay above them and handed down Eustace's trunk as if it had been an attaché case.

" Ye'll mind the bit cording for Mrs. Mackie, Donald ", he said, acknowledging Eustace's shilling with a jerk of the hand.

" I will that. Will ye tell Mr. Shand the Captain hopes to send him a haunch tomorrow or next day. I missed him about the station just now."

" He's away to Fort William to see the guidwife in the 'Firmary, puir body."

" That'll be bad, Jock ", declared Donald with a shake of the head. " She'd no go in for a trifle."

The porter shook his head and glanced up at the sky.

" It's moving round ", he said. " Ye'd best be off, Donald."

Already a slight stir was visible in the hitherto
still water of the harbour. Donald cranked a handle
and the engine burst into stuttering life. As it
moved gracefully forward Eustace slipped on his
mackintosh ; there might be a little spray if the
boat went fast, no point in getting wet.

" There's an oilskin under the seat, sir ", said
Donald, nodding to the stern where Eustace sat.

" Oh, this is quite all right, thanks ", said Eustace
confidently.

" She'll maybe take in some water presently ",
said Donald, but made no further attempt to
persuade Eustace into the thick black oilskin,
though he put one on himself. During the hour
and a half that followed Eustace learnt some
elementary lessons about the west coast of Scotland.
He learnt that a headland apparently within a
stone's throw is usually a mile or more away ; he
learnt that a launch, apparently rushing so swiftly
through the water, takes six or seven minutes to
cover that mile ; that the next headland, after a
further half hour, is just as far away as it was
before and that few headlands are less than five
miles apart, and that there is always another round
the corner, and then another. He learnt that what
seemed to him an imperceptible change of wind
could work a mill-pond up into a respectable roll
in a few minutes, and a tossing, white-capped ocean
in half an hour ; that a small open launch can be

hurled up and down, from side to side, like an eggshell and not go down ; that a man's stomach that turns queer at a slight roll in a steamer can stand anything in an open launch ; that the Scotch are an imperturbable and silent race ; that landing from a small boat on to a narrow stone jetty in a sea is a ticklish job. He learnt these and several things about himself that surprised him ; he was a very frightened man and at the same time a very brave one. He was glad, God, how glad, to get his foot on dry, firm land.

He was greeted by Blanche Hendel who, clad in tweed skirt and jumper, came down to the jetty to give him a hand.

" David's on the hill ", she said. " Have you had an awful doing, Eustace ? It did come up suddenly."

The lodge lay within a stone's throw of the sea, sheltered from the south-westerly gales by a head-land which formed a small natural harbour. Behind rose a thick belt of fir-wood and above and beyond that the heather and grass-clad slopes of the mounting hills. The lodge itself was a small stone building, severely simple, with a little cluster of corrugated iron outhouses. The accommodation, as Eustace presently learnt, consisted of two living rooms, a large gunroom, four best bedrooms, one bathroom, two servants' bedrooms, and various offices. The staff comprised one man-servant and two maids, with Donald, the boatman, lending a hand with shoes and lamps, as well as acting as supernumerary ghilly on occasions. The man-servant, Harding, and Donald slept in one of the outhouses. In addition there was a stalker, McShail, whose house was high up the glen, in the heart of the forest, and a young ghilly, Ian Cameron, who lived in the tiny village whose scattered houses bordered the shore of the little bay.

Eustace was astonished at what seemed to him the meanness of the whole affair. He had expected, if not actually a 'Scottish baronial' castle, at least a substantial stone house, with plenty of bathrooms, a full staff, and considerable comfort. For a rich man like David to live in such squalor, even for a month or two, seemed to him incomprehensible. His opinion of the ex-Guardsman sank considerably, with a compensating rise in his own self-confidence.

The sun had come out again and Blanche suggested 'lunch outside', which Eustace found to consist of pickings from a cold sideboard, eaten on a hard bench just above the shore. Blanche, who as the wife of the eldest son must have been accustomed to even higher standards of living than David, seemed to take it all as quite natural and even appeared to enjoy it. She talked to Eustace of the forest, the fishing, the stalker; told him that David had killed 'a narrow six-pointer for the larder' yesterday and was taking Joan Hope-Fording out for her first stalk to-day. Blanche herself had not yet had a stalk and was not sure that she wanted to kill a stag, though she was doing some rifle shooting and had accompanied the others on the hill the previous day.

" I couldn't manage two days running ", she said with a laugh. " It's frightfully hard work. Joan's as hard as nails ; she hasn't turned a hair. I wonder what you'll think of her, Eustace ; she's very good-looking and very nice, I think ; rather *too* masculine for my old-fashioned ideas perhaps, but I think David likes that."

Eustace wondered whether this remark had any special significance, but before he could pursue the subject Blanche had changed it.

" David wants you to try the rifle you're going to use ", she said. " I'll take you along to the range. Then we'll take the dogs for a run and after tea we might try for a trout, or a mackerel if the sea's gone down enough."

The ' rifle range ' was the foreshore, the target a large brown stag crudely painted on a rock. Eustace soon found that shooting under these conditions was a very different thing to hitting a black bull's-eye on a white ground in a sheltered gallery. Even at a bare hundred yards the brown stag had an uncanny way of fading into its background when looked at over the sights of the rifle ; even with Blanche's advice to ' follow up the foreleg till you see brown ' he found it very difficult to be sure that he was on

the heart and not the large expanse of belly behind
it. A rock was digging into his stomach, one elbow
would not fix itself on the uneven ground, grass in
front of him, blowing in the wind, distracted his eye.
To his bitter disappointment he found that in ten
shots only two bullets had ' killed '—straight through
heart or liver, two had grazed the belly below the
heart, one the spine above it, one had gone clean
over the top, while four were well back in 'the
guts'.

"David doesn't like those ", said Blanche ; " he
can't bear wounding stags. Those four shots will all
mean that the stag dies, but it would probably go a
long way first and suffer horribly. That's why I'm
not sure that I want to try. Let's go on practising."

A pot of paint was produced from behind the
target rock, the starred white splotches painted out,
and the practice went on for an hour or more, to the
annoyance of the wheeling seagulls and the frenzied
excitement of the spaniels, who had escaped from
their kennels and had to be forcibly restrained from
' retrieving ' the victim of every shot. Blanche shot
steadily and well, with an occasional wild shot that
missed the target altogether and once even the rock ;
Eustace's shooting improved as he grew more accustomed to the conditions, so that in his next ten shots
only two were slightly off the line. He became absolutely absorbed and could hardly tear himself away
for the walk, but even this hateful pastime was

changed to a pleasure by taking a glass and learning to use it. Naturally so early in the season most of the deer were on the high ground, which was hidden from them by the foothills, but they did manage to pick up one lot of hinds on the low ground ; it was fascinating to see the tiny brown objects emerging into the definite forms of living animals as his glass settled on them and his eye steadied and grew accustomed to the focus.

At six o'clock the stalking party returned, Miss Hope-Fording on a pony, David Hendel walking beside her. At some distance behind followed a second pony led by the ghilly, Ian, and bearing the body of a stag, while the rear was brought up by the stalker, old McShail, smoking a charred pipe and carrying the rifle in its cover reversed over his shoulder. David was wearing an old tweed jacket, patched knickerbockers of a different suit, and a dilapidated cap of yet a third neutral colour. His shirt was open and the ends of his coat sleeves turned up. Joan Hope-Fording was also in knickerbockers, but of a newer, smarter appearance. She was a tall, handsome girl, with auburn hair, brown eyes and flashing white teeth. Her voice was loud and confident ; she had killed her first stag, a nice ten-pointer of about fifteen stone—and naturally had a good deal to say about it. She took very little notice of Eustace, who was not attracted by her. David greeted him pleasantly enough, though without any

obvious enthusiasm. He too seemed chiefly occupied
with the prowess of his Diana.

After dinner, which consisted of mackerel, venison,
and cheese, the women retired to the sitting-room
and David, pushing the port towards Eustace, began
to expand. To the latter's intense surprise, the old
Coldstreamer was evidently intensely proud of his
forest. He had been, he said, infernally lucky to get it
when old Rodstein had crashed in the Wall Street
slump ; it was only a thirty stag forest, but the feed
was good, there were magnificent corries, a permanent herd of its own, and in a westerly or north-
westerly wind the cream of the bigger inland forests
drew up into it. He did his own stalking as a rule,
old McShail was really a watcher ; he could only put
out one rifle at a time, save at the end of the season
when the deer came down on to the low ground, or in
certain winds when it was possible for a second rifle
to work the far side from the sea. The house was just
right and there were no neighbours to bother one.
He hoped Eustace would enjoy himself.

All this was not said in a breath ; in fact it lasted
Eustace through three glasses of port, at the end of
which time he was seeing the place in a different
light from that of his first impressions and was
beginning to wonder whether he would ever be able
to persuade Jill to face such discomfort if . . .

David's slow, drawling voice went on, but Eustace
was hardly listening to it now. His thoughts had

turned to his own affairs and in his new-found confidence he wondered that only a few hours ago he should have felt such depression and doubt. A forest of his own ! He would improve the house, of course, and have a proper staff, but it looked like being grand fun !

CHAPTER IX

DEATH OF A STAG

WHY well-to-do people have beds in their shooting lodges which are so hard and lumpy that the scullery-maids and pantry-boys would not be asked to sleep on them at home is a mystery beyond comprehension ; so at least it seemed to Eustace Hendel as he tossed and turned throughout a troubled night. It was with no great eagerness that he equipped himself for the hill on the following morning, but it was at least with relief that he heard that the two women were going to spend the day sea-fishing. That would at least give him the chance of discovering whether the conditions he needed for his plan were likely to arise or not. David's remark about 'doing his own stalking' had filled him with optimism, but it remained to be seen what became of McShail and Ian when the stalk began.

At 9 a.m. Ian appeared with the two ponies, on which David and Eustace mounted. McShail would be at his house, away up the glen, whence he would have spied a great part of the ground. They had not gone far when Eustace felt he would give anything

to get off and walk; he had never before encountered a deer-saddle and its broad, hard span was
torture to his unaccustomed legs. However, David
was jogging stolidly on ahead, the covered rifle
across the saddle in front of him, while Ian strode
along a few hundred yards in the rear; better bear
the pain. The pony path followed the line of the
River Ellich up the glen, almost due east towards the
towering pinnacle of Sgurr na Gaillich; on their left,
to the north, rose Beinn Fhan, close behind the house,
a comparative pigmy of 2,300 feet; further on came
Beinn Rhoinn (2,900) merging its eastern shoulder
into the lower slopes of Sgurr na Gaillich (3,300).
South of the glen lay the long even ridge of Beinn
Meall-Dubh, its highest, eastern end 2,500 feet.*

After riding some four miles at the slow, exhaust-
ing jog of the deer-ponies the party reached the
stalker's house, which lay at the junction of the
Ellich with a lesser stream running down from the
northern ridge of hills. Old James McShail was
reclining in the heather, his back propped against a
hummock, his stick erect before him, steadying the
hand that held his spy-glass at stretch. He was
looking up towards Beinn Meall-Dubh. As David
slipped off his pony he rose to his feet and touched
his cap.

" Morning, Jim. This is Mr. Eustace Hendel."
Again the old man touched his cap. Uncertain

* See map at end of book.

about the etiquette of the occasion, Eustace touched
his. David sank down in the heather beside his
stalker, casting a quick eye over the rolling clouds
above him.

" Just south of east ? " he asked.

" About that. I'm thinking she'll shift more into
the sun."

David nodded and relapsed into silence, his glass
slowly sweeping the northern slopes of Beinn Meall-
Dubh. Although he knew perfectly well that
McShail's glass had been over every inch of the
ground he asked no question. After seven or eight
minutes he lowered his glass.

" One small lot of stags below the crest at this
end. A single stag about half a mile further on ;
not shootable, I should say. Several lots of hinds all
the way along, lower down."

" Ay, and a big lot of stags on the near shoulder of
the Sgurr ", said McShail.

David raised his glass again.

" This side of the screes ? "

" Ay, just below the patch of sunlight."

" I've got them. Same lot that we saw in Coire
Dobhar yesterday, I should think. Pity to disturb
them unless we can help it. In this wind they might
go over the march. We'll have a closer look at these
fellows on the Beinn."

He pushed his glass back into its case and rose to
his feet. Eustace followed suit ; he had diligently

swept the ground with his borrowed glass and had seen not one single beast, stag or hind. Leaving Ian with the ponies the little party left the path and, moving southwards, were soon beginning to climb. David went in front, his long slow strides seeming to skim the ground without effort ; then came Eustace, trying to follow suit but quickly dropping to a shorter step ; in the rear McShail, the rifle, still in its cover, tucked under his arm. Each man carried a long stick and his glass slung over one shoulder, Eustace in addition carried a rolled mackintosh, also slung. For half an hour they climbed steadily, Eustace panting and pouring with sweat, but sticking manfully to David's heels ; his waistcoat was unbuttoned, tie discarded, cap in his pocket, sleeves rolled up, and he was just feeling that human lungs could bear no more when David slipped down behind a large rock and again pulled out his glass and pushed it round the edge. For a minute he spied, then pulled out a cigarette and lit it.

" See 'em, Eustace ? " he asked.

" Er . . . not yet."

David extended his stick towards a patch of bright grass on the hill-side about half a mile away ; there seemed to be a few lumps of brown rock on it. Eustace put up his glass and immediately there leapt into his view a group of stags seeming so close that he could have thrown a stone at them. Instinctively he dropped his voice.

"Grand", he said. "Are they . . . are they shootable ? "

David nodded.

"Two are. That's a nice ten-pointer, Jim ; good spread. Young stag, isn't he ? "

"Ay, I'd say so."

"Better leave him then ; may be Royal next year. The light beast would be better dead ; narrow head, six or seven pointer."

"Seven ", murmured McShail. "Ugly brute."

David closed his glass.

"Got your wind, Eustace ? "

"I think so."

The breathlessness that he was experiencing was probably excitement.

"Come on, then. Stay here, Jim, will you ? "

Eustace's heart gave a quick throb. So they were going on alone. Would there be . . .? But McShail's glass was still out ; he would be watching them.

Taking the rifle from McShail, David drew it from its cover, loaded it with five rounds, and thrust it loosely back into the cover again. Dropping back down the hill for a bit he then turned up again and was soon on the flat, bare top. As they came over the crest a burst of icy wind caught them, seeming to blow straight through their heated bodies. Eustace hurriedly buttoned waistcoat and coat and put on his cap.

" Quiet as you can ", murmured David. " Keep clear of the loose stones and for God's sake don't tap them with your stick."

With quiet deliberation he moved along the top. The wind was in their right eyes and Eustace found his beginning to water. After going about five hundred yards David edged towards the northern crest and again pushed his glass round a rock. After half a minute he beckoned Eustace up beside him.

" Have a good look at him ", he whispered. " That light brute. You can't mistake him, but don't let's have any bloomer."

Eustace put his eye to David's glass. The stags were only about three hundred yards away now and about a hundred feet below the crest. Through the glass every hair on their coats stood out clear. Eustace's heart was pounding against his ribs ; all thought of his sinister objective had gone out of his mind !

" I daren't go any further along the top," whispered David ; " they might get our wind. We must get in from here."

From here ? Did that mean shoot from here ? Without the glass the stags looked horribly small. But apparently it did not.

" Leave your glass and stick and that coat," whispered David, discarding his own stick. " We shall be in view most of the way. Keep behind me, your nose against my shoes ; keep absolutely flat ; pull yourself along with your arms. If I stop, stop. Only move when I move."

He slid forward over the edge and Eustace followed suit, feeling naked and exposed to the hostile eyes of the deer. But David slid quietly along, downhill and to the right. It was easier going than Eustace expected ; no doubt the ' down hill ' accounted for that. But they seemed to go on for ever . . . crash ! Eustace's nose banged against the hobnailed soles of David's shoes ; the stalker had stopped. Smothering a cry of pain, Eustace lay still, trying to quiet his heavy breathing. After what seemed like an age, but was probably not more than five minutes, the shoes moved forward again ; then the ground rose slightly and David, leaning round, beckoned Eustace to come up beside him ; they were out of sight. A tiny ridge was before them, covered with a few small boulders. David put his mouth to Eustace's ear.

" About eighty yards ", he breathed. " I'm going up to look ; when I beckon, come up on my right."

Sliding his rifle out of its cover, David wormed his way slowly forward and in a short time was peeping round a rock. His hand beckoned and Eustace followed suit till he lay beside his host. Slowly, cautiously, he raised his head. Not sixty yards from him stood a magnificent stag, its head bristling—to Eustace's eyes—with countless points. It was feeding quietly, oblivious of danger. The light stag was the furthest of the little group ; its tail was towards Eustace, presenting no sort of a target.

" Wait till he turns broadside. Take your time," whispered David, quietly sliding the rifle up into Eustace's hands.

Breathless with excitement, his heart pounding, the blood roaring in his ears, Eustace waited . . . and waited . . . and waited. A good thing really ; he was getting calmer ; his hand would be quite steady. A half turn ; Eustace's pulse jumped up again ; slowly he raised the rifle and . . . the stag sank on to its knees and lay down.

" Curse the brute ", breathed David.

Again Eustace's pulses quietened, his muscles relaxed. The stag lay, obliquely to the rifle, solemnly chewing the cud, twitching its ears, gazing out over the glen. Another stag lay down and another ; only the ten-pointer remained on his legs and he was feeding towards them ; it looked as if he might walk right on to them. Eustace felt an overpowering temptation to change his target, to take this magnificent beast, so near to him, such a certain shot. He glanced at David, but there was no response in that still, hard face. Minutes passed ; the ten-pointer was not a chain away ; it would soon be too late. One more glance at David ; he was frowning ; would he change his mind ?

" He's up ! "

Barely a whisper, but enough to switch Eustace's eyes back to the yellow stag. It was standing up; stretching its graceful legs, body broadside on. Up went Eustace's rifle, thud! thud! went his heart; the foresight swung round in narrowing circles; it was on the body now, behind the shoulder, no, in the middle of the ribs; curse it, why wouldn't it keep still?

" Quick! He's seen you."

The ten-pointer had thrown up his head, was staring direct at the rifle. Eustace's eyes wavered, back to the yellow stag. He *must* shoot, or it would be off. The foresight was still wavering, it was on . . . bang!

As the crash echoed across the glen, Eustace saw the stag's back hump up, its hind legs drop. It staggered, walked a step or two.

" Quick! Another."

Wild with excitement and anxiety Eustace fired again, without even waiting to drop his foresight into the V. The stag turned away, took a few steps, broke into a slow trot.

Bang! Bang!

His head completely lost, the unfortunate Eustace pumped lead after the disappearing stag, saw dust fly from under its feet.

" Stop, damn you! Give it me! "

David seized the rifle, but it was too late.

Bang!

The magazine was empty and before it could be

reloaded the stag, with its fellows, had disappeared round a spur. Only waiting to cram another five rounds into the magazine, David leaped to his feet and followed. Running with bent head he slowed as he reached the spur, peered over it, ran on. Panting behind him, Eustace caught up his cousin as he again slowed at the next small ridge.

"I'm awfully sorry, David", he gasped. "Is he wounded? Where . . . ?"

David turned a set, angry face over his shoulder.

"Keep behind me!" he snapped. "And keep quiet!"

Almost crying with humiliation Eustace dropped back. Indeed he found it almost impossible to keep running. He glanced down the hill. Five stags were galloping diagonally down it toward the head of the glen; the yellow one was not with them. Further on, the whole side of the hill seemed to be alive with galloping deer, hinds rushing in panic of the unknown; but no sign of the wounded stag. The cry of a curlew came from behind them; David checked and looked back. McShail was on the skyline signalling vigorously with his arm.

"He's gone over the top. Good for you, Jim", muttered David.

He ran up the slope, Eustace plodding behind. Again the piercing wind struck them, but Eustace was too miserable to heed it now. Standing behind a large rock McShail was pointing forward down the southern slope. Eustace stared down, saw a moving form.

" There he is ! " he cried, starting forward.

" Stop, you fool ! "

David seized his arm, almost pulling him to the ground.

" If he sees us now we shall lose him."

At that moment the stag stopped, turned its head from side to side, turned it far back to look up the hill direct at the hidden watchers, as if it were searching for pursuers. Seeing nothing, it stretched its neck still further, trying to get its tongue to the dark patch which showed far back upon its belly. Then it moved on again, heading straight into the wind. Presently it disappeared into a little gully ; instantly David started forward, running with astonishing speed and sure-footedness down the rocky hillside ; doggedly Eustace followed, determined not to fall out of the hunt, remembering only that he must stop when David stopped. The stag reappeared, nearer now ; the two men dropped. Slower now, faltering a little, but moving over ground too open to allow of close pursuit, the stag made down the hill. At the bottom it stopped, looked back, licked its side, staggered on a step or two ; its knees dropped and it lay down, head to wind, but turning from time to time to look back the way it had come.

Slowly, cautiously David crept nearer, followed closely now by Eustace. A hundred yards away they checked in a little hollow.

" Let me have the rifle ", whispered Eustace. " I won't miss again."

" No ", said David curtly. " He's nearly on the march. Stay here."

Sullenly Eustace obeyed, watching his cousin creep forward up the little slope, drop to his knees, then to his belly, draw his body forward a foot or two, quietly raise his rifle.

Bang !

For a moment or two David lay, still covering the stag with his rifle, then rose to his feet and walked forward. When Eustace joined him he had already taken off his coat and was unhitching a long knife from his belt. With a flutter of excitement Eustace watched him. David looked at him.

" You might get back up the hill and show Ian where we are ", he said coldly. " Then you can take the other pony and get home."

Eustace hesitated. God, how he hated the fellow ! Sneering, superior brute ; he could kill him now with pleasure. But that damned stalker and his glass. . . .

" Won't McShail fetch him ? " he asked, clinging to a faint hope.

" He'll be signalling him up now, but I want him here."

Signalling him up ? What did that mean ? Would he be out of sight ? and for how long ?

"Go on, will you ? It'll take the hell of a time to get him out from here. It's damn rough going for the pony—if it ever gets here."

David leant down and with a quick movement thrust his knife into the stag's throat. Dark blood gushed out. Eustace watched fascinated, hesitating. If only they had been alone—alone for the day. David put his foot on the stag's shoulder, pressed on it, trying to squeeze more blood out of the neck wound ; but little came.

"Damn ; bleeding inside ; that'll spoil the flesh. Look sharp, for God's sake."

Angrily Eustace turned away. He wanted to help ; why could not McShail bring the boy and the pony down ? He wanted to see just what was done, but the fellow's boorishness made it impossible. Reluctantly he turned away, began to walk up the hill.

"Here, take the rifle, will you ; we may have to drag if the pony gets stuck."

Eustace picked up the rifle, thrilling at the sense of power—of deadly power—which the weapon gave him. How easy now ! He walked away, stopped and looked back. David was bent over the stag, skilfully running his long blade up the skin of the belly. How easy it would be from here ! Impossible to miss. But impossible to explain away under such circumstances. No, he must wait ; he knew just what was needed now ; the chance might come yet. He was not going to throw his own life away.

Climbing slowly up the hill he found McShail at the top, watching the slow approach of the pony. The stalker had a clutch of sticks, Eustace's glass and coat, the rifle cover. He handed Eustace his possessions without comment. Was there contempt in that cold grey eye, or was it philosophical detachment ?

" Captain Hendel wants you down there to help him ", said Eustace. " I'm to show Ian where you are."

" Ian could no' get the poany down without me ", said McShail. " The rocks are bad on that slope ; the Captain knows it well."

Eustace flushed angrily. Damn the fellow ! So he had sent him away just to get rid of him ! Didn't want his help or his company ! All right !

McShail took the rifle from him.

" I'll take that ", said Eustace sharply.

The stalker threw open the breech, ejected the four cartridges and picking them up put them calmly in his own pocket.

" Maybe it'll be better unloaded ", he said, handing it back.

Sick with anger and mortification, Eustace

watched the man turn to join the pony and ghilly,
leading the way down the slope towards the dead
stag. Eustace turned on his heel and strode down
the other side.

CHAPTER X

A STALKER'S PERIL

EUSTACE'S depression and resentment lasted all the rest of the day. He had got home early in the afternoon and found that the women were still at sea, so that he had plenty of time in which to chew the cud of his mortification. The sea-fishers returned in time for a late tea, full of eager enquiry; Eustace's tale was not an easy one for a man with an inferiority complex to tell. Blanche was sympathetic and consolatory, but Joan, secure in the assurance of her own prowess, was patronising; she was, felt Eustace, of the very kidney of David—the Etonian type that he most loathed. David himself, with the stag, got back only just in time to have a bath before dinner. He said very little about the day's stalking, made no unkind criticism of Eustace, was perfectly civil to him, but the unfortunate tyro felt that he could more easily have borne any amount of chaff, or even abuse; it was the air of superiority that he could not endure.

On the following day Eustace found that he was so stiff and tired that he could hardly move. He was glad to stay behind and laze while David took the two women out on the hill. They returned at

110

six, without having had a shot, but all three seemed very happy and pleased with themselves, a fact which did not make Eustace feel any more at home with them. On the following day David asked Eustace if he would care to go out with McShail; he himself must attend to letters and business that was accumulating. Joan Hope-Fording at once announced that she too had a lot of letters to write, and Blanche, realizing that Eustace would feel he was being 'left out', asked him if he would mind her coming too. Eustace eagerly accepted and thoroughly enjoyed his day, though he had no shot, refusing to take one at two hundred yards, which was the closest that McShail said they could get in to the stag they were after. McShail's quiet: "It's as Misterr Hendel pleases" might have made Eustace again suspicious if Blanche had not at once said: "I think you're perfectly right, Eustace", putting him on terms with himself and the world at large.

On the way home Eustace tried to find out from Blanche whether she too thought that Joan Hope-Fording was after David. Blanche was discreet, but Eustace had little doubt that his guess was right. It gave him a savage sense of satisfaction that what he was going to do—if he got the chance—would have the secondary effect of putting a spoke in that wheel. The trouble was that time was passing; here it was Thursday and he was due to leave on Monday ; he could hardly hope to have more than one more day on the hill with David, and how was he to be alone with him for long enough . . . ?

There were other possibilities, of course, now that he was in close touch with him, but none of them looked so good. On the previous day, when he had been alone in the house, he had taken the opportunity to examine David's room and had found no patent medicines or special foods that might be doctored, and how else could he ensure that David and only David took the stuff ? Or there were other forms of accident ; for instance, if they found themselves high up on Sgurr na Gaillich, above that precipitous face, it might be possible to stage something in a comparatively short unwatched spell. He would have to trust to something turning up.

Friday threw everybody's calculations out of gear ; mist came down early and lay on the hills all day, putting all thought of stalking out of the question. That left only Saturday for Eustace, and he felt sure that David would want to get the Hope-Fording woman another stalk that week ; she hadn't had a shot since Monday. It was not till bedtime on Friday night that Eustace realized that the weather had played right into his hands in a way that was little short of miraculous. As he lit the candles David announced his plans ; Joan and Blanche should go up the glen with McShail to-

morrow, Eustace and he would go round by boat
and try the northern slopes of Beinn Rhoinn and
Sgurr na Gaillich ; so long as there was no north
in the wind that would give both parties a chance
of a stalk. The girls would have McShail and Ian
and the two ponies ; if Eustace and he got a stag
they would easily be able to pull it down to the
launch.

Eustace got very little sleep that night. First
excitement and then nerves kept him awake. The
opportunity was to his hand ; he could have chosen
no more ideal conditions for his plan ; would he
have the nerve to carry it out ? It would require
nerve. For quite a long time the situation would be
most uncomfortable—at the very best. So Eustace
tossed and turned and woke in the morning
exhausted and depressed.

The wind was right, just east of south. McShail
would have the whole of the glen, all Beinn Meall-
Dubh, all the Sgurr except its northern slopes ; he
was sure to find deer. David and Eustace would
first spy Coire Bheach from the launch, and if there
was nothing there, move on to Coire Esdaile, at the
top of which or on Beinn Rhoinn there would almost
certainly be stags. The two men saw the pony
party off with many expressions of ' good hunting '
and then boarded the launch. They had thick
coats for the return journey ; after a sweaty day
on the hill, two or three evening hours in an open

boat strike chill. Donald was in charge of the
launch and the voyage was a silent one; David
was by nature not a talker, and Eustace, who never
felt at home with him, now added nervousness to
shyness.

The voyage to Coire Bheach took fifty minutes;
nothing was spied from the launch but there was a
slight swell, so David landed and climbed a foothill
so as to get a good look at the north-western slopes
of Beinn Rhoinn. There were stags almost on the
summit, but they were on the move, feeding over
the crest. David eyed the clouds and, returning to
the launch, consulted Donald; the boatman, whose
judgment of wind was seldom wrong, opined that
it would swing round into the west within a couple
of hours.

"Then we'll go on to Coire Esdaile and work
back", decided David, and on they went. The far
corry, stretching right up into the grim darkness of
Sgurr na Gaillich, was reached by eleven o'clock,
and the two men landed. In addition to their
usual impedimenta each carried a coil of thick cord
for pulling; David had the rifle in its cover slung
over one shoulder. Donald was to take the launch
to Mallaig to do some shopping; he would not be
back for five hours at the earliest, and was to keep
a look out for smoke signals anywhere along the
northern slopes.

The climb up Coire Esdaile seemed to Eustace

terribly severe and almost interminable. Actually it was less than half an hour before they reached a point from which a good view of both Beinn Rhoinn and Sgurr na Gaillich could be obtained. In silence the two men sat, backs propped against rocks, slowly swinging their glasses over the massive heights. To his delight, Eustace actually picked up a lot of stags on the Sgurr and eagerly pointed them out to David, whose only answer was a grunt. Finally the stalker condescended to explain his plan of action ; the lot of deer which Eustace had found contained some shootable beasts, but they were on a very rocky bit of ground ; to pull down from there would be no easy matter ; another lot on Beinn Rhoinn were just as accessible and there was a reasonably good grass slope all the way down to the sea ; they should be the objective.

There were several parcels of hinds about on the slopes they had to cover. One lot was circumvented, and passed by crawling up the bed of a tiny burn—a wet and painful process ; one lot deliberately ' put off ' by giving them their wind ; Eustace was too inexperienced to realize the skill of his host's leading. He felt much less excited to-day, partly because it was not his first stalk, but principally because he had grimmer business in hand ; he felt strung up, but cold and almost uncannily calm.

Once past the hinds the stalk was simple ; very

soon they found themselves lying within a quarter of a mile of the stags, calmly picking their beast. David realized the importance of choosing a stag which could easily be identified by his inexperienced guest ; it is all too easy—and regrettable—a matter to shoot the wrong one. As there was no shootable beast either much lighter or darker than the rest, he chose the nearest, an eight-pointer which should scale well over fifteen stone. Then the ' crawl in ' began ; it was not possible to get so close as on the previous occasion, but presently they were on a little ridge which offered a good position.

" Can you manage from here ? " whispered David.

" About a hundred and forty. Plenty of time."

Eustace nodded. He felt quite calm and steady. After waiting a minute or two to get his wind after the crawl he raised his rifle ; the foresight came straight to the spot behind the shoulder of his stag, rested there. . . .

Bang !

The animal lurched, plunged forward a few strides, and then stood swaying unsteadily on wide-spread legs.

" Neck, I think ", said David ; " better give him another, behind the shoulder if you can."

As he spoke the stag's forelegs buckled and it crashed forward on one shoulder and lay still. Eustace heaved a sigh of relief.

" Thank God ", he said. " I thought I'd bungled it again."

David laughed.

"He turned a bit just as you fired", he said. "Never mind; you've got him all right; he won't get up again."

They walked forward and stood looking down at the stag. A small patch of blood showed on the shoulder. The beast was not quite dead; an occasional gasping breath shook its body, but otherwise it lay quite still and its eyes were already glazing.

"Cut the windpipe, I think", said David; "smashed the shoulder too; wonderful how he stood up at all."

He tapped the stag's horn sharply with his stick; there was no sign of feeling.

"Unconscious. The knife'll do it."

He clapped Eustace on the shoulder.

"Good for you. Nothing wrong with your aim, but it went in at an angle because of his turning—just missed the heart but cut the windpipe. You'll have to be blooded."

Eustace started. His heart began to quicken now; the time was coming.

"I'd like . . . I'd like to gralloch him if you'll show me", he said.

David looked at him with surprise.

"Would you really? It's a messy job, you know. Got a knife?"

Eustace shook his head and David unhitched his own long knife from his belt and opened it.

" Coat off. Sleeves up ", he said, setting the example.

Eustace felt the point and edge of the knife on his thumb. Perfect. His eyes, if he could have known it, were glittering with excitement. David took hold of the stag's horns and pulled the head round, stretching the neck for the ' bleeding ' thrust.

" Just above the breast-bone ", he said.

Eustace took a step forward, struck his foot against a rock and stumbled against David, thrusting the knife into his groin. The unfortunate man staggered back.

" God ! You've stuck me ! " he cried. " Pull it out ! "

Eustace gave a sharp tug and the blade, which had not gone in very far, came out. A gush of blood spurted out on to his hand. With a groan of pain David sank back on to the heather, clutching at his knickerbockers.

" Oh Lord ! Oh David ! I'm . . . I'm frightfully sorry . . . what have I done ? "

Eustace was overwhelmed with delight at the success of his thrust ; he felt certain that he had severed the femoral artery, just at the junction of thigh and abdomen. It would be almost impossible to stop the hæmorrhage, even if he had wanted to. Completely confident and master of himself now, his acting was superb. Dropping his knife, he sank down beside his cousin and stared in horror at the flowing blood. David glared at him, white-faced.

" What the hell were you doing ? Here, we must stop this. Fold up your handkerchief ! Tear up your shirt ! Quick, man ! Bandages ! We must make a tourniquet somehow or I shall bleed to death."

With fumbling hands he tore open his knicker-bockers, thrust them down, then placed Eustace's folded handkerchief against the wound and pressed it tight. Eustace had wrenched off his shirt and, as he tore it into strips, David bound them tightly round his thigh. Eustace's fingers itched to do the job properly, but he could not help admiring the way this layman set about the work—these war soldiers knew too much. Still, the wound was too high up for easy bandaging with such inadequate material. His aim had been a shade too low ; his intention had been to sever the artery at the base of the abdomen, perhaps half an inch above the crease of the thigh ; then the abdominal muscles would have made it impossible to keep pressure on the artery. As it was, the wound was exactly on the crease, where bandaging, even with a tourniquet, was intensely difficult.

" Break the end off my stick and shove it through the bandage ; only a short bit. That's it, now twist it. God ! Now tie the ends above and below.

That's the best we can do. God knows if it'll stop
it. Or how I'll ever get down from here."

"I'll go and get help", said Eustace
anxiously.

"There's no one to get; the launch is the only
hope and it won't be back for hours yet. I can't
wait here alone. It might start again and I'm
getting weak. I might not be able to stop it. You
must stay with me. When Donald comes in sight,
light three smoke fires; there's paper and matches
in my pocket; collect bracken and heather and get
them ready. He'll put his glass on them and you
must semaphore. *Can* you semaphore?"

"No", lied Eustace. "I'm afraid not."

"I'll teach you. S.O.S. is all he'll want."

Cool and indomitable, the old Coldstreamer showed
Eustace the arm-positions for the three vital letters,
showed him how to make the smoke fires, sent him
for water, ate his own lunch, drank a little whisky
from his flask.

"That's all we can do for the moment", he said.
"God, Eustace, what were you up to?"

"I . . . I stumbled. I completely lost my
balance."

"It seems impossible. Why were you holding the
knife so high as to get me there?"

"I'm most frightfully sorry, David. I can't tell
you . . . I can never forgive myself."

David stared at him, a frown on his face.

" I can't understand . . ." he began, then suddenly collapsed in a dead faint.

Instantly Eustace leapt forward, thrust his fingers under the bandage and pulled apart the lips of the wound. He felt the warm blood well over his fingers. Gently he moved the leg, increasing the flow of blood. Suddenly David's eyes opened, stared at him. Taken by surprise, Eustace recoiled with a gasp. With an effort David sat up, looked down at his disarranged bandage, then back at Eustace, suspicion blazing in his eyes.

" God ! You did it on purpose ! You're trying to kill me ! You bloody murderer, if I could get at that rifle. . . ."

Eustace jumped back, picked up the rifle. But the effort had been too much for David ; he had fainted again. Eustace kept his distance, afraid to get into the grips of this desperate, dying man. He picked up the knife and hid it behind a rock. Time passed ; it was two o'clock. Again David opened his eyes ; as consciousness returned to him he looked at Eustace with a cold fury of rage, at the same time trying to press the tourniquet down into position. Eustace knew that a steady drain of blood must be going on now, that it was only a matter of time—an hour or two. But he could not face those fierce, implacable eyes ; he moved round behind David ; the dying man tried to follow him with his head, as if suspecting an attack from behind. Eustace walked over the crest and sat down, staring out to sea.

Now that the thing was done, reaction began to set in and he found himself trembling. It was an awful thing to have done. Accustomed as he was to blood and the horror of approaching death, he thought he would never get the look in David's eyes out of his mind. He couldn't face them again while the man lived. While he lived ? God, supposing he recovered ? In sudden panic Eustace sprang to his feet, crept back to the ridge to see. . . . David had disappeared !

With a stifled cry Eustace looked wildly round. Impossible that . . . ah, there he was, ten yards down the hill, lying on his face. He must have been trying to crawl down and have fainted again. Cautiously Eustace approached, the rifle in his hand. Could this be a trick to get him within reach ? No, there was no mistaking that look ; the man was out. Not dead yet ; there was a flutter in the pulse ; but it was very unlikely that he would ever regain consciousness. Taking the heavy body under the arms, Eustace dragged it back to its original position by the stag, arranged it as comfortably as possible ; examined the wound—yes, there was still a slight steady ooze.

Eustace looked about him. It was getting on for three ; Donald might be back before long ; he must tidy up before anyone came. In the first place, the stag ; he had forgotten all about it. Now he found that the poor beast had died without the aid of the knife-thrust that had found a different billet. Never mind ; a thrust must be made—a partial thrust—to support his story. That done, Eustace wiped his own fingermarks from the handle of the knife, clasped David's hand round it, let the knife drop beside him. He examined the ground and found smears of blood on the grass and stones where David had dragged himself along ; he obliterated them. That was all. He sat down to wait. Four o'clock came ; no sign of the launch. David's pulse still fluttered, but only a doctor could have found it now. 4.30. Ah, there was the launch, just coming round the point. In a minute Eustace had the three fires burning, tall columns of smoke rising, bending as they came into the wind. Through his glass he saw Donald reach for his own, direct it on the smoke. Eustace jumped up and signalled. S.O.S. . . . S.O.S. . . . went his arms. He saw Donald jump up, signal R.D., then swing the launch in towards the nearest point of the shore, drop anchor, leap into the dinghy and pull furiously for the shore.

As he watched the man come bounding up the hill Eustace realized that the crisis had come. Could he make them believe his story ?

" Ma God, sirr, what's happened to the Captain ? "

Panting and pouring with sweat, Donald stood

staring at the white still face, the blood-stained bandages.

"There's been a dreadful accident, Donald", stammered Eustace, real agitation now helping him to play his part. "He was just starting to bleed the stag when it struck out—drove the knife into his leg. It must have cut an artery or something ; we couldn't stop it bleeding."

Donald examined the bandage.

"Ye've made a fine tourniquet ; that should have done the trick. He's no deid ? "

"No, I don't think so, but he's fainted several times. I'm afraid he's very bad. We must carry him down."

With the help of the two sticks and the coats they made a rough stretcher, slung the rifle and glasses over their shoulders and made off slowly down the hill. Donald had picked up the knife, folded it and put it in his pocket. Fortunately the going was smoother, or their frail stretcher would not have stood the strain. It took them an hour to get down to the shore ; they lifted the stretcher into the dinghy and a minute or two later from the dinghy into the gently swaying launch, placing it on the floor. While Donald turned his back to start the engine Eustace bent down and felt for the pulse ; there was no longer even the faintest flutter.

CHAPTER XI

THE voyage in the launch back to Glenellich was a terrible strain upon Eustace's nerves. The sight of the dead man lying on the bottom of the boat, covered only with a tarpaulin, was bad enough, but it was Donald's persistent questioning that nearly drove him to distraction. Not that the boatman showed any sign of being suspicious ; he was merely curious and excited ; at their first meeting Eustace had thought him calm and imperturbable but now he talked incessantly, having to hear the story over and over again, airing his own theories, recounting the experiences of others—the ' accident lore ' of the west coast.

It was nearly seven o'clock when they got back to the little harbour, and to his dismay Eustace saw that Blanche and Joan, with old McShail, were waiting for them at the pier, the stalker scanning them through his glass. Suddenly Eustace realized what had happened ; the officious Donald had lowered the launch's red ensign to half-mast and McShail had instantly spotted it. The landing, the explanation of the accident, the carrying of David's body into the house, all these were a long-drawn-out nightmare to Eustace, who was already exhausted by what he had been through. Joan Hope-Fording was white and hysterical, Blanche much the calmer of the two, though she obviously felt the shock terribly. McShail was respectfully sympathetic, but full of technical inquisitiveness ; Eustace managed to put him off on to Donald.

It was Blanche who took charge of the situation. A doctor must be sent for, and as there was no telephone at Glenellich Donald would have to run across to Mallaig in the launch. At the same time the police had better be told. She did not know what Scottish procedure was or whether they had Coroners, but the police would deal with that. Eustace had better have a bath and some dinner before anyone started worrying him with questions. Eustace had already given her a brief account of the accident and was intensely thankful to be left in peace for a while. He lay for half an hour in a boiling mustard bath—without shirt and jacket, his heavy overcoat had not saved him from getting terribly cold in the launch—and gradually his nerves calmed down and he was able to think. He knew that he had a severe ordeal in front of him— the questioning that was bound to come from doctor and police—but he believed he could outwit them and the great, triumphant fact remained that he had done what he came up to do ; David was out of his path, and as soon as old Barradys and the invalid Desmond went their inevitable way he would reap his rich reward.

It was ten o'clock before they heard the sound of the launch returning. There was fairly bright moonlight and in it Eustace could see that there was a second, larger launch behind the Glenellich boat. In a few minutes two figures came ashore, one of them in police uniform. The other, a sturdy little man, at once approached Eustace and introduced himself.

" I'm Dr. Kennedy ", he said. " No doubt you'll be Mr. Eustace Hendel that Donald was telling us about. This is a terrible affair, sir. I have brought over Police-Constable Laing of the County Constabulary. You understand that there'll have to be an enquiry, of course. Everything will be done to avoid distressing you and Captain Hendel's relatives and friends, but there are certain inevitable formalities."

Eustace nodded to the policeman, and led the way to the gun-room, in which David's body was lying. The two men stood looking down at the tragic figure. Dr. Kennedy bent down and undid the tourniquet, which was still in position.

" You made a good job of that ", he said. " That would have stopped it if anything could."

" He showed me how to do it ", said Eustace. " He was wonderful."

There was an effective catch in his voice. He

really did feel admiration for David . . . now that he was dead.

"Ay, he would be. I know his sort. Donald told us what happened but no doubt Laing will want your own account. I'll make a short examination here, but of course there'll have to be a P.M. Just tell me this ; did the knife stay in the wound ? How far did it go in ? "

"I don't really know ", said Eustace. "I was a yard or two away. I saw him bend down to bleed the stag and the stag strike out with its fore-leg. David fell back clutching his leg and then I saw him throw the knife on the ground. I think he must have pulled it out."

Dr. Kennedy nodded.

"It looks like that ", he said. "It's a nasty wound with a blade that size, even if it isn't very deep."

By the light of his torch he carefully examined the wound, clucking his tongue as he did so.

"Severed the femoral artery at the base of the abdomen ; half an inch lower and your tourniquet might have saved him. Well, I can't do any more here. You'd like to hear what happened, I expect, Laing."

The constable pulled out a massive note-book.

"If Misterr Hendel will give me a full narrrative for ma reporrt ", he said.

Slowly, with long pauses while the constable

scribbled, Eustace told his tale, described shortly the voyage round, the stalk, the shooting of the stag.

" My cousin took off his coat to gralloch the stag ", he went on. " I was a few yards away, unloading the rifle. I saw him, as I told you, bend down to put the knife in its throat and as . . ."

" Half a minute ", said Dr. Kennedy. " Was the stag dead then ? I'm no deer-stalker myself ; I don't know what happens."

" I thought it was dead ", said Eustace, who realized that this was thin ice, " but apparently it wasn't, because as the knife pricked its throat it struck out with its foot. It must have been not quite dead."

" Not necessarily ", said the doctor. " There was a case in this country not long ago where a man was killed by a blow from an ox he was actually skinning. And I've even heard of a surgeon doing a post-mortem getting a slog in the eye from the dead man's arm."

He chuckled, quite unmoved by the presence of the body on which he was to do just such an examination tomorrow.

" Ay, I mind that slaughterhoose case ", said Laing. " And A've hearrd tell of a case just like this, of a stalker being wounded by a stag he was bleeding. Likely Jim McShail would mind who it was."

There was a step in the passage, the door opened,

and in walked the stalker, carrying the two rifles which he had been oiling. Dr. Kennedy winked at Eustace, as if to show what he thought of the coincidence.

" We were calling to mind yon case of a stalker who had just such an accident as this ", said Laing. " Do ye mind who it was, James McShail ? "

McShail methodically put away the rifles before answering.

" There was Angus McDonald o' Glenfarran that was struck in the face by a staag as he took hold of its fut ; he lost an ee. An' there was yon Adams up at Runie, a daft fellow. He put his blade into the ghilly's wrist."

" Na, na, James ; I didna mean them. There was a case away back, I've heard ma faither speak of it. A case like this where the staag strruck the knife into a stalker's leg."

Eustace was not sure whether to be pleased or anxious at this delving into the past. No doubt it was the case of the Fannich stalker that Laing had in mind. But McShail had not heard of it, and Eustace was allowed to continue his story.

" I saw the stag's leg jerk out and David stagger back. His back was slightly towards me. I saw him throw the knife on the ground and then collapse. I ran up to him and found him holding his hands against the wound. We bandaged it as best we could—as you saw, doctor—but we couldn't stop the bleeding. The launch had gone to Mallaig; I wanted to try and get back here for help but David didn't want to be left. We waited for the launch. He was gradually getting weaker all the time and he was unconscious before Donald got back with the launch. I think he was dead before we got him down; I couldn't feel his pulse at all when we got him on board. I'm afraid that's all I can tell you."

" And a very clear account ", said Dr. Kennedy. " If you don't want to ask any questions, Laing, I'd like to be getting home. I've got a confinement I'm expecting some time tonight."

Police-Constable Laing closed his note-book.

" I'll no ask any questions now ", he said. " The Inspector will be along in his car from Fort William tomorrow, and likely he'll be bringing the Procurator Fiscal with him. Maybe they'll have some questions to ask. Ye'll understand, Mr. Hendel, that we must take charge of the boady till the Registrar gives his certificate and that'll no be till the Fiscal's satisfied. We'll tak it along in the launch now and then it'll be ready for the post-morrtem tomorrow."

" I expect the Procurator Fiscal will bring a surgeon along from Fort William ", said Dr. Kennedy. " That's the usual practice. Of course, I shall be present."

" What about the staag, Mr. Hendel ? " enquired McShail anxiously. " Did ye gralloch it ? "

"No, I'm afraid I didn't. I was so taken up with my cousin. Besides, I don't know how to."

"T, t", clucked Jim. "That'll be good meat spoilt. I'll be along first thing the morn, but I doobt it'll be too late to save the meat."

"Na, na, James McShail; ye mauna touch it", declared the police-constable. "The *corpus* must remain *in loco* until the Inspector and the Prro-currator Fiscal have viewed it. I doobt it ought to be under police superveesion."

"I'll be up there first thing in the morning", said McShail. "If ye like, I'll watch over it till ye come. It'll be the Saabath, but the Meenister will no raise his voice against my doing that for the Captain."

"That's kindly, James. I must get back to Mallaig myself with the boady and to notify the Inspector. There's no other Constable nearer than Fort William. If ye'll mind the staag for me it will all be ship-shape for the Inspector and the Fiscal when they come along in the morning."

So it was arranged, and within a quarter of an hour the big launch had gone chugging off in the moonlight. Eustace and Jim McShail stood on the beach and watched it out of sight. The old stalker shook his head.

"I always told the Captain to approach a staag wi' mair caircumspection", he said. "'Tis a peety ye didna gralloch the beast ; 'tis a sad waste of guid meat."

*   *   *   *   *

On the following morning the launch returned at about half-past one, bearing P.C. Laing, a uniformed Inspector, and two gentlemen in plain clothes. The older of these two proved to be Captain Buchanan, Chief Constable of Inverness-shire, while the other, thin and clean-shaven, was the Procurator Fiscal of the district.

Once the necessary introductions had been effected, the Chief Constable and the Police-Inspector remained quietly in the background, leaving the task of interrogation entirely to the Procurator Fiscal. And very thoroughly he set about that task. Once again Eustace had to tell his story, and this time he realized that he was up against the critical phase of his ordeal. No easy acceptance of statements here, no slurring over of awkward facts, no chance of evading exact questions. A trained lawyer, Mr. Hannay was there to investigate the cause of death ; he was perfectly polite but he took nothing and nobody for granted. After half an hour's rigid cross-examination Eustace thought his story was unshaken—but he was not too comfortable about it ; the Procurator Fiscal gave no indication of his feelings. Having finished with Eustace, he proceeded to question Blanche, then Joan Hope-

Fording, Harding, Donald, and finally even the ghilly, Ian. Having spent nearly two hours over all this he announced that he was ready to go and see the *locus*. The whole party climbed into the launch and soon after half-past five they joined McShail beside the dead stag on Beinn Rhoinn.

It was here that Eustace was made to realize the astonishing thoroughness of the Scottish methods of investigation. Inspector Wainwright produced a camera; the dead stag was photographed from several angles; Eustace was invited to place himself where he had stood when David Hendel approached the stag; then he was asked to show David's attitude when the stag struck him, and was photographed in that attitude from the position at which he himself had been standing. Fortunately he had thought all this out before giving his description to Laing; if he had made a slip, if—taken in conjunction with the stag's position—David could not have been standing as he had described, the camera would have found it out. Then he showed where David had lain, where he himself had knelt when bandaging him. The ground was searched— Eustace thanked his stars that he had obliterated all trace of David's crawl downhill. The position from which he had fired was asked for; McShail had already found that and showed the spent cartridge case and even the slot of the stag where it had plunged on being struck, the marks of its few staggering strides before it fell. That produced technicalities about the effect of bullets upon various parts of the stag's body.

Finally, by the Procurator Fiscal's direction, the stag was gralloched by McShail, helped by Police-Constable Laing, who had been a ghilly in his younger days. The beast's lacerated windpipe was produced—and photographed! At this point Captain Buchanan took a hand. He had personal experience of deer-stalking, which the Procurator Fiscal had not. Eustace was questioned as to the actual movements of the stag after being struck by the bullet. Mr. Hannay expressed incredulity at the beast being able to remain on its feet for even a moment, let alone move an appreciable distance, with a smashed shoulder and a severed windpipe, but the Chief Constable assured him that such vitality in stags was not only possible but common. The stag, he said, could not have lived many minutes, but till it had drawn its last sobbing breath it would be capable of striking a blow in self-defence.

Eustace was intensely grateful for this unexpected advocacy. He was thankful that he had stuck to the literal truth regarding the stag's condition. If he had lied, or prevaricated over the effect of his bullet, he would have been found out for an absolute certainty.

At last Mr. Hannay was through, and McShail

and the constable, attaching ropes to the stag's head and fore-feet, began to pull it down the hill. The rest of the party followed ; as they approached the shore Eustace realized that he and the Procurator Fiscal were some distance behind the remainder. Mr. Hannay stopped to light a cigarette.

" I understand, Mr. Hendel ", he said, carefully burying the match in the earth, " that there are now very few male members of the senior branch of your family left ? "

Eustace felt his heart check.

" There's old Lord Barradys ", he said, " and Desmond Hendel—Captain Hendel's son. And there are sons by the female lines."

" Ah, yes, but they cannot succeed . . . to the title at any rate."

Who had been putting him up to this ? Not Blanche, surely. That Hope-Fording woman, it must have been.

" I'm not very well up in the family tree ", he said carelessly.

" And yet, if anything were to happen to Mr. Desmond Hendel, you would in due course become Lord Barradys."

" Is that really so ? A couple of months ago there were a whole packet of them. Extraordinary, isn't it ? "

In desperation, Eustace felt that recklessness was his only line.

" A most tragic business ", said Mr. Hannay quietly. " The father and son being drowned together. You weren't there ? "

Eustace stopped dead.

" What the hell are you getting at ? " he asked angrily. " Certainly I wasn't there. I hadn't seen Howard for years—didn't even know where he lived."

There could hardly be any mistaking the ring of truth in his words. In any case, it could easily be proved.

In silence they walked on. As they approached the launch Eustace asked :

" When'll the inquest be ? "

Mr. Hannay smiled.

" There are no inquests, such as you mean, in Scotland ", he said. " I am making the enquiry now."

Eustace stared at him.

" Then there is no . . . ? "

" No verdict ? No, Mr. Hendel, either there is a criminal prosecution . . . or there is not."

CHAPTER XII

It was a gloomy dinner that Eustace, Blanche and Joan Hope-Fording sat down to that Sunday evening at Glenellich. Blanche did her best to appear natural, but this was the second shock that she had suffered in a few weeks, and the close questioning of the Procurator Fiscal could have left her little doubt of what was in his mind. She did her best to let Eustace see that she herself entirely accepted his explanation of what had happened. It was otherwise with Joan Hope-Fording; the girl was morose and silent, spoke little, and never to Eustace. There could be little doubt as to who had been suggesting things to Mr. Hannay. As for Eustace, he was utterly exhausted after two days of incessant nervous strain. He was almost too exhausted to feel anxious—and Heaven knows he had good reason to be.

As he drank his third glass of port, after the women had left him, he thought over the day's events—and the more he thought the less he liked them. His story had not been shaken, he had not been caught out in any lies, but under the close scrutiny of the Procurator Fiscal it had worn extremely thin. There remained the undoubted fact that extraordinary accidents do happen, that there was precedent both for serious injury being caused by a dying stag and even for the actual severing of a femoral artery by a stalker's knife. This, coupled with the fact that there was, and could be, no direct evidence against him, made Eustace hopeful—after the third glass of port—that his story would, however reluctantly, be accepted by the authorities. It was a comfort to him at least to know that it was accepted by Blanche ; that being the case it was unlikely that there would be any public suspicion—the Hope-Fording woman could hardly draw attention to herself and her thwarted aspirations by spreading rumours.

So it was in a more cheerful frame of mind that Eustace went into the sitting-room. He found Blanche alone.

" Joan's gone to bed ", she said ; " got a headache. I'm rather glad ; I wanted a chance to talk to you, Eustace."

Eustace wondered anxiously what was coming. He didn't want another cross-examination.

" It's about poor David ", she went on. " I wrote to Desmond to-day and asked him what he would like done about the funeral. Personally I feel that as they haven't a family home—they've only been at Clarge a few years—and with all the delay and the post-mortem, it would be much best for him to be buried here. He loved Glenellich; it was the one place where he seemed to be natural; I don't want to seem to criticize my husband's family, but they were rather overbearing in some ways, both Howard and David. I never saw their father, but of course old Lord Barradys is too. Up here David seemed to drop all that."

Eustace thought that that was not his impression, but he was prepared to admit that he had not seen David under the most favourable circumstances; the chap had, at any rate, been decent yesterday when he did kill his stag.

"I quite agree, Blanche", he said. "Will Desmond be coming up here, d'you think?"

"Oh, no, he couldn't possibly stand the journey, poor boy. He lives most of the time in London, you know, so as to be near doctors and treatment. It's a terrible life for him."

"It must be, poor fellow. I've never met him. Do you think he'd care for me to go and see him?"

"I'm sure he would, Eustace. He's very lonely, I think. He's got a sort of superior nurse-companion; she's very nice but . . . he doesn't see many men. He writes, you know; he's rather a poet."

"What about David? I wonder he left the poor boy alone like that."

"Well, one can hardly blame him, Eustace. He couldn't bear London after the war; hunting and shooting and fishing—things like that were all he

cared for, especially after Beryl died.   He was always
very nice to Desmond but . . . I suppose it was
natural that he should feel disappointed ; he wanted
a son to do things with him.   I don't think they
understood each other very well."

Eustace thought there were probably not many
people in the world who ' understood ' others as
Blanche did.   She always had a good word for everybody—saw the best side of them.   That probably
accounted for his being asked up here—an ironic
twist !

" I hope they'll get through with that post-
mortem quickly ", he said.   " I don't like to think
of the poor chap lying on some cold slab in Mallaig."

Early bed that night and Eustace slept more
soundly than he would have believed possible on
that excruciating mattress.   The following day was
a complete blank ; nobody came near Glenellich.
The police had ' released ' the body of Eustace's
stag on the previous evening, after it had been
skinned and closely examined, and McShail spent
the morning cutting it up and distributing it, by
Eustace's orders, to crofters along the shore.   Joan
Hope-Fording had also killed a stag on Saturday
and this would be used in the house or for sending
away, though one haunch was spoilt by a bullet
that had necessitated quick action by McShail.
Eustace felt childishly pleased to hear the stalker's
account of how he had snatched the rifle from ' the

leddy' and dropped the stag with a neck shot just as it was disappearing over the sky-line.

On Tuesday came Police-Constable Laing, bearing the Registrar's certificate and asking for instructions about the body. In the mail-boat that brought him came a telegram from Desmond agreeing to Blanche's suggestions as to the funeral, and a further telegram from Mr. Christendome to say that he was coming north that night and hoped to arrive on the following day. Eustace was slightly perturbed at this prospect ; he remembered having made rather indiscreet attempts to pump the old lawyer about the family affairs.

However, when he arrived, Mr. Christendome was the embodiment of polite sympathy to Eustace ; evidently he had no suspicions at all. Fortunately Joan Hope-Fording had left on the previous day, her departure being unwept by either Eustace or Blanche. There was no further sign from the Procurator Fiscal nor from the police, save that Laing had done everything in his power to help with arrangements for the funeral.

David was buried on Wednesday and both Eustace and Blanche were touched by the way in which every man, woman and child in Glenellich came in ' decent black ' to see the laird laid to his last rest by the Presbyterian minister. Eustace was aware that he himself was the centre of a good deal of interest, but it was not hostile ; evidently in this quarter, at any rate, his story had been accepted without question ; no doubt the reminiscences of Donald, McShail, Dr. Kennedy, and Police-Constable Laing had helped to this end, and Eustace was grateful to the Chief Constable and the Procurator Fiscal for keeping any doubts which they might have harboured to themselves.

No other relations came to the funeral ; it was hardly to be expected that they would. Lord Barradys and Desmond were prevented by age and infirmity, Henry Carr telegraphed that he was alone in the office and could not get away for so long, for the rest . . . it was a far cry for any but the nearest to come to the west coast of Scotland. Eustace was the sole male representative, and he was conscious of a first-stirring of self-importance as he played his future part as ' head of the family '.

Harding, Donald, and the two maids, helped by Blanche, had been busy packing for two days ; on Thursday the whole party, including Mr. Christendome, left Mallaig at 2.15 p.m., reaching King's Cross early on the following morning.

Only returning to his lodgings to dump his luggage, Eustace hurried round to Pearl Street. Jill was still in bed, but she bustled out of it at once and in ten minutes was eating, in pyjamas and kimono, the breakfast that Mrs. Hollebone had obligingly prepared for them both.

" Quite like a married couple ", said the good-natured landlady with an affectionate smile at her pet lodger. " I can't think why . . . oh, well; there's them as knows their own business best."

Jill listened to Eustace's story with eager excitement and brushed aside his doubts about the Procurator Fiscal's opinion of the story.

" They'd never have let you come away like this if they really thought you'd done it ", she declared. " Why, they couldn't get you now if they wanted— not without an extradition or whatever it is."

Eustace laughed.

" Scotland isn't such a foreign country as all that ", he said, " even though it has got its own way of doing things. Rather a smart way, too, to my thinking ", he added with a grimace. " However, I daresay you're right. All the same, I shall keep a sharp look-out for being shadowed for the next week or two. And look here, my girl, no talking about this in public—Valtano's or anywhere like that."

Jill kissed him vigorously.

" Of course not, idiot. Never another word about it—from either of us. We'll just lie back and wait for the plums to fall. But talking of Val's, what about a spot of celebration to-night ? "

These were both good ideas and the celebration at Valtano's could be carried out without further thought—and was. As for the plums, all was now ready for them, but there remained the question of how to carry on until they actually fell. The £50 legacy from Howard had gone ; nothing else would come in until that poor chap Desmond actually passed out, and Eustace was uncertain when that was likely to occur. He would follow Blanche's advice and go round and see him—see for himself just what the position was. In the meantime money must be raised. With such a future before him Eustace did not intend to go on living in his present squalid manner ; in any case, something had got to be done about Jill, otherwise she would have to take an engagement.

There was, of course, his small stock of capital, from which he drew his only fixed income. With the future assured, or practically assured, that capital might now be realized and used for current expenditure until ' the plums ' came along. But . . . a streak of North-country caution in Eustace warned him not to part with his one sheet anchor. After all, to say that the future was ' practically assured ' was not *quite* the same thing as knowing, with good legal statements in black and white, that it was *absolutely* assured ; in any case, the period during which assurance must do duty for fact was an uncertain one—it depended upon the ' expectation of life ' of Desmond Hendel—and Eustace knew from experience that dying men often take an unconscionable time about their going.

No, it would be unwise to sell capital ; far better raise another loan. Now that David was dead

Isaacson would surely see that the security was
there. Other money-lenders had seen it, shrewd
fellows. On his return from Scotland Eustace had
found two letters awaiting him, offering to advance
any sum up to . . . the usual stuff, but the point
was that it was several years since any such offer
had been made to him ; these fellows had been
cute enough to spot the change in his circumstances.
They were the wrong sort, of course ; the letter-
writing, touting fellows with good old Scottish
names who charged scandalous rates of interest
and gave you no rope if things went a little wrong.
Nothing like Isaacson, who had been fair and decent
enough . . . up to a point.

From Isaacson, however, he had heard nothing,
rather to his disappointment. Well, he must go
round and see him ; that was all there was to it.
So thought Eustace, but it appeared that he was
wrong. Following his usual practice of acting
directly a decision was taken, he went round that
same afternoon—the Monday following his return
from Scotland—to Jermyn Street. He learnt that
Mr. Isaacson was engaged ; he would wait ; Mr.
Isaacson regretted that he was engaged all the
afternoon. Surprised and angry, Eustace banged
his way out of the office and down into Jermyn
Street. What the devil did it mean ? It was
impossible that the fellow could be engaged for the
whole afternoon, could not even do him the courtesy

of one minute's conversation in which an appointment could be fixed. No suggestion, even, of an appointment on another day. What was behind it ? Impossible that he could suspect. . . . Impossible !

None the less Eustace was worried as well as anxious as he turned into the Jermyn Club, ordered a double-whisky and picked up the evening paper. The double-whisky improved things. He strolled into the little bar—modern addition much frowned on by the older members—and ordered a dry Martini. Here was George Priestley, with others of his type, who greeted him with acclamation and definite signs of a desire to toady. George, of course, had spotted what was up, what his position was now. What was it he had said, that day the news of Howard's and Harold's death came in ? 'Two steps nearer the throne '; that was it, wasn't it ? Well, now he was another and much more vital step nearer. George would have realized that—and told his cronies. In any case, the very fact that he had been staying with David—a Guardsman—the very fact, even, that he had been deer-stalking, would send him up in their estimation.

Well, that was all pleasant enough . . . but just a trifle dangerous. He didn't want any talk about the prospects of his succession to the title ; he didn't want attention drawn to it. His conversation with the Procurator Fiscal on the subject had been unpleasant, decidedly awkward ; he didn't want anything more like that. Better keep quiet, keep out of the way, until in due course—not too soon, he hoped—Desmond died and he succeeded in a perfectly natural way.

In any case, pleasant or not, this sort of toadying wasn't going to bring him in any immediate shekels. Indirectly it might, of course, because it would probably lead to more poker-playing, meeting more of the right sort of young fellows from whom shekels could, without undue risk or difficulty, be extracted. That aspect of the position must be attended to, but in the meantime the wind must be raised, even if it only amounted to a hundred, or even fifty. For a small sum like that it wouldn't do any harm to go to one of those touting fellows who had written to him : ' Angus McPhamish ' or the ' British Loan and Mutual Assistance Society (Manager, J. Levy) '.

Preferring the titular pretentious to the pseudo-Scotch, Eustace wrote to Mr. Levy and in the course of post received a polite invitation to an interview ; the interview was so satisfactory and the terms so reasonable that Eustace found himself going a good deal further than he intended, eventually leaving the office with five hundred pounds in his pocket, which he promptly proceeded to deposit with a surprised but gratified banker of the established order.

After a further celebration Eustace and Jill proceeded to plan for the future. Eustace had said nothing about matrimony, had hardly given the

subject serious consideration ; Jill for her part was
too shrewd to start the subject at this stage ; that
could and should come later on, as opportunity
arose. For the meantime she was comfortable
enough where she was ; all she wanted was money ;
not a lot, she was not extravagant, had no urge for
jewels or a lot of expensive furs ; just enough to
make work unnecessary, some decent clothes, of
course, a good dinner and an evening on the tiles
every now and then ; a bit lazy, perhaps a shade
greedy—those were the only vices with which Jill
Paris could consciously debit herself.

Eustace's requirements, on the other hand, were
rather greater. A decent flat again ; that was what
he wanted, first and foremost ; it was really a *sine
qua non* if he was to have a chance of making any
money, quite apart from the question of comfort.
Not St. James's ; he had no idea of returning there
just yet ; that would be making himself too con-
spicuous, drawing attention to his altered circumstances just at the very time he didn't want to ;
Bloomsbury would do, but the real Bloomsbury,
not this edge of Finsbury where he now lived ; or
better still, something in the neighbourhood of
Covent Garden, handy but inconspicuous. Some
new clothes—couldn't afford to look shabby. A
man-servant. Live like a gentleman again ; that
was all Eustace asked, and it was not asking much
after all he had been through.

CHAPTER XIII

LORD BARRADYS

On the morning following his satisfactory interview with the Managing Director of the British Loan and Mutual Assistance Society, Eustace paid his promised visit to his cousin, Desmond Hendel. The boy lived in a flat overlooking Regent's Park; with—as Blanche had told Eustace—a Mrs. Toumlin, a nurse-companion, to look after him. It was Mrs. Toumlin who greeted Eustace in the small sitting-room into which he was shown. She was a tall, thin woman of about fifty, with kindly eyes and a gentle voice, but there was a certain tightness about her mouth which suggested to Eustace that she might be firm, even grim, on occasion. Mrs. Toumlin had been a hospital nurse, had married a doctor, and on the latter's death had been compelled to earn her living again, but she had had no difficulty in finding well-paid posts such as this. Her gentleness, combined with her trained skill and efficiency, made her an ideal companion for a sick person.

Eustace explained who he was and Mrs. Toumlin, who had probably heard of him from Blanche Hendel, showed no hesitation in talking to him about Desmond. He was fairly well at the moment.

His father's death had been a shock to him, of
course, but he had lived for so long outside the
world and the lives of other people that they were
probably less of a reality to him than they would
be to a healthy, normal boy, so that their lives and
deaths, their successes and tragedies, passed him by,
almost untouched, in this quiet backwater of life.
Desmond would miss his father, but the death would
have very little effect on his own life. Mrs. Toumlin
did not think he even contemplated any change,
whatever the material alteration in his position and
prospects might be. He was quite happy here, with
his books, his wireless, his own poetry, a few friends.
At the present moment he was out on the balcony
overlooking the park ; that balcony was one of the
reasons why the flat had been chosen ; facing
slightly west of south, it was ideal for an invalid and,
unless he was feeling too bad, Desmond spent most
of his daylight hours on it, enjoying the view and
such occasional sunshine as the climate allowed.

That one little sentence—' unless he was feeling
too bad '—was the only direct reference to
Desmond's illness, and Eustace did not like to ask
any pointed questions. It was a pity the boy was
out on a balcony ; to a doctor his bedroom would
have told a good deal more. Still, he could come
again another time, after dark. So Eustace followed
Mrs. Toumlin out on to the broad balcony and at
once all doubts about the future passed from his

mind. One glance at the pale, emaciated face of the boy lying on the bed was enough ; Eustace knew that he was in the presence of death, and of death hovering at no great distance away.

It was curious how quickly that first, unmistakable impression disappeared under the charm of Desmond Hendel's manner, the friendliness of his smile. Desmond was twenty now and sufficiently man of the world, for all his illness, to realize that visitors are often embarrassed in a sick-room, to know how to put them at their ease. As he talked to Eustace, about his father, about Glenellich—which he had never seen—about Blanche, whom he undisguisedly loved, his face lit up and Eustace saw no longer that mask of death but a handsome, obviously Hendel face, with none of the haughtiness that marred the elder branch of the family but with a softened, wistful expression that was infinitely appealing.

The two cousins talked together for more than an hour, chiefly about the Hendel family. Each approached it from a different, rather detached point of view and they found that their impressions had much in common. Apart from Blanche, Desmond was most attached to Henry Carr ; the solicitor came frequently to see him, especially in the summer when he snatched an hour or two to watch cricket at Lord's but always found a fraction of those precious hours to come and cheer up the young invalid ; he generally brought books or news of books, talked to Desmond of what was going on in the world, treated him as a man, naturally and without the scarcely-veiled pity which invalids find so hard to bear. He seldom announced his visits beforehand, for fear that some business, preventing him, might disappoint Desmond of a pleasure which both shared. Eustace was surprised to hear this version of a character which had struck him as self-centred, though hospitable and friendly enough.

Eustace went away, feeling really sorry that this nice boy, so brave and cheerful in spite of his suffering, would have to die before 'the plums' could come to Jill and himself. Thank goodness, nature would do that tragic work ; it would not fall to him. The removal of a disagreeable fellow like David had been unpleasant enough ; to do the same with Desmond would be . . . however, he need not bother his head about that.

When he returned to his rooms that evening Eustace found a letter in a sprawling, unknown hand awaiting him. The envelope was of thick, good-quality paper ; the impression it gave him was much the same as that made by that other letter which he had received only five short weeks ago, the letter by which his cousin, David Hendel, had signed his own death-warrant. And here—as he discovered on opening it—hardly less surprising, was a letter from David's grandfather, old Lord

Barradys, whom Eustace had never met and who had never previously shown any sign of being aware of Eustace's existence.

> Derrick House,
> Barradys-on-Tyne.
> *September* 18th, 1935.

DEAR EUSTACE (it ran)

I shall be grateful if you will put yourself to the trouble of coming North to see me. There are one or two matters which I should like to talk over with you. If you will let me know what day and at what hour you will arrive at Newcastle, my car shall meet you. As it is a long journey I hope that you will stay here for the night.

> Yours truly,
> Barradys.

Eustace felt himself flushing with excitement as he read the letter. Here was proof indeed that his position was changed, that he was now someone of importance in the family. Old Barradys had the reputation of being a hard, plain-spoken man, with very little use for polite manners or conventional family ties. Witness the fact that he had never before shown any sign of interest in Eustace's existence. But now, not only was he recognizing his existence, but doing so in an extremely courteous, hospitable letter. Things were moving! George

Priestley would know what interpretation to put on that letter—if he showed it to him—which of course he would not.

He showed it to Jill though, and she was not less pleased and excited than he was, urging him to catch the first train to Newcastle, telling him what clothes to wear and what to take—she would have packed for him if the Drages would have allowed her inside their house, which Eustace knew only too well that they would not. The trains to Newcastle were awkward; the journey was too short to be done comfortably at night; there was a 'sleeper' at 10.45 p.m. but it reached Newcastle at 5.10 a.m., an unconscionable hour. Finally it was decided that Eustace should travel in comfort by the *Flying Scotsman* the following Friday morning, arriving at Newcastle at 3.8 p.m.

It was a dull journey. Even the pleasurable pastime of making plans for a golden future could not fill those five tedious hours. A hunting man can often amuse himself by picking a line of country as the train flashes past meadow and stream and fence, but Eustace was no hunting man, for all his two horses at Bicester in bygone days, and in any case this was September and the country still 'blind'. As the hours dragged on the golden dreams of the future inevitably changed to uncomfortable memories of the past. Those four grim days in Scotland would not pass easily from any man's mind, even from the memory of so volatile a person as Eustace Hendel.

That cross-examination by the quiet, relentless Hannay would cling to his memory, thought Eustace, until his dying day. The whole story as he told it then, as it revealed itself under the questions, the reconstructions, the photographs of the Procurator Fiscal, had sounded so terribly thin, so suspicious ; it had seemed impossible that the police would accept it. And yet, they had taken no action ; here it was, a fortnight after the accident and, since the Registrar's certificate had been given, they had shown no further sign of interest in the case. The post-mortem must have borne out his story ; the Procurator Fiscal must have reported to whatever authority decided those things in Scotland that the case could be considered closed. Well, thank God for it ; it had been an anxious time.

The train drew up in York Station. Eustace looked at his watch—it was half-past one. On again, the twin towers of the minster gleaming in the afternoon sun. Another hour and there sprang into his view the one unforgettable sight of that two hundred and seventy mile journey, the superb mass of Durham Cathedral, the lesser profile of the Castle, perched almost in mid-air above the cañon of the river Wear. Twenty minutes later they were in Newcastle.

A smart chauffeur, in white collar and short coat,

greeted Eustace as he followed his porter out into
the porticoed entrance of the great station. A
Daimler limousine rolled him luxuriously through
the narrow streets, up the long hill, past the pits,
out into the open country north of the Tyne. In
half an hour he was being ushered into a square
stone mansion overlooking the river, through a
large hall, into a long book-lined room where a fire
crackled cheerfully in the big hearth.

His Lordship, said the sleek, black-haired butler,
begged Mr. Hendel to excuse him. He had been in
Newcastle on business all the morning and was now
resting. He hoped to meet Mr. Hendel at dinner.
In the meanwhile, would Mr. Hendel take tea ?
Mr. Hendel would, he thought, take a whisky and
soda. Left alone for a minute, he looked about
him, noted the solid mahogany furniture, the thick
velvet curtains, the prints on the dark red walls—
heavy perhaps, old-fashioned, much of it, but good,
unmistakably good. He regretted now, with this
superior butler, these silent, well-trained footmen,
that he had not had time to get the new clothes
that he had promised himself. His outer man was
passable, but his underclothing was definitely
shabby. Servants noticed these things ; were
inclined to judge a man by them. A bit undignified,
for the future. . . . Pity.

Eustace spent the next hour or two wandering
about the well-stocked, well-kept garden. There

was money here, money in every well-pruned fruit-
tree, money in the weedless paths, the long expanse
of glass, the golden vines. Eustace licked his lips
as he inspected it all. Whether Derrick House was
included in the entail he did not know, did not
really care ; he would certainly never live there
even if it came to him ; but the signs of wealth
were unmistakable ; no man in these days kept the
staff of gardeners that this perfection demanded
unless he was rolling in money, and that must be
reflected in the entailed estate.

Dressing for dinner, he felt a first qualm of
nervousness. What would this old peer, head of a
great business, autocratic ruler of a proud family,
what would he be like ? What did he want to talk
about ? He, Eustace, must mind his p's and q's ;
it might be important for him to make a good
impression. If the old man liked him he might, in
view of the position that was coming to Eustace,
be willing to settle something on him straight away,
enable him to take his proper position in the world
as heir presumptive . . . well, no ; not yet ;
Desmond was still that, on paper . . . as inevitably
the future head, should he say, of the Hendel
family. It was more than possible ; indeed it was
the obvious thing for him to do ; Eustace wondered
that he had not thought of it before. There was a
sparkle of excitement in his eyes as he walked down
the thickly-carpeted stairs and entered the library.

Lord Barradys was sitting in a stiff high-backed chair on the far side of the fire. He was looking towards the door and as Eustace approached him he hardly seemed aware of his visitor's presence ; he did not smile nor make any sign of greeting. Lord Barradys at this time was ninety years old ; he was a small man and was now slightly bent ; he had the hooked nose of all the Hendels, but his thin white hair and withered skin cancelled the usual identification marks of the elder or the younger branch ; his face was deeply lined, his hands thin and wrinkled ; only his grey eyes seemed alive and they were fixed now upon Eustace's face in a penetrating stare. Eustace held out his hand, muttered an uncomfortable : " How are you, sir ? " Lord Barradys did not at first appear to see the hand, but at last his own rose slowly, touched it, and fell into his lap.

" How d'ye do ? Had a tiring journey ? "

The voice was harsh, louder than seemed possible in that frail body. Eustace felt as if he were talking to an old mummy fitted with a mechanical voice ; it was uncomfortable, uncanny.

" Not at all bad, sir. Fine place you've got here."

Not quite tactful, that ; looked as if he'd been measuring up. Still, it was awkward, this, difficult to know what one should say.

Lord Barradys appeared to take no notice. A gong rumbled ; the butler entered the room, helped his master from the chair and gave him an arm, leading him across the hall and into a dining-room hung with full-length portraits of, Eustace did not doubt, Albert, Chandos himself, Bevis, and old Andrew, first Lord Barradys. The likenesses were unmistakable, the fair Hendels of the elder branch, no dusky cadets of Augustus's line sullied this room, only Eustace himself, sinking nervously into the great leather-covered chair at the heavy, gleaming mahogany table.

Dinner was an ordeal through which Eustace felt he would not pass again for untold gold. It was of full length ; clear soup, turbot, saddle of mutton, a trifle, angels on horseback ; rich, well-cooked, admirably served. Lord Barradys ate none of it ; he took what appeared to be some gruel from a silver bowl, some dry toast, drank half a glass of water, while the butler plied Eustace with sherry, hock and burgundy. Eustace tried his best to talk, not of the family—he hadn't the nerve to do that—but of such topics of the day as he had read about in the paper coming up. Lord Barradys' responses were occasional and often bore no relation to the subject mentioned by Eustace. He croaked out a sentence or remained completely silent, staring in front of him. Fortunately the continuous presence of the servants made the strain just endurable, their swift, silent service kept the thing going ; otherwise, Eustace thought, he must have screamed.

The table was cleared, fruit and nuts offered to and declined by Eustace, a salver of thin wafer biscuits laid before Lord Barradys, the large port glasses filled from a great cut-glass decanter, itself then placed carefully before the host. The servants, extinguishing all but the picture lights and the candles on the table, left the room. The old man, sipping his port, seemed gradually to warm into life. Eustace, giving up all attempts at conversation, watched him in silence, savouring the bouquet of the vintage wine.

"Cockburn '96", croaked the old man, though his voice seemed to Eustace already to have mellowed with the wine. "Ye're not drinking; fill that up."

He pointed to the decanter. Eustace filled his glass, made the conventional half-circle, and replaced the decanter. Lord Barradys, with an effort, lifted it and filled his own glass. For a time he sat, sipping, colour creeping into his withered cheeks. A second time the big glasses were refilled. Then Lord Barradys, shifting slightly in his chair, turned his grey eyes upon his guest. Eustace was startled to see how keen, how alive, they were now.

"So ye're Eustace, eh? Grandson of Clarence, son of that young rip, Victor."

The voice, too, was fuller, less creaking, than before.

"Ye've got the looks of both of them, the whole

rotten line. Loose mouth ; vicious ; I know you. Women, eh ? Wine, too."

He jerked his finger towards the decanter. Eustace, flushing with anger and embarrassment, stared back at him.

"I sent for you because I thought ye might be different. Times change, lines change, sometimes. But ye're not, ye're the same. Useless, vicious, good for nothing. And you'll be Lord Barradys, eh ? That poor boy, David's boy ; he's going, they tell me. They're all gone now ; only me and that poor boy left. After that—you."

The withering contempt in that last word made Eustace shrink back in his chair as if he had been struck. Instantly the old man leaned forward, striking the table with his thin hands.

"But don't think because ye're going to be Barradys that ye'll get Barradys's money. Don't deceive yourself, Eustace. Better for you to know now. The title you must have ; I can't prevent ye. But nothing more, nothing more."

He sank back in his chair, exhausted, the blood drained from his face. Eustace, seething with anger, not knowing how to deal with the old madman, watched him, wondering if he were going to faint. He looked so white and still, so lifeless . . . an anxious thought flashed into Eustace's mind. Good Lord, he wasn't going to . . . ? That would be . . . frightful, most damnably awkward. He leaned forward and pressed the electric bell which lay on the table in front of his host. The butler appeared, gave one quick look at his master, stepped forward quietly and gently raised him from his chair. Without another glance at Eustace, without a word, Lord Barradys tottered slowly from the room, clutching the butler's arm.

CHAPTER XIV

GEORGE HENDEL

EUSTACE saw no more of his host that night. He retired, considerably agitated, to the library, where later the butler visited him with an A.B.C., asking what train he would wish to catch in the morning. Much as he disliked early rising, Eustace chose the 9.15, feeling that he would do a good deal to avoid meeting that infernal old maniac again. At 8.45 a.m., therefore, he was rolled away in the stately Daimler, leaving behind him a superbly munificent tip ; his departure, he felt, might be in the nature of a retreat, but at least it should be dignified.

If the journey north had been dull, the return was depressing to a degree. After a night's sleep in an extremely comfortable bed, Eustace had been able to shake off the greater part of his agitation, was able now to convince himself that all that talk last night had been the bluff of an angry, disappointed old dotard, who, knowing himself powerless, wanted still to give an impression of omnipotence. Because it was perfectly clear from what both Christendome and Henry Carr had said that old Barradys was only tenant for life of the entailed estate; he could not dispose of it, one way or the other, whatever his

feelings and wishes might be. No doubt he had a
good deal of personal property which he would not
now leave to Eustace, whatever might have been
his original intention ; that was tiresome enough,
but it did not affect the main issue ; the bulk of the
estate was entailed and it would inevitably pass to
him with the title.

A faint stirring of uneasiness passed through
Eustace. Was that right ? Did the entailed estate
inevitably pass with the title ? What was it Henry
Carr had said ? 'Lord Barradys had only a life
interest in the estate ; it was bound to pass to his
lineal descendants, just as his title was bound to
pass to them'. That was it, wasn't it ? Wasn't
that good enough ? The title *was* bound to pass to
him now, so the estate. . . . Wait, though. Did
that follow ? Did what Carr said apply to the subsequent tenants of the estate, or only to the original
tenant for life, old Barradys ?

Eustace racked his brains, trying to remember
exactly what Henry Carr had said, wishing he had
had some legal training, wondering whether he could
find out from some book. It would be risky to ask
questions now. He must try to remember. Carr
had said something else, something about 'barring
the entail'. Was that the expression ? 'The
tenant in tail could bar the entail with the consent
of the tenant for life'. Wasn't that it ? It seemed
to be coming back to him now. Then what did that

mean now ? Desmond was now tenant in tail.
Then it meant that Desmond could bar the entail
with the consent of Lord Barradys ; and Barradys
had just declared . . . !

Eustace flung himself back in his seat, sweating
with anxiety, struggling to understand a legal
problem for which he had had no training. Why
should Desmond bar the entail, why should he cut
him, Eustace, out ? He had been very friendly
to him, seemed to like him. Besides, who else
should it go to if not to him ? The one clear Hendel
rule, so both Carr and old Christendome had said,
was to keep the estate in the family ; that was the
whole object of entailing it. Who else, but he,
would keep it in the family ? None of those children
descended through the Hendel women would do—
they weren't Hendels. Young Dick Carr, Julia's
boy, or Bernard Stone, who had been at the funeral
with his mother—what was her name . . . Patience.
They weren't Hendels, there was only himself . . .
oh, and his cousin George ! He had forgotten him ;
George and his father, William Hendel, the wine
merchants ! Forgotten all about them.

As the train rushed through Peterborough Eustace
stared, unseeing, at the towering chimneys of
' London and Forder's ' brick works. Why should
old Barradys prefer George to him, Eustace ? Why
should Desmond ? His past record ? Well, what
was wrong with it ? He had come in for money and

lived an independent life, perfectly respectable, not a breath against him—well, not a breath that would reach old Barradys up at Newcastle or Desmond on his sick bed. And George ? He was a correct little wine-merchant. Nothing startling about that ; nothing against either of them, nothing to choose between them—except the one outstanding fact that Eustace was the senior and would be Lord Barradys.

What was it that had made old Barradys rave against him ? The Lord knows. Merely the fact that he came of the junior line—' the whole rotten line ', he had condemned, silly old fool. That included George, didn't it ? Wait though ; the old man had said : ' grandson of Clarence, son of that young rip, Victor '. His commination didn't go back to Augustus, the common ancestor of Eustace and George. It was Augustus' son, Clarence, who had been supposed to be a bad hat, he and poor Dad ; though what Clarence and his son Victor were supposed to have done beyond blueing their money, a bit of horse-racing, well, perhaps, a bit fond of women—small blame to 'em—Eustace did not know. Augustus' other son, Hubert, had not, so far as Eustace had heard, been tarred with the same brush of disapproval, while his son William was now the respectable wine-merchant, with *his* son George conveniently in tow. Respectable, worthy people ; perhaps that was what old Barradys wanted to inherit the blasted family estate, thought Eustace bitterly ; people who wouldn't have the faintest idea what to do with the money when they got it.

The train swept through the suburbs of London, and Eustace, beginning to collect his things, tried also to collect his thoughts, recover his *morale*. After all, this was pure imagination on his part ; he had no real reason to suppose that Desmond had any such intention. Still, it would be worth keeping in touch with Desmond.

The week-end, which Jill and he had contemplated spending in a burst of extravagant luxury at Brighton, to celebrate the triumphant acceptance of Eustace as his ultimate heir by the head of the family, was, under the altered circumstances, declared to be a wash-out. Jill, in consequence, was sulky, though trying to be sympathetic, and Eustace had little else to do but brood over his troubles.

On Monday morning, as a result of these broodings, he went round to see Desmond but was told by the maid that Mr. Hendel was indisposed and not seeing anyone ; on enquiring for Mrs. Toumlin, he learnt that she was out. Disappointed, and feeling vaguely uncomfortable, Eustace made his way back to his own part of London and began a desultory search for a flat. As he hunted through the quiet streets which even now an expert can find round Covent Garden, he began to warm to his task.

House-hunting had always had a great attraction for him ; he had a vivid imagination and was able to picture what even the barest or most ill-furnished room would look like with his own decoration, his own furniture. After a sandwich and a glass of Munich beer at Appenrodt's he decided to call Jill into partnership and this move was a success, for Jill had been bored and rather depressed, wondering whether Eustace's fine ideas would ever come true, wondering whether she would be able to get him to do something permanent for her if they did ; this activity on his part revived her confidence in his star and she flung herself into the game with a zest that quickly communicated itself to him.

At first their enthusiasm met with no great reward ; most of the flats they saw were dark and dingy, or the street was too noisy, or if flat and street were satisfactory the rent was invariably too high. Just as they were thinking of knocking off for the day, however, they came across one that really seemed made for their purpose. It was in a fairly modern block of flats within a few minutes' walk of the Opera House. It had been done up by (or for) its present occupant, a Mrs. Oliphant, only a year previously, but for reasons of her own she now wished to leave it in a hurry and would pass on the remainder of her three-year lease without premium. It had one good living-room, two bed-rooms—one of them large and airy—a bathroom, kitchen, etc., and accommodation for maid or man on the top floor. The decoration was sufficiently recent and in good enough taste to call for no further expenditure.

Eustace's imagination at once began to fill it with the excellent furniture which had adorned his St. James' flat, and which for two or three years had been languishing in store. Jill, with a shrewd judgment of 'atmosphere', sensed that this block of flats was of sufficiently free and easy a character to allow her to have a more than academic interest in the *ménage* of Mr. Eustace Hendel; she strongly suspected that Mrs. Oliphant had been 'provided for' by someone who was going to provide for her no longer; that meant that the management was 'not too damn particular'.

Even without a premium the rent was higher than Eustace had intended to pay, but it was just within reason, and, after taking the evening to think it over, he clinched, made the necessary legal and financial arrangements for transfer of tenancy, and gave orders to Maple's Depository to deliver his furniture on Monday morning. That gave him nearly a week in which to find a 'man' and it took him only twenty-four hours to do that. The very first registry-office he applied to had on their books 'the very man he wanted', an interview followed, and James Hamilton, at one time valet to Lord Cockspur but since then engaged in a private enterprise—a small valet-service affair—which had not prospered, took the oath of allegiance and established himself in the already vacant top-floor room at Brandford Mansions.

On Thursday Eustace, his spirits largely restored by the excitement of his approaching change of environment and circumstance, decided to look up his Uncle William, take a glass of sherry off him, and see for himself what possible attraction young George might have for old Barradys and Desmond, in case they ever really did contemplate preferring the young prig to the prospective peer.

The office of Hendel and Son, Wine Merchants, was in the City, and as in September the City has not completely come to life again after its summer holiday, business was not brisk. Mr. William Hendel was disengaged and received his nephew in the tiny office-within-an-office, which looked out upon a backyard. The wine-merchant carried the Hendel nose, the dark colouring of the younger branch ; in the earlier fifties he was still vigorous and bore the stamp of *bonhomie* so necessary to his trade.

" Come in, Eustace ", he exclaimed, holding out a pudgy hand. " Haven't seen you for a month or more. Not since all these tragedies in the ' Baron's Branch ', eh ? That was a terrible business up in Scotland, terrible experience for you. You must tell me all about it. But you'll take a glass of sherry, eh ? Not too dry ? An Amontillado ? Or there's an Oloroso '80 I'm just sampling, if you prefer that. An after-dinner wine, really, but very pleasant at middle-day on occasions."

Eustace preferred the Amontillado and over a glass or two told again the story of David's death. With continued practice it had developed into a fairly convincing tale, but Eustace was uncomfortably aware that it took on a different hue when regarded, as it inevitably must be, in the light of his own change of fortune. However, Mr. William Hendel was too polite to show any sign of doubt or incredulity, whatever he may have felt. He commiserated with Eustace and enquired after David's son. After telling all he knew in that respect, though minimizing the seriousness of Desmond's illness, the prospect of his early death, Eustace enquired after George. The wine-merchant beamed.

" Ah, George ", he said. " George has had a very pleasant surprise. Lord Barradys has very kindly invited him to go up to Derrick House. He went north yesterday by the 11.20 from King's Cross. The first time cousin Chandos has ever shown a sign of being aware of our existence, to tell you the truth. A very courteous, very friendly letter. You know him, no doubt, Eustace ? "

Eustace had felt himself flushing as the proud father retailed his news. So it *was* serious ; there *was* something behind this idea of his . . . about

George. Curse it, what could . . . ? He pulled himself together; mustn't let old William see how annoyed he was.

"Oh, yes", he said airily. "As a matter of fact I was up there myself last week." (That would take some of the wind out of uncle William's sails.) "I thought the old man rather shaky. Not surprising, really; must have been a great shock to him, losing two grandsons and a great-grandson all at once. No doubt that's why he sent for George; wanted to see what the younger branch of the family was like."

Eustace was surprised at his own coolness. No chance of Uncle William realizing what a shock it had been to him, hearing of George being sent for by the old man. Because it was a shock; there was no use blinking the fact. It proved that he had been right—or at least that there had been some basis to his imaginings in the train on the way down from Newcastle. Whether or not the old man would be able to persuade Desmond to cut him, Eustace, out of the entail, it showed which way the wind was blowing; it showed there was danger.

Taking leave of his uncle, Eustace walked back to the West End, chewing again the cud of those uncomfortable reflections which had bothered him on the way down from Newcastle.

He spent the afternoon supervizing the cleaning out of his new flat, which 'Mrs. Oliphant' had

already vacated, and in mentally arranging the
furniture and pictures which would come in on
Monday. In the evening he went to the Jermyn
and set about organizing a poker party at the flat
on the following Wednesday; George Priestley promised to come, Freddie Gallater—another Jermyn-
ite; each thought he knew of a young fellow who
would care to come along and have a flutter. That
was the sort of house-warming he wanted; the
inaugurating of a new series of such events, which
was to keep him in funds until . . . the plums fell.
If they did; damn it, it didn't look such a certainty
now.

There was to be a different sort of house-warming
on Tuesday night, organized by Jill. Jill's friends
that time, actresses and young men of some kind—
actors or hangers-on. Eustace didn't care for Jill's
friends, had never been attracted by the theatrical
profession, only by one or two of its individual stars.
Jill for instance—not a star in the accepted sense,
not a planet, but still one of the glittering millions
that went to make the Milky Way of Theatreland.
Jill, to his mind, the brightest of them all. Of
course she must have her party—but it must not
get too rowdy—no use starting a tenancy on the
wrong note—she had promised to see to that. But
she would not be at the Wednesday house-warming;
no women at that; pure business.

Still, that was all laid on on Thursday and there

was nothing more to be done at the flat. He regretted now that he had not ordered the furniture to be delivered sooner; he had not expected Mrs. Oliphant to get out quite so promptly.

Feeling at a loose end on Friday, he decided to go up to Regent's View Mansions again and see how Desmond was. It might give him an idea of how the wind was blowing in that quarter; it would also give him a chance of counteracting any ill-effects which an unfavourable opinion from old Barradys might have had; in any case, he liked the boy and would be glad to try and cheer him up. After lunch, therefore, he mounted a 53 bus and was soon making his way to the entrance of the block of flats. As he approached the lift, the iron gate opened and out stepped Henry Carr.

At first glance Eustace thought the solicitor was looking old and careworn, but as he recognized Eustace, whose back, of course, was to the light, his face brightened with a cheerful smile.

" Eustace, by all that's lucky. I'm glad to see you ", he exclaimed. " You've had the devil of an awkward time since I saw you last, I'm afraid ; worse even than I had down at Coombe. I want to hear all about it. Come and dine with me at the Club one night, will you ? You're going to see Desmond now ? I've just been lunching with him. I won't keep you now. What about Monday ? I've got to be in town that day."

" Do me well ", said Eustace, making a note of time and Club. " How's Desmond ? "

Henry Carr shook his head.

" Not too well, poor chap, I'm afraid. Amazingly cheerful, though. Brave as a lion. Well, see you Monday."

Eustace stepped into the waiting lift and was whisked to the fifth floor. The door of the flat was opened by Mrs. Toumlin, who seemed slightly taken aback at seeing him. She did not move back from the doorway to admit him.

" Good afternoon, Mrs. Toumlin ", said Eustace, " can I come in and see Desmond ? "

" I'm very sorry, Mr. Hendel, but really I'm afraid I must say ' No '. Desmond is not at all well to-day."

Eustace looked curiously at her. Why did the woman seem so embarrassed ?

" I'm sorry to hear that ", he said. " But he was able to see Henry Carr, wasn't he ? "

" Yes, but . . . that's really why I must say no. Mr. Carr's been lunching here and, much as Desmond likes him, I think he's made him rather tired. He always enjoys it tremendously at the time. Mr. Carr is so cheerful. But there's always a reaction."

" I see. Well, of course, if you say so, I must go. I should very much like to see Desmond though. When can I come ? "

Mrs. Toumlin hesitated ; then, after a moment's thought said :

"Will you come in on Sunday morning ? At about half-past twelve ? But only for a little while."

And she firmly closed the door.

CHAPTER XV

A SHATTERING BLOW

PUZZLED, and not a little disquieted, Eustace made his way slowly down the stairs. It was not so much that he had twice in the last two days been denied access to Desmond, though that seemed rather odd, especially in view of Henry Carr having just lunched with him, but why had the companion, Mrs. Toumlin, looked at him so oddly, seemed so uncomfortable? Eustace shrugged his shoulders, decided to try again in a day or two, turned the last flight that led into the hall, and found Henry Carr still waiting there.

" Hullo ", he said. " Why . . . ? "

" I thought you might possibly not be allowed to see him ", said Henry. " Thought, if that was so, you might care to stroll across the Park with me."

They went out into the sunlight, heading for the nearest entrance to Regent's Park.

" But why did you think I mightn't be allowed to see him ? "

" What reason did Mrs. Toumlin give ? "

" She said he wasn't feeling well—that you had tired him ", said Eustace bluntly, irritated that Carr should know he had been turned away.

"I thought that might be so", said the solicitor quietly. "Have you got time to spare? I've an appointment at the Temple at half-past three; that'll give me plenty of time for a walk if you care for one."

Eustace had plenty of time too, and could hardly be so boorish as to pretend he hadn't. Besides, this might give him a chance to sound Carr about that entail—if he could do it not too obviously.

It was hot walking in the blazing September sun and presently Carr suggested sitting for a bit; two chairs under a thorn tree offered rest, shade, and—as it happened—isolation. Eustace had no excuse for not telling once again his story of the death of David. He did not want to; this man was a lawyer; he might ask the same sort of questions that that infernal Procurator Fiscal had done. Eustace thought he was prepared for all emergencies, but he would have much preferred the whole thing to be forgotten; however, he could not well refuse. Henry Carr listened in silence, asked a question or two about the investigation, points about procedure, explained to Eustace about the Crown Office, the Judge Advocate, the Advocates Depute, the Procurator Fiscal, commiserated with him on his trying ordeal, and fell silent.

After a minute or two he turned to Eustace with a smile and said:

"Well, Eustace, there's no concealing the fact

179

that these last two months have altered your own position a bit. I suppose you realize that when poor Desmond goes you will be heir presumptive to the Barradys peerage ? ''

Eustace, his heart beating a little faster, nodded. " Yes, I realize that ", he said. " It's rather extraordinary, isn't it. I've never given the possibility a thought."

" Naturally ; there were so many of them."

Henry took a long pull at his cigarette, inhaling and letting the smoke trickle out of his nostrils.

" I wonder if I might venture to offer you a word of advice ", he went on after a pause, " as a friend, but with the experience of a solicitor ? "

He looked at Eustace, who nodded, wondering what was coming.

" When Desmond dies you'll be inundated with letters from money-lenders and touts of every description, offering you everything under the sun, on no security at all. They're very tempting gentry."

" I suppose so ", said Eustace. " And after all, if that ever does eventuate, it wouldn't be so very unreasonable to borrow a bit on one's expectations ; after all, old Barradys is ninety ; he can't go on for ever . . . and I've lived in a lodging-house long enought to want to get out of it."

Henry Carr carefully ground the stub of his cigarette under his heel.

" This is where it gets difficult ", he said. " It's easy enough for me to come the heavy lawyer and say : ' don't borrow on your expectations ' ; your answer, naturally enough, is : ' why not ? ' Now, I have got a reason for saying what I did, beyond the ordinary lawyer's caution. The question is, (a) do you want to hear it ? (b) ought I to tell it you ? You see, it came to me more or less in confidence—not professional confidence, of course ; that would settle the thing. Ordinarily I should play for safety and keep my mouth shut, but you might get badly landed and . . . well, I don't want that to happen."

" You sound very mysterious ", said Eustace. " So far as I'm concerned, I certainly want to hear your extra-special reason."

" All right. Let's approach it this way : what *are* your expectations ? "

Eustace stared at him.

" Why, you've just been telling me ", he said. " That I'm likely to succeed to Lord Barradys."

" Yes, but succeed to what ? "

" The title and the . . . the entailed estate, I suppose. You explained that to me down at Coombe. Not about me, that is, but about the entailed estate. You said it passed with the title."

" Surely not ? " said Carr. " That does not necessarily follow, though, speaking generally, that might be considered a very usual line for it to take. Without bothering about generalizations, though, the position in this case now is that Lord Barradys is tenant for life, Desmond tenant in tail; Lord Barradys cannot himself interfere with the entail, Desmond can; he can bar it, he can end the entail, he can resettle the estate in a fresh entail; he has, with certain qualifications, to get the permission of the tenant for life to do these things. So you see, Eustace, it does not follow that because you succeed to the title you will succeed to the estate; your money-lending friends may or may not realize this, but those who do will tighten their terms very much as a result of their knowledge."

Carr paused to light a fresh cigarette. Eustace, realizing that this was confirmation of his uncomfortable reflections in the train, sat glumly poking at the ground with his umbrella.

" I see that ", he said. " But after all, isn't that all rather hypothetical? Desmond *can* resettle the estate, but is there any reason to suppose that he will? Old Christendome said that it was practically a certainty that the family estates would remain entailed, that old Lord Barradys would never agree to the entail being broken."

A slight smile appeared on Henry Carr's lips.

" I think Christendome would have rather a shock if he heard that interpretation of his very guarded remarks on the subject. But, Eustace, whatever he said, he was referring to a different set of circumstances from the present; when he spoke the direct succession of the elder line was still more or less assured ; David was alive and in a position to marry again ; quite apart from Desmond, there was every reason to suppose that an heir would be forthcoming. Now David is dead and there is no heir of the direct line ; only poor Desmond who cannot be said to count."

" You mean, now that I'm practically the heir ", said Eustace, forgetting his resolutions of caution, " that they might want to cut me out ?—resettle the estate on someone else ? "

Henry Carr looked at him carefully, as if sizing him up. Then he took a decision.

" Desmond told me this morning ", he said, " that his great-grandfather had written and advised him to resettle the estate upon your first cousin, George."

Eustace felt the blood drain out of his face, saw the trees slide away into a dim and hazy distance, heard the blood drum in his ears, felt himself sick and faint. It was like a knock-out blow on the point of the jaw, paralyzing him with its suddenness and force.

Probably it was only for a few seconds that consciousness wavered in Eustace Hendel. He clung to it, dimly aware that Carr must not see, must not notice, what his words had done to his companion. Then, beyond that thought, flickered the other : ' all for nothing, all for nothing, murder . . . for nothing '. The news, he realized as reason returned to him, was only a confirmation of his own fears, but it was none the less shattering for that ; one can bear a lot of doubts and fears, but certainty may mean smashing disaster. For this was disaster ; if Desmond broke the entail, settled the estate on George instead of him, of what use was the title ? Without money a title was a handicap—well, no ; it might be used as a bait, but . . . Eustace sickened at the thought ; was that all that he had got by what he had done, by that awful time in Scotland, by the frightful risk he had run ?

These thoughts flashed through his brain as he recovered control, as the blood flowed slowly back into his cheeks. Henry Carr seemed to have noticed nothing ; he was watching a nurse-maid trying to catch a flying two-year-old.

" That's rather extraordinary ? Why should he do that ? "

Eustace's voice was commendably firm.

" Apparently Barradys wants the estates to pass in the male line, but has a prejudice against your particular branch. They had very rigid ideas, those old north-countrymen ; Barradys himself was brought up on the strict traditions of non-conformity ; he was brought up to regard your grandfather, Clarence, who was his contemporary, as little less than a child of the devil. Clarence's son, Victor, your father, apparently displeased the non-conformist conscience too ; so you have been hung for someone else's bad name. Unfortunately Clarence's brother, Hubert, was a model of the virtues and old Barradys now regards his descendants as the only proper successors to the Hendel estates ; he can't stop your getting the title, but he *can* see that George gets the estates."

" But can he ? Surely Desmond isn't going to be bullied by that old lunatic ? " demanded Eustace angrily.

Henry Carr shrugged his shoulders.

" I'm afraid it looks like it ", he said. " He regards the old man as the family Patriarch and his word as law. He likes you, he told me—Desmond, I mean. But he'll do what Barradys tells him."

With difficulty Eustace fought back his indignation, stifled the fury that was raging in him. What was the good of letting Carr see it ? He couldn't do anything. Or could he ? Desmond liked him ; he had influence with Desmond. Was it any good . . . ?

" It seems a bit hard ", he said, speaking as calmly as he could. " Is it absolutely certain ? Do you . . . do you think it's just ? If you think it's unjust, couldn't you . . . say something **to** Desmond ? "

He looked anxiously at the solicitor, who shook his head.

" I'll do my best, certainly ", he said, " but I've got no official standing. Christendome does the family business, as you know, and unfortunately the old man has got . . . well, he doesn't seem to have got a very favourable impression of you."

Eustace stared.

" Old Christendome ? Why on earth not ? What can have . . . what have I . . . 'oh ! ' "

" Can't imagine ; old man's prejudice against the unemployed young, probably ", said Carr, ignoring Eustace's closing exclamation—a quite involuntary exclamation wrung from him by the sudden realization of what Christendome's prejudice might be based on. He had been up at Glenellich, at the funeral ; he might have talked to . . . the police ! Or, even possibly, that damned Procurator Fiscal might have got hold of him, wanting to pump the family solicitor.

This idea started all Eustace's worst fears into existence again. Had Christendome put ideas into Hannay's head ? Well, hardly that ; because they were there before the lawyer arrived in Scotland— put there, Eustace had guessed, by that damned Hope-Fording woman, vindictive at being done out of her coveted husband ! But Christendome might have told the Procurator Fiscal about the settled estate. That would be news to him ; Joan Hope-Fording couldn't have known about that. Then why had Hannay done nothing ? Why had he let him leave Scotland ? Had he realized that there was no evidence to support a charge of murder, or was he . . . ?

Eustace shuddered as the horrible thought struck him :

. . . was Hannay waiting for more evidence ? Was he watching him, waiting for him to make a false step ? Was he being watched now ?

With difficulty Eustace restrained himself from looking round ; with an effort he forced his thoughts back to his companion.

Carr was looking at his watch.

" Time we strolled on ", he said, " or I shall be late for my consultation. I wish I could help you, Eustace. Julia took a great fancy to you when you came down to Coombe, and the kids too. We should all like to see you come into a fortune. But I doubt if any influence I may have with Desmond will go very far. It's difficult for us to realize the position that old Lord Barradys holds in that branch of the family. He's been the Patriarch now for so long ; they've all been brought up to regard his word as law. If he has decided that the estate is to go to your cousin George, to George, I'm afraid, it will go."

Curse the old fool ! Curse him ! And I was afraid he might be going to die that night ! God, if he only had died, this wouldn't have happened !

CHAPTER XVI

SENTENCE OF DEATH

ALL for nothing. All for nothing. That frightful day. Watching David die. That terrible voyage back in the launch. Arriving at Glenellich with the body. A nightmare of a day. And then the police; the questioning, the reconstructing, the photographing. The strain of it all. Waiting that next day, while nothing happened. Waiting for the police to . . . what were the police doing? Were they watching him, following him?

Instinctively this time Eustace looked over his shoulder. There was nobody. He was walking alone through Golden Square, on his way back to his lodgings. Why should there be anyone? What earthly point could there be in following him? What evidence could the police hope to collect against him? However much they might doubt his story, the only possible evidence against him would be that of someone who had actually seen him drive the knife into David's leg. No good looking for such a witness in London; a fisherman with a telescope in the Sound of Sleat, perhaps, or a poacher with a spy-glass on the forest itself—those were the only two remote possibilities of evidence against him.

Then why worry ? If the Procurator Fiscal had disbelieved his story he would have acted at once— he or the Crown Office or the police or whoever's job it was to take the initiative, to charge him. No ; they had made up their minds either to believe him or else that there was not enough evidence on which to charge him.

But that did not alter the appalling fact that if Desmond did what the old man wanted him to do it would all have been in vain, not only in vain, but worse than in vain, because he had borrowed more money on the strength of it, taken an expensive flat, engaged an expensive man. How could he pay for them now ? How could he meet the interest charges on his loan, let alone repay the capital ? It meant disaster, ruin, the loss of Jill ; it meant going downhill with a rush, without hope of recovery. No, not while he'd got a brain and courage ! He was not going down ; he would fight to his last gasp. He would . . . God, if he had known, he would have killed that old lunatic in the north before he could write his infernal letter to Desmond. He had killed one man to get this estate ; he would kill another, willingly, without a quaver, to save it from slipping from him.

Was it too late ? Even now, if old Barradys died, Desmond might give up the idea. Why hadn't he done it when he was up there ? How could he do it now ? It might be possible if he were staying in the house ; something to make him sleep and then a prick of morphine or cocaine ; it wouldn't take much with an old man like that. But how was he to get back into the house now ? Write and ask for an interview ? Barradys would refuse it. In any case, an interview would be no good ; he must be staying in the house to have a chance of killing him without being suspected. Even so it would be difficult enough, especially if he were already suspected of killing David. Better to get into the house unbeknownst—break in—and kill him in his sleep—one prick of a needle would be enough. But how could he break in ? That sort of old man's house was always hermetically sealed at night. If only he had thought of it while he was there he could have reconnoitred, found a way in, at least have found out where the old man slept, whether anyone slept next door to him ; he didn't even know that. Why, the old man, with one foot in the grave, might have a night-nurse, or a pet pug-dog sleeping in his room— anything. It would be an appalling risk, without knowing.

But risks must be faced ; the prize was enormous, failure would be . . . worse than any penalty of discovery. Better to be hung, thought Eustace, in his blackest mood of depression, better to be hung and done with it than to go down hill, through the dreary, squalid stages of cheaper lodgings, worse food, shabbier clothes, to the inevitable, ghastly end.

In the meantime, a drink. He couldn't stand his own gloomy thoughts any longer. No good going to Jill—only depress her. No good going to the Club, couldn't face George Priestley in his present mood. ' Julian's ' ; that was the place ; better drinks and more amusing people.

' Julian's ' had the desired effect, at least of clearing off the worst of Eustace's depression. It even set his brain working again in a more rational fashion, though the thoughts which emerged were perhaps unduly tinged with rose. He had jumped too quickly to the worst conclusions, had let Carr put the wind up him ; these lawyers were all alike, pessimistic devils, always looking on the gloomy side of things. Ten to one Desmond had not the smallest intention of being dictated to by his 'ga-ga' old grand- . . . no, great-grandfather. Anyway, he would find out something about that on Sunday when he went round to see the boy.

Saturday passed slowly. The effect of Julian's wizardry had worn off and depression returned ; not quite so black as before, more reasonable, more controlled, but still . . . depression. Eustace was glad when Sunday came and he could go round to Desmond's flat and find out for himself how the wind blew.

Punctually at half-past twelve he presented himself at the door of the fifth-floor flat and was admitted by Mrs. Toumlin herself.

"The girl's not back from church yet", she explained ; "I always let her go in the mornings once a month and when there are five I let her have the fifth as well."

"What the hell does that matter to me ? " wondered Eustace. "Why's she talking as if she was nervous or excited. She was like that on Friday ; she wasn't the first time I came here."

"I'm afraid I shan't be able to let you stay very long ", continued Mrs. Toumlin. "Desmond hasn't been at all well this week. He seems so nervy and gets so tired. Of course you won't let him know that I've said that ; it's not good for him to know I think he isn't well. But if you won't mind going when I give you a little hint ? I'll blow my nose, shall I ? "

How irritating women were, with their little plots and subterfuges. It never paid, that sort of thing ; always made people suspicious of something worse than you were trying to conceal ; much better to be frank and open. However, one must do what she wanted.

He followed the irritating woman through the sitting-room onto the balcony. Desmond was lying, as before, on a couch, with a light rug over his legs. Eustace was struck by the change in his looks. He seemed more haggard, his eyes deeper sunk into his skull, than when Eustace had seen him last ; they were restless, too, those deep, violet-coloured eyes ; they did not rest on one with the calm peacefulness that had so much impressed him before.

To Eustace's intense annoyance Mrs. Toumlin took a seat on the other side of Desmond, picking up some needlework on which she had evidently been engaged before the visitor arrived. Why on earth couldn't she clear out and let him talk to Desmond alone, as she had done on his first visit ? It would be almost impossible to find out anything worth knowing with that woman listening to every word. How was he to get rid of her ? Tact ? Subtlety ? Downright rudeness ?

Nervous and uncertain, Eustace's eyes wandered from one to the other of his companions, noting the nimble working of Mrs. Toumlin's fingers, the restless movements of Desmond's blue-veined hands ; noting, too, the details of furniture, the table with its books and flowers ; noting the absence of the usual invalid paraphernalia—no bottles or pill-boxes or thermo-meters here, only a box of cigarettes—for his guests ; Desmond did not smoke himself—a box of chocolates for himself.

Mrs. Toumlin, placid again now, kept the con-versation going, neither of the men seeming to have anything to say. She was one of those women who made a point of ' knowing men's subjects ' ; she talked about the situation in Abyssinia, the state of the Funds, about horse-racing, dog-racing, about hunting and—finding neither Eustace nor Desmond responded to these subjects—switched back to the Government and the prospects of a General Election. Eustace, whose ideas on women were curiously old-fashioned, found himself growing more and more irritated ; he couldn't stand this yap ; he must get rid of her somehow.

With cumbersome tact, he devoted his attention to Mrs. Toumlin for a minute and then said, heartily :—

" Now, Mrs. Toumlin, why don't you trot off for a bit of exercise before lunch ; it's a lovely morning. I'll look after Desmond."

Mrs. Toumlin's hands checked for a minute at their work, then went on as steadily and surely as before. She herself had not taken her eyes off what she was doing.

" Thank you, Mr. Hendel ", she said, " but I had my walk before Gladys went to church. Now *do* you think France will go off the gold standard ? "

Hell ! She wasn't going to budge ; that was plain as the nose on her face ; it didn't take a psychologist to see that. These nursing women, when they turned obstinate, were worse than ten mules. Very well ; she must stay. But he would come some time when she was out and have his talk to Desmond then. Desmond would be glad enough of a quiet talk with him ; no two men could ever talk comfortably in front of a woman. He would find out somehow when the old hen did take her exercise and he'd slip in then ; tip the girl, Gladys, if necessary. In the meantime, do what he could to amuse poor Desmond.

The attempt was a failure ; Desmond was ill-at-ease, nervy, quite different to the smiling boy he had first met. Before long Mrs. Toumlin produced a substantial square of ' sensible linen ' and trumpeted into it. Vindictively, Eustace ignored the signal, took a fresh cigarette, lit it, and began a dissertation on Hungarian cooking—of which he knew nothing. Mrs. Toumlin trumpeted again, saying : " I really think I'm catching a cold ; there's quite a draught coming round the corner ", and rose to her feet. Eustace was compelled to follow suit and soon found himself being shepherded through the sitting-room. As he emerged, in Mrs. Toumlin's wake, into the little hall, he noticed that the door opposite the sitting-room was ajar, which it had not been when he arrived ; the maid, Gladys, must be back from church—or wherever she had elected to spend her ' fifth Sunday ' morning.

" Well, good-bye, Mrs. Toumlin ", he said. " I'll come in again in a day or two ; perhaps be able to relieve you for a proper afternoon off ; I expect you find it difficult to leave Desmond for long unless you know someone's going to be with him."

Mrs. Toumlin held out her hand.

" That's very kind of you, Mr. Hendel ", she said,
" but just at the present, you know, I think it would
be better if you didn't come and see Desmond. You
can see for yourself that he's not the thing ; I'm
really rather worried about him and I'm thinking of
asking Sir Horace to come round and advise me ;
such a kind man, and so wise."

And there he was, out on the mat again.

It had been a frost, Eustace told himself as he
walked down the stairs. Apart from the continued
presence of the Toumlin woman the change in
Desmond himself would probably have made the
visit a failure. He was so obviously embarrassed,
no doubt as a result of old Barradys' letter ; poor
boy, he probably felt a sort of guilty conscience at
what he was doing . . . well, contemplating doing
. . . to upset Eustace's apple-cart. No wonder he
felt uncomfortable ; it was a rotten thing to do to
anyone, let alone to somebody he had no reason at
all to dislike. However, next time, when he got
Desmond to himself, thought Eustace, he would get
things back on a more natural, friendly footing, and
very likely be able to knock the whole idea of re-
settling the estate on the head. Of course he was
not going to be put off by the Toumlin. For some
reason or other she had got her knife into him. He
would just old-soldier her ; watch her times of going
out and slip in.

Walking away from the flats, deep in thought, Eustace nearly ran into a young woman, neatly dressed, who was turning the corner from St. John's Wood Road. Her face was vaguely familiar; he half raised his hand to his head; she gave a nervous smile and hurried on. Who on earth? Why, of course, the maid Gladys. Then she had not been back at the flat when . . . he must just have been mistaken about that door. Should he follow her, call to her, question her about Mrs. Toumlin's exercise hours? Rather awkward to do that here; rather awkward to follow her, call to her, in the street; it might look . . . better wait and have a talk to her in the flat some time.

Eustace was not unduly disappointed by the fruitlessness of his visit; he was not going to be deterred by a small set-back; his blood was up now, his fighting spirit roused. Once the first shock of Henry Carr's news was over, once he had conquered—with 'Julian's' aid—the black depression caused by that shock, he had made, he flattered himself, a good recovery and was not going to allow anything now between him and his goal. Guile, in the first place—to get a quiet talk with Desmond; then tact—to find out what he intended to do; finally, skill, charm, whatever it needed, with the help of Henry Carr and possibly Blanche—good idea that—whatever was needed to checkmate the machinations of that old maniac up at Newcastle. If the worst came to the worst, he would deal with the old devil himself—but that would be risky and he wanted no more risks than were necessary.

To-morrow he was dining with Henry Carr ; not a bad chap Henry ; rather an odd mixture of the cautious lawyer and the oncoming, hearty good fellow. Of course, he had had a chance to see both aspects ; no doubt most people saw only one or the other. Henry might have heard a bit more by then, be able to suggest a line of country. Till Monday then . . .

The Junior English Universities Club is probably the least select and at the same time the most prosperous of all the University Clubs in London. By keeping its subscription low it had attracted a vast number of men from many Universities who either could not have afforded or would not have been eligible or acceptable at the more dignified clubs. It had three Squash Courts, a swimming bath, a notable bar, many bedrooms, a grill-room as well as a dining-room ; it only narrowly escaped the ultimate horror of a ' bell-hop '—that buttoned imp who wanders about the huger caravanserais singing in a nasal falsetto : ' Meester Laizenby '. And as a result of its popularity it was able to produce an extremely good dinner, one of a character not to be found in the dignified brethren that turned up their noses at this vulgar upstart.

" I had to chuck my old Club when my firm

smashed up in '21 ", explained Henry Carr, leading
Eustace to the white-tiled, chromium-plated lavatory. " Did without one for five years, but it was
devilish awkward. Then someone suggested this,
I had a look at it, thought I could manage the subscription . . . and haven't regretted it. It gives
me a game or a swim, both of which I love ; the
food's good ; there's always a bedroom when I
want it ; most of the members are appalling, but
there are one or two good fellows."

Henry Carr was a good host. He no doubt
realized that Eustace was going through a trying
time, as a result of the news he had given him on
Friday, and he set himself to entertain and amuse his
guest, on the principle that it does one good to
forget one's worries even for an hour. The dinner
was excellent ; more like that of a high-class
restaurant than a club.

" What about coffee and a cigar on the terrace ? "
asked Carr at the end of it. " It's quite warm still
and yet not hot enough to attract a crowd ; we shall
have a chance of a quiet talk."

That was exactly what Eustace wanted and he
wasted no time in getting down to business. He
told the solicitor frankly that since David Hendel's
death he had assumed that he was bound to succeed
to the estate as well as to the title, that he had
already borrowed money, incurred extra expenditure, on the strength of that assumption, and that

the news of old Lord Barradys' advice to Desmond had come as a complete and very severe shock to him.

" Can't it be stopped, Henry ? " he asked eagerly. " Surely you—perhaps Blanche too—can stop Desmond doing this, breaking the entail, resettling on George ?   Why should he have it ?   You don't think it's right, do you ?   No, I know you don't. And I don't believe Blanche would either if she knew.   I believe she likes me ; she was very kind to me down at Coombe and at Glenellich too ; I believe it was she who got David to ask me up there.   Desmond is devoted to her—and to you.   I am sure that if you two talked to him he would give up the idea."

He looked anxiously at Carr, trying to read his expression in the darkness. A sudden glow from his cigar threw a faint light on the solicitor's face ; Eustace saw that he was smiling slightly—though there seemed nothing to smile at. There was an appreciable pause ; then Carr leant forward, gently tapping the ash from his cigar as he did so.

" I don't think any good will be done by beating about the bush, Eustace ", he said quietly.   " I sympathize very much with your position, but it is facts that we have got to face. I saw Desmond this afternoon. He told me that he had definitely decided to carry out Lord Barradys' wish and to resettle the estate upon your cousin, George."

Hope died in one moment in Eustace's heart, the optimistic imaginings of the last three days faded away, never to reappear. This, he recognized, was final. The tone of Henry's Carr's voice told him that. It was like receiving, at the hands of some doctor, sentence of death.

Minute followed minute on leaden feet. Eustace sat motionless, his cigar dying to cold blackness in his fingers, just as his hope had died. He made no attempt to speak, no pretence of hiding his feelings. It was K.O. He was ' out '.

Henry Carr watched him, that same smile, now hidden in the darkness, still curling the corner of his expressive mouth. At last he spoke.

" There's only one fact that qualifies what I've told you ", he said. " Desmond cannot break the entail until he comes of age. He is still a minor. He is twenty-one on the fifteenth of November."

CHAPTER XVII

BEATING A BLANKET

IT must be Desmond, then. That fact stood out, ice-clear, in Eustace's mind. Desmond must not live to make that change in the entail. That was the only hope. It was too late now for persuasion or dissuasion. He had decided, definitely ; so Henry Carr said. Then—he must be stopped. There was no time to try any other alternative ; there were just six weeks. Desmond, poor, sick, suffering Desmond, must die before he came of age, before he could legally bar the entail and re-settle the estate upon George. George ! Why on earth George ? What was the attraction in George ? A young prig in a port-shop !

A sudden gust of rage shook Eustace as he thought of the monstrous injustice that these people were contemplating—old Barradys and Desmond. Even Desmond did not escape that anger and Eustace almost welcomed the fact ; it made the decision to put Desmond out of the way a little less unpleasant. Because he had got quite fond of Desmond in the short time he had known him and it was a disagreeable thought that the poor boy would have to die. But after all, he had got to die before very long anyhow and it would really be a kindness to put him out quietly and quickly now ; brave and cheerful as he was, life could be no great pleasure to him. Yes, really a kindness ; nothing to regret at all.

The extraordinary thing was that he hadn't thought of it before. Why had he gone to all the trouble of trying to think of a way of killing the old fool up at Newcastle, when all that that would do would be to eliminate an influence—an influence which might already have proved decisive, so that the elimination might already prove too late ? Whereas by eliminating Desmond he went straight to the crux of the matter. Extraordinary that he should not have realized that before. Why hadn't he ? Interesting psychological problem that, and Eustace, as a doctor, knew something about psychology. Probably the reason was simply that he had *wanted* to kill old Barradys—had leapt at an excuse to get his own back on the old maniac who had been so offensive to him. Just as he had been quite glad to kill David, whom he had disliked at sight. Whereas Desmond he had liked—and so the idea of killing him had not entered his mind ! Interesting.

And not only was the elimination of Desmond so much more direct and effective a way of achieving what he wanted, but it would be so much easier.

Desmond's case presented all the favourable conditions that he had wanted when he first thought about how to kill David. The boy was an invalid; he would have medicines, probably some form of hypnotic drug; there should be no great difficulty about substituting a lethal for a harmless dose; it was only a case of finding out what the drug was and how it was administered.

Even if it proved impossible to find out, it should not be impossible to guess; there are not many ways of treating a sarcoma of the spine. Apart from any question of radium or deep X-rays, the boy would certainly be having a fairly frequent administration of some hypnotic; morphia was the most probable—morphia injections, but there were some men who had a passion for giving veronal or luminol in the form of a mixture, often with some form of opium as a sleeping draught. There were patients, too, Eustace knew—cancer patients—who hated the impression of being doped which the morphia prick inevitably gave them; for them, no doubt, a mixture at regular intervals was more suitable. Whatever it was, there was the groundwork on which to build. If Desmond was taking some such mixture, then an added dose would soon break him up; best of all, of course, if one could ensure its being taken with the last dose before the sleeping draught; that would mean a concentration of drug very difficult for a weakened constitution to

resist, even though it had gained some immunity
from constant administration. That was what he
wanted ; a gradual, though fairly rapid, breaking
up ; far less dangerous than one lethal dose, which
in any case would be difficult to administer.

The one essential was access ; he could do nothing
without that. Even if it was safe to assume that
Desmond was being treated with a hypnotic, it was
imperative to discover how that hypnotic was being
administered; if the hypnotic was being given sub-
cutaneously—and with a nurse in the house that
was quite likely—then there would be practically no
chance of monkeying with the dosage ; on the other
hand, if it was being given in liquid form, then he
must find out where the bottle was kept and how to
get at it. All this would need careful reconnoitring.
Mrs. Toumlin was the snag ; there was no getting
away from the fact that she was a watch-dog whom
it would not be easy to get past.

The whole thing would take time, and there was
little time to spare—six weeks. Not only time, but
infinite care. There must be no breath of suspicion
against himself ; it would be too dangerous after
that business in Scotland. Eustace did not know
how much *liaison* there was between the Scottish and
English police—whether any report of David's case
would have reached London. Probably not, but the
English police had an uncanny knack of knowing
everything about one and if suspicion touched him

over Desmond's death they would be sure to think about David's—and then they would put two and two, or rather, one and one, together !

Eustace had not stayed long at the Junior English Universities Club after Henry Carr had thrown that bombshell at him. He had made no attempt to hide from his host what a shock that news about Desmond's definite decision had been, and Carr had behaved very decently—left him alone, fetched a couple of brandies, and raised no objection when he said that he thought he would be getting home. Henry Carr was all right, a good fellow really, but no use to him now ; he had got to act for himself— the lone hand. As he walked home—to his first night in the new flat—Eustace had thought out all the implications of Carr's news, had come to his decision that only the death of poor Desmond could save the situation now.

As he had discovered before, when deciding to kill David, it was a very different matter to carry that decision into effect. All the difficult and tedious details must be thought out and executed, all the risks actually faced. Waking in the grim, grey light of early morning, Eustace found himself dreading this second terrible task which he had laid upon himself. He would have given anything to turn away from it, but the alternative was ruin.

Flinging himself out of bed, Eustace dressed in a mood of gloomy determination. He had got a job to do that very morning ; there could be no more delay. He had got to find out how he could get into Desmond's flat and have a good look round, without interruption. Obviously Mrs. Toumlin must be out of the way and the only practical way of discovering when she would be out of the way was to watch her get out of it. Probably she would see Desmond comfortably settled on the balcony and then go out and do her shopping. Eustace was vague as to what that shopping might be or even whether a woman in Mrs. Toumlin's position would do it, but somehow he had a feeling that she would leave nothing of that kind to a servant—she would choose even the Brussels-sprouts herself. No time to be lost, then ; it was already nine o'clock.

An hour later Eustace was ensconced behind a *Daily Telegraph* on a bench in the churchyard close to Regent's View Mansions. He could not actually see the entrance to the flats, but it was a monkey to a mouse-trap that anyone bent on shopping would come this way ; anyhow, it was the best he could do ; he couldn't hang about on his feet outside the entrance—it would be far too noticeable. Fortunately it was a pleasant day and there were other people on the benches, either reading or thinking or just sitting, so that he was not at all noticeable. His patience, however, had begun to wear thin when, just after the church clock had sounded eleven, he saw the erect figure of Mrs. Toumlin, with two books and a basket, come round the corner and, a minute later, board a south-bound bus.

Nothing could be better. The books probably meant a library, the basket other shopping, and the bus at least some distance—and consequently time. Giving her five minutes' start, Eustace handed his paper to a neighbour and made for the flats. The porter knew him by sight now and touched his cap, whisking him up to the fifth floor without enquiry. Gladys opened the door and at once showed signs of the embarrassment which Mrs. Toumlin had displayed on the occasion of his last visit. What was the matter with the women ? Surely Desmond couldn't have told them of his great-grandfather's disapproval ? Anyhow it was no use wondering ; he'd got to keep his wits about him and needed all his attention for the work in hand.

" Good morning ", he said. " Can I see Mrs. Toumlin ? "

Eustace was aware that he possessed good looks of the type which appeals to many women—the dark, rather sinister type so much in demand for film lovers. He put across his most charming smile and was gratified to see the girl, who was herself not unattractive, blush and drop her eyes.

" I'm afraid Mrs. Toumlin's out, sir ", she said in a low voice.

" Oh, what a pity. I thought I should be sure to catch her. Does she always go out about this time ?"

" Generally at eleven, sir ; she'll be in at twelve for sure."

Admirably done. What could have been more natural or more completely successful ?

" Well, I daresay I can have a talk with Mr. Desmond then ", said Eustace.

The blush had disappeared, but the embarrassment was if anything greater.

" Oh no, sir ; I'm afraid that wouldn't be possible. Mrs. Toumlin never allows anyone to visit Mr. Hendel when she's not here."

Confound the woman, with her rules and regulations. However, regulations have been broken before now. Eustace gently clinked the silver in his pocket and produced another smile.

" That can hardly be applied to me, Gladys, eh ? " he asked in a confidential voice.

But the girl's mouth hardened. She stood her ground.

" I'm afraid so, sir ", she said firmly.

Another rock. Try a fresh tack.

" Oh well, I must just wait for her, then. You won't mind my coming in and sitting down, I suppose ? "

Gladys hesitated. This was evidently a problem outside her instructions. Her natural sense of hospitality made it difficult for her to refuse such a harmless request.

" I . . . well, I'm afraid I couldn't show you into the sitting-room or the dining-room, sir ; they both open on the balcony and Mr. Hendel would know you were here."

" That's all right ; I'll sit in the hall."

Eustace walked in and sat himself firmly down on a wooden chair. The hall would do admirably ; easy access to Desmond's bedroom from there— and the medicine cupboard. Or to Mrs. Toumlin's, if that was where it was.

Gladys, still uncertain of her duty, hovered for a moment and then made her way along a short passage into what was evidently the kitchen. A murmur of voices reached Eustace and presently Gladys returned.

" I'll just send a message and let Mrs. Toumlin know you're here, sir ", she said. " I think I know where to get her."

She approached the telephone.

" Oh no, please don't do that. I wouldn't for the world bring her back till she's ready. Really, I can quite well wait. I'm in no hurry at all."

This really was maddening. Why couldn't they leave him alone ?

" It's quite all right, sir. I know Mrs. Toumlin would wish to know. Welbeck 3781. No, 3781, please."

" But look here, really . . ."

Eustace was conscious of a feeling of helplessness. Men one could deal with, but these obstinate women. . . .

" Is that the Times Book Club ? Will you give a message to Mrs. Toumlin, please, when she comes to change a book for Mr. Hendel ; yes, Guaranteed Subscriber. Please tell her that Mr. . . . er . . . er." The maid broke off, eyeing Eustace uncertainly. " Mr. Eustace Hendel, isn't it, sir ? "

Eustace nodded gloomily.

" . . . that Mr. Eustace Hendel has called and will wait till she comes back. Yes, that's all, thank you."

Gladys hung up.

" I don't think she'll be long, sir ", she said. " There's a 53 bus all the way to the corner. Would you like a paper, sir ? "

" Thanks."

Still a chance. The woman couldn't get back in less than a quarter of an hour at the very earliest. Once this silly girl was back in her pantry. . . .

" Thanks. Don't you bother about me. I'll be quite all right."

Eustace opened the paper and over the top of it watched the maid disappear through the door just opposite the sitting room—probably the pantry. But she did not shut the door ; it remained ajar, as it had been on that previous visit when he came out of the sitting-room. Why on earth couldn't servants learn to shut doors properly ? He must give her a minute or two to settle to her work and then . . . reconnoitre.

There was no sound of work, no clink of plates, no running tap. Perhaps she was sewing, or polishing silver ; that wouldn't make a noise. Quietly Eustace folded the paper and laid it on the floor, rose, and was tip-toeing towards the door of what he took to be Desmond's room when he saw a shadow move on the thin patch of pantry wall that was visible to him. Instantly he checked, holding his breath, watching that strip of wall. Yes, there it was again—a slight movement, but clear enough now to show that someone—no doubt Gladys—was standing just inside the door, listening, watching. No, not actually watching him, because the way the door opened made it impossible for her to do that ; but she was there on the watch, none the less ; if she heard him move, heard a door open, she could easily peep out and see that he had left his seat. It wouldn't do. It was too risky. He simply could not afford to be seen doing anything even faintly suspicious.

Eustace slipped back onto his chair, picked up the paper, cursing the whole regiment of female busybodies. Curiosity, of course ; there couldn't be any earthly reason for Gladys to watch him ; just downright busybodying curiosity—'rubbering ', as the Americans so expressively put it.

As he turned over the pages of the ' Morning Post ' with unseeing eyes, Eustace experienced an uncomfortable feeling of doubt—almost of despair.

How was he going to defeat these female watch-dogs? One on guard had been difficult enough, but evidently there were two, like parent eagles guarding their precious young. It was all very admirable, of course—protecting the invalid from undue disturbance or worry—but surely this was overdoing it. How was he going to evade this watch? How get into Desmond's room, how find . . . ?

A faint whirring sound announced the rising of the lift, the clang of a gate, a shadow on the glass panel of the front door, the scratch of a key . . . and Mrs. Toumlin walked into the hall. She was flushed and breathless, but at sight of Eustace rising, paper in hand, from his hard wooden chair she pulled herself together. Out of the corner of his eye Eustace was aware that Gladys had looked out of the pantry, withdrawn her head, and shut the door.

" I'm sorry that you should have had to wait for me, Mr. Hendel ", said Mrs. Toumlin, putting down her two books and a still empty basket.

" I am still more sorry that you should have hurried back on my account ", Eustace assured her. " I told Gladys that I could quite well wait."

" Gladys was right to tell me. You will excuse my not asking you to come into the sitting-room, Mr. Hendel, but I do not want Desmond disturbed."

" Is he seriously ill, Mrs. Toumlin . . . worse, I mean ? "

" I trust not, but . . . I have to be most careful that he should not get overtired."

" Surely you will let me have a little talk with him ? I promise I won't tire him."

Again Eustace experienced the sensation of helplessness in face of female obstinancy; it was like beating at a blanket.

" I'm very sorry, Mr. Hendel, but that is quite impossible. Desmond has visitors to lunch and he must rest quietly all this morning."

" Visitors ? "

" Yes, his cousins, Mr. William Hendel and his son."

CHAPTER XVIII

ANOTHER HENDEL DIES

EUSTACE had little heart for the first of the house-warming parties that night—Jill's party. He played his part as a host, distributed drinks, flirted with the young women, refrained from kicking the young men ; but at the back of his mind all the time he was conscious of the gnawing thought that he was up against a bigger proposition than he could manage. How to get past those two women ; that was all. A nurse and a parlourmaid. He was check-mated—or at least in danger of being checkmated—by just that—Queen's Bishop and Pawn.

Force was no use to him, violence out of the question. Even the passive, persuasive force that he had used that morning—his attempt to bribe Gladys—had been dangerous, and it had been unsuccessful. Mrs. Toumlin was hostile to him already—heaven might know why ; he simply dared not try to force his way past that blanket again. He must lie low, till the attempt had been forgotten. In the meantime, the precious hours were flying. Only six weeks—and he was already forced to ground, to lie low, like any hunted fox. No, that was an exaggeration. There was no question of being hunted. It simply was that he must avoid calling attention to the fact that he was the fox!

The last and noisiest of the guests departed soon after half-past one, and Jill joined him in a final drink before taking her own departure.

" What's biting you, darling ? " she asked, ruffling his hair. " Haven't you liked my little friends ? "

" It's not that ", said Eustace ; " they're all right. Only . . . I'm rather up against it."

He explained as best he could the difficulty in which he found himself. Jill listened in silence, her mouth hardening as she heard his decision to ' lie low for a bit,.

" Are you backing out of this, Eustace ? " she asked when he had finished.

" No, of course not, but . . ."

" ' No . . . but ' nothing ! "

Jill sat up straight and taking the lapels of his coat in her two hands gave him a shake.

" If you back out of this now I'm through with you ", she said sharply. " I refused a good cabaret engagement this morning because I thought you meant business. If you . . ."

" Of course I mean business ", he retorted irritably. " It's just that I don't see how I'm going to get at him now. Those two women never take their eyes off him."

"Those two women! You make me tired!"

Jill's eyes flashed angrily.

"Why don't you use your brains? You can't expect to walk in on him and hand him the stuff in a glass! They're looking for you; you mustn't go near him."

Eustace stared at her.

"Looking for me?" he stammered.

"Of course they are! Isn't it obvious? You've got your head in the sand. If anything happens to Desmond now they're bound to suspect you."

"Then how on earth can I . . .?"

"Why, send it to him, of course. Patent medicine, fruit, chocolates. There are dozens of tricks. Don't you ever read anything? That's always being done. Didn't someone send poisoned chocolates to Lloyd George?"

Chocolates! Desmond's table flashed into his mind; the box of cigarettes for his guest, the chocolates for himself. Eustace had wondered at it at the time, but soon realized that many men who did not smoke had a passion for chocolates. Peppermint chocolates; the big round ones in the well-known cream and gold box—Dudeville's. Just such a box lay on the table now amid the wreckage of the refreshments.

Eustace rose to his feet, his brain beginning to spin. Excitement always had that effect on him.

"You'd better be off now, Jill," he said curtly, fetching her coat.

Jill looked at him curiously. A smile slowly spread over her face. She pulled his face down to hers and kissed his lips; then without another word let herself out of the flat. Eustace stood for a moment listening, then walked to the table and picked up the box of chocolates. It was a two-pound box, bought only yesterday; now there were only a dozen or so chocolates left in it—a mixed lot, hard and soft, among them one large round peppermint cream. Eustace picked it up and examined it carefully. It was beautifully made, smooth and glossy; it would be a very difficult matter to open it, remove and replace the contents, and reseal the chocolate without obvious signs of interference. It would certainly be necessary to experiment, but that could probably be done on an inferior brand; it would certainly be unwise to buy any more of Dudeville's if it could be avoided.

The remaining peppermint cream in this box of Dudeville's assumed a special value now; it would not do to leave it to the tender mercies of Hamilton, whose particular line in petty theft had not yet disclosed itself. Instead of returning it to its fellows, therefore, Eustace locked it up in a drawer of his writing-table, a drawer which contained a tiny, thin glass bottle. Then, feeling dead tired, but slightly less depressed, he went to bed.

In spite of his tiredness Eustace found great difficulty in getting to sleep. It was only the second night in his new flat and he had always had difficulty in becoming acclimatized to new surroundings. The noises were different, the window was in a different place ; even the bed, though he had slept in it for years in his St. James's flat, felt strange to him now, after its long sojourn in Maple's Depository. Worse still, his brain had begun to work again at the very time when it is better inactive ; the problem of the chocolate, the problem of lethal dosage, the problem of substitution, one after the other, raced through his brain, becoming more and more confused as he grew more weary. The grey rectangles of the windows were lightening, noises were increasing in the outside world, when at last Eustace fell into the drugged sleep of utter exhaustion.

It was with difficulty that he struggled back to consciousness, aware that something unusual was happening. At first he thought it was a dream and allowed himself to slip back into sleep ; then the disturbance became too acute to be ignored and he realized that he was being shaken. With an effort he opened his eyes and saw the barely familiar face of his new man-servant, Hamilton, close to his own.

" Wake up, sir ", the man exclaimed. And again, monotonously : " Wake up, sir."

Was this the fool's idea of calling one ?

" G' 'way ", growled Eustace. " . . . sleep."

He closed his eyes, but Hamilton renewed his efforts.

" Wake up, sir." Shake. " Wake up, sir."

Eustace roused himself and sat up.

" What the hell's the matter ? " he asked irritably, aware now from the man's expression that something *was* the matter.

" There's a police-officer asking to see you, sir."

" Police . . . ? "

A cold sponge could not have wakened Eustace more thoroughly. He stared at Hamilton.

" What sort of police-officer ? "

" Plain clothes, sir. Didn't give any rank."

The man was clearly thrilled, as well as anxious. It wouldn't do to let him see what an unpleasant shock his news was.

" All right ; I'll see him. Some silly fuss. Give me my dressing-gown."

Having brushed his hair, Eustace lit a cigarette and strolled into the sitting-room.

" Where is he ? "

" In the hall, sir. Very insistent ", murmured Hamilton.

" Show him in here."

Hamilton opened the door and with a slight cock of the head indicated to the visitor that he could come in but that he was not going to be announced as a gentleman would be. A burly figure, clad in dark clothes and carrying a bowler hat, came into the room.

"Good morning, sir."

The big policeman paused and eyed the door till Hamilton had reluctantly closed it behind him. He was, thought Eustace, almost too like a policeman to be true; heavy in build and expression; nothing to be afraid of so far as a battle of wits was concerned.

"I'm sorry to disturb you, sir. I'm Divisional Detective-Inspector Wennessy."

He held out a warrant card for Eustace's inspection.

"I have been instructed to inform you that your cousin, Mr. Desmond Hendel, died at seven o'clock this morning."

Desmond! Dead! It was impossible to conceal altogether the tremendous effect of this astonishing news. Eustace drew a deep breath of smoke into his lungs and exhaled it through his nostrils. Walking to the fire-place he stubbed out the cigarette against the grate. When he turned towards the police-officer his face and voice were under control.

"Poor chap," he said. "That's very sad, though it's only what was expected, isn't it? I don't quite understand why you should have been troubled to come and tell me."

The detective looked at him stolidly.

" Mr. Hendel's death was not quite what was expected, sir," he said. " The doctors think he died of an overdose of a drug."

He stopped, as if expecting some comment. Eustace felt his heart pounding. Overdose of a drug ! What could it mean ? There had been no . . .

" I don't quite follow," he said. " What drug ? "

" That's not known at the moment, sir, of course, though it will be after the autopsy. It may be the drug that he was taking for his complaint. You don't happen to know what that is, do you, sir ? "

" I ? The drug ? Why should I ? "

" I just thought you might happen to know, sir. You've visited Mr. Hendel fairly frequently, haven't you, sir ? "

" Fairly, yes. After all, he's my cousin."

" Quite so, sir. That would be only just recently, though, wouldn't it ? That you've visited him, I mean."

The man's expression and demeanour were as stolid as ever, yet Eustace felt a faint stirring of uneasiness. What was the point of these questions ? The death must have been accidental—or natural. Why should he be questioned about it ?

" It does happen to have been only recently," he replied, " but I don't see what that's got to do with

222

it. As a matter of fact I had seen nothing of that branch of my family since I was a boy. I met them again—some of them, that is—at the funeral of Mr. Howard Hendel and his son."

" Ah, yes, sir; very sad case, I remember. Accidental death, of course."

" Of course; they were drowned down in Cornwall."

" And you met Mr. Desmond Hendel then, sir ? "

" No, not him; he's been practically bedridden for some time. I met his father and some other cousins; through them I subsequently met Desmond."

The large detective drew a note-book from his pocket and turned over the pages till he found a blank.

" You'll excuse me if I just jot some of this down, sir ? " he asked.

" Of course; but I don't know what on earth it's all about."

Inspector Wennessy made no attempt to answer that point, but renewed his own questions.

" And the first date you met Mr. Desmond Hendel, sir ? "

" I don't know exactly; about a fortnight ago; after I got back from Scotland, anyhow."

" After the death of the young gentleman's father, that would be ? "

"Yes," replied Eustace shortly.

"And that was . . . accidental also, sir ? "

Eustace felt a cold shiver of apprehension run through him. There was something behind all this aimless questioning ; that was quite obvious. But what could it mean ? Desmond's death at least must have been accidental, if not actually natural. Why should the police question him like this ? Mercifully, he had nothing to hide ; his conscience, so far as Desmond was concerned, was clear. He did not answer the last question and apparently Inspector Wennessy did not expect an answer ; at any rate he did not repeat the question.

"Now your visits to Mr. Desmond Hendel, sir," he went on. "The first was on the 19th September, I think you said."

"I didn't say anything of the kind. I don't remember the exact date. It was about a fortnight ago."

"Does not remember exact date," murmured Inspector Wennessy, scribbling in his note-book. "And since then, sir, ? Fairly regular visits ? "

"Not regular, no. I've been two or three times. But why on earth do you want to know about that ? "

"Mere matter of routine, sir," replied the Inspector blandly. "And would I be right in saying you visited him again on Monday 23rd, Friday 27th, Sunday 29th, and yesterday ? "

Eustace stared.

" Where on earth did you get all those dates from ? " he asked.

" Information received, sir. Would that be about right ? "

" I've only seen my cousin twice. On Sunday was the last time. I've called once or twice besides, but he wasn't well enough to see me."

" I see, sir ; anxious about the young gentleman's health, no doubt ? "

Damn the fellow's impertinence. What *was* he getting at ?

" And on two of those occasions the companion-lady was out ? Is that right, sir ? "

" Yesterday she was. I don't remember any other time. She came back soon after I got there."

" And till she came back you were alone in the flat, sir ? "

Eustace felt a cold sweat break out all over him. There was danger in this question. How could he say that he had known he was being watched ? It would look as if he had a guilty conscience. What *had* happened to Desmond ? Why was he being questioned like this ?

" Certainly I was not alone. Apart from Mr. Hendel there was the maid who let me in and I believe another maid. I heard them talking. I waited in the hall for Mrs. Toumlin to return, as the maid thought she wouldn't like my cousin to have any visitors in her absence."

" Quite so, sir. So you waited in the hall. And the maid ? She went back into the kitchen, I suppose ? "

" She did for a minute or two. Then she came out and telephoned—a message for Mrs. Toumlin. Then she went into another room, just off the hall ; the pantry, I think."

" I see, sir. And you remained in the hall till Mrs. Toumlin returned ? "

Eustace nodded.

" How long would that have been, sir ? "

" Ten or fifteen minutes, I suppose."

" You didn't go into any other room, sir ? Mr. Desmond Hendel's bedroom, for instance ? "

Eustace frowned angrily.

" I told you I remained in the hall."

" You did, sir. I just wondered whether it might have slipped your memory. Well, I think that's about all I need bother you with just now, sir. The inquest will be to-morrow, I fancy ; you'll be notified about time and place by the Coroner's officer."

" But I've got no evidence to give the Coroner."

" You never can tell, sir. No doubt he'll like to know about your interest in the young gentleman and your visits and all that. If you'll excuse my suggesting it, sir, I think it would be as well if you

were to rub up your dates—when you visited Mr.
Hendel, when the companion-lady was out, and
so on."

Eustace's nerves were fraying ; it was all he could
do to keep his temper.

" I've no idea about dates," he said shortly. " I
don't keep a diary."

Inspector Wennessy closed his note-book, took a
comprehensive look round the room.

" Nice place you've got here, sir. Not been here
long, I understand ? "

" I've been here two days and I should like some
breakfast if you've nearly done asking irrelevant
questions."

The detective rose to his feet.

" Very sorry to have kept you, sir, I'm sure," he
said. " Having mine early made me kind of
inconsiderate."

He moved towards the door. Eustace would
have liked to follow the dignified course of ringing
for Hamilton to show him out, but he did not want
any gossiping on the landing. He went out into the
hall himself and opened the outer door. Inspector
Wennessy paused on the threshold.

" And there's nothing you wish to tell me, sir ? "
he asked, his small eyes seeming to bore into
Eustace's brain.

" I've told you all I know . . . and that's
nothing."

" Very well, sir. Good morning."

He stumped slowly down the stairs, ignoring the lift. After waiting to make sure that he was gone, Eustace closed the door of the flat and returned to his sitting-room.

CHAPTER XIX

G O L D E N D R E A M S

EUSTACE hardly knew whether to be most alarmed or elated by the startling news brought to him by Detective-Inspector Wennessy and his subsequent interrogation. The supreme fact emerged that the way was now clear for him to succeed to the Barradys title and estates, that the last obstacle had been removed without any action on his part. He was innocent of poor Desmond's death, and that was a real relief to Eustace; he had liked the boy and the idea of killing him, even though death would be a merciful release, had been definitely repugnant to him. Not only was he now relieved of that unpleasant task, but he was also saved, almost miraculously saved, from the appalling risk which that task would have involved.

But was he saved ? That was the other side to the picture, the alarming aspect of the detective's visit. There had been some unpleasant, even sinister, meaning behind all those questions. The inspector himself was a fool, but he had almost certainly been acting under instructions. Why ? What had the police got in their minds ?

As he shaved, Eustace turned the problem over

in his mind and before long he thought he saw what had happened. Desmond had come to the inevitable end which, sooner or later, awaits all the unfortunate victims of that terrible disease. No constitution, undermined by shock and suffering, can stand up indefinitely against the effects of hypnotic drugs, however carefully administered. His end had probably come sooner and more suddenly than had been expected, but Mrs. Toumlin herself had said that the boy had been unwell during the last week ; no doubt that had been the symptom of break-up. The death was natural and inevitable, but the police had jumped to the conclusion that there was something sinister behind it. Why ? Obviously because of what had gone before. Within little more than two months there had been four sudden deaths in the Hendel family, as a result of which he, Eustace, from the position of rank outsider, had moved up to first favourite. Odds on favourite now ; in fact, dead certainty. And so the police, muddle-headed idiots, had jumped to the conclusion that he must, or at any rate might, be responsible for what had happened.

It was rank injustice, but it was a disquieting idea. Obviously the Scottish police had had suspicions about the death of David, even though they had evidently decided that they had insufficient evidence on which to proceed. They must have communicated their suspicions to the English police, and

Scotland Yard had evidently, as Eustace had more than once feared they might, put one and one together and were jumping to an entirely erroneous conclusion. Not only one and one, but even two and one and one, making four! That fool detective had even questioned him about the accidental drowning of Howard and Harold! It was preposterous, and of course there was no danger in that, because he could easily prove that he had not set eyes on them for years. But there was danger in the other idea—Desmond. There was danger because, innocent as he was, there was some foundation for their suspicions in that case.

Eustace cursed his own persistence in trying to get access to Desmond's flat. Five times in a fortnight; it did seem rather a lot, rather odd, considering that he had never before been near the boy. There was a good, and perfectly innocent, reason for that, but Eustace was broad-minded enough to realize that the police had some grounds for raising their eyebrows.

If only he had waited! There was this gift from the gods waiting to fall into his lap and he, like a fool, had gone fussing round, drawing attention to himself, pushing his head into an entirely unnecessary noose. Attention? Was it more than that that he had drawn? Had he actually made them suspect *before* the death? It was a disturbing thought. Eustace recalled Mrs. Toumlin's odd

behaviour on the occasion of his last two visits.
She had been normal and pleasant enough the first
time he called, but after that she had been decidedly
queer. He remembered that she had seemed
embarrassed, even nervous, that day when he had
met Henry Carr coming out of the flat and when
she had said that Desmond was not well enough to
see him. Then, on the Sunday when, by arrangement with her, he had had his second talk with
Desmond, she had been the same, had never left
him for an instant, and had hustled him out of the
place as quickly as she possibly could. Why was
that ? Was she suspicious of him then ? Had the
police . . . ?

With a shock Eustace remembered the incident
of the pantry door that day, the door opposite the
sitting-room. It had been shut when he arrived,
open—or rather, ajar—when he left. At the time
he had thought that the parlourmaid must have
returned from church, but he had met her outside.
He had assumed that it must have been the cook,
though cooks do not usually go into a pantry in the
middle of a Sunday morning. But was there
another explanation ? Was it conceivable that
Mrs. Toumlin, warned by the police, had notified
them of his intended visit and that they had put a
man there—in case anything happened ? That
indeed was a truly alarming idea ; if the police had
been so suspicious of him as all that, he had indeed

been walking on the edge of a precipice. What a merciful dispensation of providence that he had done nothing to incriminate himself, that Desmond had died naturally and that he, Eustace, was absolutely innocent of that death.

With a sigh of relief Eustace finished his second cup of coffee and rose to his feet. Better forget all about the appalling risk he had run and concentrate on the wonderful fortune that had befallen him. Heir presumptive to one of the richest peers in England and bound inevitably by law to succeed! Always provided, of course, that he survived Lord Barradys! And as the old man was ninety, that seemed something worth betting on. How the money-lenders would pester him now! How that fellow Isaacson would kick himself for not accommodating him the last time he had wanted money, for being actually rude about it! The fellow would come cringing now, as soon as the fact of the now-unbreakable entail became known, as it almost certainly would. Well, Isaacson would get no more business from him. Indeed, it would be unnecessary to deal with any money-lender; his bank would be only too glad to lend him all he wanted on that security.

Eustace stretched his arms luxuriously. It was a glorious prospect. Unlimited money, luxury . . . and Jill. Jill must be told at once; he would go round now and break the glad tidings to her. No need to worry her with that detective's silly questions. All that would be put right by the inquest, after the P.M. had cleared up the cause of death. Dear, lovely Jill; he wasn't going to worry her; love and happiness were all that she must have, and by God, she should have them now.

Filling his cigarette case from a fresh box, his eye fell on the depleted box of Dudeville chocolates which had barely survived the previous evening's party. The sight of it reminded him of that other chocolate, the peppermint-cream, which he had locked up in his writing-table, intending to experiment on it to-day. Thank goodness, that necessity was washed out. It had been a mad idea, really, the sort of thing one only thought of late at night after a good deal to drink and invariably discarded in the morning. It would have been appallingly difficult and risky, even if it had been even possible. Thank God, it was no longer necessary even to try. All the same, the thought of that chocolate reminded him of what lay beside it in that locked drawer— the little glass tube of morphia tablets.

A qualm of uneasiness passed through Eustace. That detective had been sitting within a foot or two of the writing-table; if he had known what was in that drawer it might have been very awkward. He had not of course been alone in the room . . . at least . . . Eustace remembered that Hamilton had taken some time to wake him, that though the detective had been left in the hall there might possibly have been time for him to come in here and snoop round. The drawer was locked, but detectives, in books at any rate, had skeleton keys . . .

Quickly Eustace unlocked the drawer and sighed with relief when he saw the little bottle lying there beside the chocolate. He picked it up and put it in his pocket ; it would be wiser to get rid of the thing ; there was no need for it now and there was no point in running unnecessary risks. The chocolate he put back in the Dudeville box, then, with an odd feeling of repugnance at the idea of Jill eating something that might have contained death, he picked it out again and threw it into the waste-paper basket. Taking the Dudeville box with him—Jill adored the things—he walked round to Pearl Street.

Jill was still in bed, reading the *Daily Mirror* with her morning tea and toast. She received Eustace's news with a delight that enchanted him. After the first rapture had subsided, the two of them settled down to discuss the golden future. Jill had set her heart on a cottage on the river at Maidenhead and Eustace, who had by now discarded the alarming aspect of Inspector Wennessy's news, willingly entered into the spirit of the game and promised to hire a car and take her down there for an exploration that very afternoon. The talk then turned to clothes and Eustace realized that he would have to make arrangements for increasing his bank balance

at an early date. He was a little bit doubtful as
to what evidence of the security of his position the
bank manager would want. It would hardly be wise
for him to display too accurate a knowledge of the
affairs of the elder branch. He would have a talk
with Henry Carr about it ; Henry was interested
and friendly ; he knew Eustace's position and
would be able to advise him.

The happy couple motored down to Maidenhead
and lunched at Skindles. Their search for a river-
side cottage was not actually successful, as nothing
of the right size was at the moment available, but
the agents thought that it would not be too difficult
to find one. Nothing had so far been said between
Eustace and Jill about marriage but there could be
very little doubt but that things were tending that
way ; the future Lord Barradys would have to
mind his social p's and q's ; unless he was prepared
to give up Jill altogether he would almost certainly
have to marry her. And why not ? He genuinely
loved her and wanted no one else. Besides, though
he did not consciously admit this, even to himself,
she knew too much about him and his recent doings
to be antagonized.

Eustace drove Jill back to Pearl Street and then
returned to his own flat to prepare for his second
house-warming. This was to be a bachelor affair
and one designed strictly for business. George
Priestley and Freddie Gallater, both of the Jermyn

Club, were coming, and each was bringing a young friend who liked a game of poker and was not too devastatingly clever at it. Young men of this type had kept Eustace in comfort for two or three years in his St. James' flat ; it was only when they began to tail off, as a result of ill-natured rumours, coupled with the universal shortage of money, that Eustace's troubles had begun. Now he was on the rise again and a new *clientèle* could be expected to gather round him.

At first Eustace had thought of dining at a restaurant—the Café Royal, perhaps—but he had decided not to court any kind of publicity. Hamilton had the character of being a good cook and he was to be given a chance to show what he could do ; nothing elaborate, turtle soup from Fortnum's, a mixed grill, a cheese *soufflé*. Eustace had not yet laid down a cellar, but his wine-merchant—*not* Cousin William—was arranging to provide him with decanted claret and port of respectable lineage. These, with not too old and mild a brandy, should do the trick.

George Priestley, whose amusement it was to disregard the ordinary canons of tact, irritated Eustace at the start by introducing his guest, one Selwyn Battie, to ' the future Lord Barradys.' It was exactly the sort of thing that Eustace wanted to avoid at the present stage of affairs. George, however, thought it was funny, and after he had

drunk his second glass of 1893 brandy and had won
a thumping ace-pot, he gave his humour free rein.

" You know, Eustace," he said, dealing a fresh
hand, " your luck is positively uncanny ; (are you
coming in, Freddie ?) how many embryo barons
have faded out of your way ?   Four, isn't it ? "

" You're dealing, George ; I want three.   And
you're not funny."

" Here's a fellow, Battie," continued Priestley
imperturbably, " who's positively wading through
the blood of cousins to the throne.   (Dealer takes
two to a busted straight).   Positively indecent, I
call it.   I wonder the Yard haven't pulled you in
already.   (And five's ten ; up to you, Freddie.)
Come to think of it, I did notice a large man in a
bowler hat lurking in a doorway when I arrived."

Eustace's heart missed a beat.   Probably this
fool Priestley was romancing but his remark was an
unpleasant reminder ; it brought one back to grim
possibilities.

With an effort Eustace threw off these disquieting
thoughts and concentrated his attention on the game.
It was going well.   He himself was losing steadily
as he had intended, though not heavily.   George
Priestley, after a run of luck and consequent garru-
lity, was now overplaying and would soon be in
trouble unless he stopped talking ; he was a good
card player but he fancied himself as a talking
card player and in that he overestimated his own

skill. Selwyn Battie was comfortably up and was clearly enjoying himself. Freddie Gallater was about square and was probably pulling a bit, while the young stockbroker he had brought, Thornton Rush, though obviously an inexperienced player, had not lost enough to worry him ; in fact, one or two well-lost coups by Eustace would send him away happy.

It was an auspicious opening of the new *régime*. Eustace felt sure that these two young men would come again and bring others with them. Eventually, of course, he would not need their money, but until old Barradys died they would be extremely useful.

The party broke up soon after midnight. As they were putting on their coats the young stockbroker asked Eustace if he were a relation of George Hendel, the wine-merchant.

" I thought you must be," he said ; " there's a family likeness. I meet him in the City fairly often and we play golf together sometimes. He's been rather pleased with himself lately."

Eustace smiled. He knew what George had been pleased about ; poor George, who would never now inherit the Barradys fortune. It gave an added zest to Eustace's own good fortune to think of the bitter disappointment that Desmond's death would bring to those smug cousins of his.

He accompanied his guests downstairs and walked to the corner of the block with them. There was no sign of any 'large man in a bowler hat' any-where. Obviously George Priestley had been pulling his leg. Anyway, why should there be ?

Eustace returned to his flat and prepared to sleep the sleep of the just, the innocent, and the blessed of fortune.

CHAPTER XX

THE following morning Eustace attended the inquest, to which he had been summoned. He found himself sitting next to Henry Carr, beyond whom were his wife, Julia, Blanche Hendel, and William and George, the wine-merchants. They all greeted him with subdued but friendly smiles, while Mr. William Christendome gave him a formal bow. The Coroner, Mr. Ellinstone, who sat with a jury, announced that he had viewed the body and that the jury might do so if they wished. They did not. Mr. Ellinstone then explained that he only intended to take formal evidence of identification that day, as it would be some little time before the report of the Home Office Analyst, to whom, by his direction, the organs of the deceased had been sent, would be ready. At this point a good many people in the court wondered why, in that case, they had been summoned to attend, and one among them, an elderly gentleman with a white moustache, wearing well-cut London clothes, put his feelings into words.

" I am Sir Horace Spavage ", he said, rising to his feet. " I am the physician in charge of this case and I desire to give my evidence to-day. I am expecting at any time now to be summoned to Scotland in consultation in connection with the . . . er . . . with the case of a Royal Personage. It would be most inconvenient and it might even be impossible for me to attend an adjourned inquest. My evidence is important but it is quite formal, and I can see no reason why it should not be given to-day."

Sir Horace sat down, well pleased with the effect of his words upon the room in general and the Press in particular. Pencils were flying over paper. Mr. Ellinstone glanced across at a uniformed police-superintendent who was sitting not far from him ; a slight shrug of the shoulders seemed to indicate lack of objection rather than acquiescence.

" Very well, Sir Horace ", said the Coroner quietly. " I will call you as soon as I have taken evidence of identification. I quite appreciate that your time is not your own. Call Julia Carr."

Henry gave his wife's hand a squeeze and she moved forward to the witnesses' chair, took her oath, and sat down.

" You are Mrs. Henry Carr and the nearest relative of the deceased, Mr. Desmond Hendel ? " the Coroner asked courteously.

" Yes ; that is, except his great-grandfather, Lord Barradys."

" Quite so. Lord Barradys," Mr. Ellinstone explained to the jury, " is a gentleman of great age and was unable to make the journey from his home in Northumberland. With that exception you are the nearest relative, Mrs. Carr ? "

" Yes ; I am his first cousin, once removed. I am the only surviving grandchild of Lord Barradys."

" You have been shown the body on which this enquiry is being held. Can you identify it ? "

" Yes. It is my cousin, Desmond Hendel."

" Thank you, Mrs. Carr."

Julia was succeeded by Mr. William Christendome, who, as family solicitor, corroborated her evidence.

" Now, Sir Horace."

Sir Horace Spavage took the oath and having explained, without unbecoming modesty, who and what he was, proceeded with his particular evidence.

" I have been in general charge of Mr. Desmond Hendel's case since he first developed symptoms of the disease that has just resulted in his death."

" That has yet to be proved, of course ", murmured the Coroner.

Sir Horace frowned.

" Of course, of course ; technically. The time to which I refer is July 1933. The boy had been complaining for some time of pain in the thigh ; there had also been loss of weight and of tone generally. I at once suspected a sarcoma of the femur and on my advice, after X-ray photographs had been taken, Captain Hendel took the boy to see Sir John Phillidor, senior consulting-surgeon at St. Christ-

243

opher's, a colleague of mine and a man of the highest distinction."

" Scratch my back ", whispered Henry Carr.

" We never advertise ", murmured Eustace, then bit his tongue. Fortunately, Henry appeared not to notice the pronoun.

" Sir John confirmed my opinion and agreed with me that the disease had passed the stage when treatment by radium or deep X-rays might be expected to check the growth. It was decided that the only hope of saving the boy's life was by amputation at the hip. This was done, by Sir John, of course, in . . . er . . ."

Sir Horace consulted a card.

" . . . in September of the same year. The operation was entirely successful. For a year all went well. There was of course some prostration from shock and the heart gave a little trouble, but the patient began to pick up after a time and I had hope, the highest hope, that the disease had been scotched. Unfortunately, in October of last year there were signs of a recurrence, this time in the spine. As soon as this was confirmed we knew that there was no hope. Everything, of course, that could be done was done, but . . ."

Sir Horace shrugged his fine shoulders.

" I gave him a year, at the outside eighteen months, in my mind. The boy had great courage, remarkable vitality. I had begun to think that the longer estimate would prove correct, but, as so often happens, the end has come quite suddenly."

Mr. Ellinstone waited to see whether the great physician had anything to add, then began to ask his own questions.

"You say, Sir Horace, that everything that could be done was done. Does that refer to active remedial treatment or to medicines designed merely to relieve pain?"

"There was remedial treatment, if by that you mean what I take you to mean. Deep X-rays were applied. One had no real expectation of a cure, but of course it does not do to appear to give up hope, either in the interest of the patient or . . . er . . . the relatives."

"Or . . . er . . . the profession", murmured Henry Carr.

"And there were medicines as well, perhaps", suggested the Coroner.

"Certainly. There was a mixture, containing veronal, a hypnotic drug, taken in regular four-hourly doses throughout the day, and the last thing at night a sleeping draught containing opium."

"And the effect of these hypnotic drugs would be . . . what?"

"To relieve pain and to induce sleep."

Mr. Ellinstone thought for a while. Then:

"You said just now, Sir Horace, that as soon as the disease recurred in the spine you knew there was

245

no hope, you gave your patient eighteen months at the outside. That means presumably that you expected death to occur some time within that period. Will you tell the jury what, in the normal course under such circumstances, would actually cause death ? "

Sir Horace Spavage tapped his pince-nez against his well-trimmed finger-nails and frowned in thought.

" I take it that the jury will not want a highly technical dissertation ", he said at last. " Putting it quite simply, death would follow from exhaustion of the vital centres."

" What would cause the exhaustion ? "

" Primarily, of course, the disease itself. There would be a steady drain of vitality by reason of the malignant growth."

" And the drugs ? Would they contribute to the exhaustion ? "

" In a sense, yes. The effect of the drugs would be to a certain extent contradictory ; by inducing sleep they would stimulate the vital centres, but they also possess in themselves a depressive effect."

" On the whole, would you say that the effect of hypnotic drugs is destructive ? "

" I should make no such general statement."

The Coroner allowed a slight smile to cross his lips. He knew that he was treading on delicate medical ground, but he had his own very strong opinions, based on long experience, on this subject.

" Let us confine ourselves to the particular case, then ", he said. " In your opinion, would the hypnotic drugs which you prescribed contribute, on balance, to the exhaustion of the vital centres which you say you would expect to be the cause of death ? "

Sir Horace flushed angrily.

" That is a very misleading question, sir ", he said. " You ignore the fact that without such drugs the patient would suffer terribly ; it would be inhuman to deny him the relief which these drugs give."

" I am not ignoring that fact at all, Sir Horace ", said Mr. Ellinstone quietly. " I entirely appreciate the reason for administering hypnotic drugs in a case of this kind, but I have a reason for wishing to know whether, in your opinion, such drugs are directly contributory to the exhaustion which would normally cause death. May I take it that that is so ? "

" Yes ; it is ", said Sir Horace shortly. " Hypnotic drugs, taken in the potency required in a case of this kind, would have a toxic effect and contribute to the exhaustion to which I have referred."

" Thank you, Sir Horace. Now may I ask you . . . you have of course seen the deceased since his death ? "

" I was present at his death. I was sent for by the nurse in charge of the case.

" That would be Mrs. Toumlin ? "

" Yes."

" And you formed an opinion as to the cause of death ? "

" Certainly. There is no doubt about it. Death was due to exhaustion of the vital centres arising from a sarcoma of the spine. I should have been prepared to give a certificate to that effect but you, sir, directed that a post-mortem examination should be made and it does not therefore fall to me to give a certificate."

" Quite so. But I take it that you consider the cause of death to be what all along you have anticipated."

" Certainly."

" You have no reason at all to doubt that ? "

" None whatever."

" Thank you, Sir Horace. That is all I have to ask you, unless . . ." he turned to the jury. " Has any member of the jury any question to ask the witness, through me ? "

A large red-faced man, who had evidently been on the point of bursting for some time, now relieved himself in speech.

" These 'ypnotic drugs ", he said, glaring at the Physician-in-Ordinary, " to my mind they're the cause of 'alf the trouble an' suicides we're always reading about. When doctors like you . . ."

" I said ' through me ', sir ", said the Coroner firmly, " and that is not a question."

" Well, I mean to say, Mr. Coroner, 'e says 'imself

they was the cause of death. What I want to know is, why do these slap-up, three-guineas-a-time doctors use the nasty stuff ? "

" Sir Horace made it quite clear, I think, that in this case the drugs were necessary to relieve suffering. We are only dealing with this case. Thank you, Sir Horace, we need not keep you any longer."

The ruffled physician walked out of court, while the Coroner whispered to the uniformed police-superintendent. After a short pause, he collected his papers.

" I shall adjourn the enquiry until this day fortnight, when the report of the Home Office Analyst will be available ", he said. Then, turning to the jury, he added gravely, " I must remind you, members of the jury, that you must not discuss the case with any outside person, nor make any communication to the Press. Thank you."

" What on earth were we called for, if that's all that's going to happen ? " asked Eustace, as he and Henry Carr settled themselves in a taxi. Julia had gone off with Blanche to do some shopping.

" It's a little way they have ", replied the solicitor. " Coroners are a law unto themselves. They're going to be tightened up though ; Departmental Committee sitting now."

Eustace thought for a while. There had been nothing disquieting about the inquest so far, but he felt vaguely uncomfortable.

" Why does he adjourn for as long as a fortnight ?
It doesn't take that time for the Analyst to do his
job . . . surely ? "

The ' surely ? ' was a hasty afterthought.

Henry Carr looked curiously at his companion.

" That's quite a normal adjournment " he said,
" when the police think they want to make any
enquiries."

Eustace stiffened. So that was it. The police
were still sniffing up the wrong tree. No need to
worry, of course ; Spavage had had no doubts about
the cause of death. Still, it was . . . disquieting.

The two men lunched at the Jermyn and Eustace
found himself more than ever drawn to Julia's
husband. There was no nonsense about him. He
did not pretend to ignore the astonishing good
fortune that had fallen to Eustace, nor yet the
awkwardness of the circumstances attending it. He
was both friendly and sympathetic. Eustace asked
him what he should do about arranging a loan with
his bank and Carr advised him to wait until after
the adjourned inquest. Something might come out
there which would make his position as heir-presump-
tive clear without any effort on his part.

Feeling relieved by this sound advice, Eustace
returned to his flat and was received by Hamilton
with the news that another police-officer had called
just before one. The man-servant had explained
that his master was at the inquest and might not

return till late in the day; Inspector Darnell, as
he had called himself, had said that he would wait a
while on the chance of Mr. Hendel coming back for
luncheon. No effort of Hamilton had been able to
dissuade him; he had stayed for half an hour and
then taken himself off, promising to call again.

Again Eustace felt that little shiver of disquiet.
Another policeman; why another? What on earth
was there for the police to investigate? Evidently
it was something which they considered important
or the man would not have waited all that time.
Well, it was no good speculating; he would know
soon enough. In the meantime, he was not going to
wait in for the fellow. Giving orders to Hamilton
about dinner he let himself out of the flat and found
a small, neatly dressed man upon the mat.

The man raised a bowler hat.

" Mr. Eustace Hendel ? " he enquired.

This was unpleasant. This opportune arrival
looked as if the fellow had either waited for him or
followed him.

" Yes. What is it ? "

" Just a word with you in private, sir; if I may
come inside."

CHAPTER XXI

CHIEF-INSPECTOR
DARNELL

AGAINST his will, Eustace found himself back in the flat and, in another moment, in the sitting-room. On closer inspection, his visitor appeared to be not so small after all; no doubt the excellence of his figure had given that impression.

" I am Chief-Inspector Darnell, sir; Criminal Investigation Department. That is my warrant card."

' Chief Detective-Inspector ', it said; Eustace's knowledge about the higher ranks of the police force was vague, but this sounded a big noise. He handed back the card, with as careless an air as he could muster.

" I have to ask you one or two questions in connection with the death of your cousin, Mr. Desmond Hendel, sir ", he said.

" But there's already been one of your fellows round here ", said Eustace.

" Ah, yes, sir; that would be the Divisional Detective-Inspector. I am from the Yard."

An ugly sound, ominous.

" I can't think what you want to find out from me.

I've only known Desmond a fortnight. I know nothing about his illness."

" Nothing, sir ? "

" Nothing except what Mrs. Toumlin told me and what I heard to-day at the inquest."

" You took a great interest in your cousin, I understand, sir—in the last fortnight."

The words were simple enough, but there was an unpleasant implication behind them. This man, shrewd, quick-witted, was obviously a different proposition to the clumsy Divisional Inspector. It would be no use trying to shirk his questions ; better take the bull by the horns.

" You're asking me the same sort of questions as your colleague asked yesterday ", he said. " It's quite obvious that there's something behind them. I think I'm entitled to ask what it is."

Chief-Inspector Darnell nodded.

" That's quite reasonable, sir ", he said, " and I'll be perfectly frank with you. Four deaths— sudden deaths—have occurred in the senior branch of your family within the last two months. As a result of those deaths, from having been, if I am rightly informed, in some financial difficulties, you find yourself the heir to a considerable estate. Now that may be perfectly natural and straightforward, but there are circumstances which compel us to investigate the position. There is nothing to connect you with the death of your cousins in Cornwall, but you alone were present with Captain David Hendel when he met with a very remarkable accident in Scotland, and for the fortnight before his son, Mr. Desmond Hendel, died, you have made repeated attempts to visit him and to see him alone; that last fact in itself is too significant for us to pass it over without investigation. There, sir; I think that puts my cards fairly on the table, as you wished."

Chief-Inspector Darnell leaned back in his chair and smiled pleasantly at his companion. Eustace was surprised to find that, now that he knew exactly how things stood, he felt quite calm and even confident.

"I see", he said. "Thank you for telling me. You'll forgive me if I say that I think you're talking a lot of nonsense, but I suppose you're only carrying out your orders."

"That's right, sir. Now may I hope that you will be as frank with me as I have been with you."

This conversation was following a line so different from what he had imagined would happen that Eustace was almost amused.

"But oughtn't you to warn me that anything I say will be taken down in writing and used as evidence against me?" he asked.

"Not 'against you', sir; that's out of date; 'may be used in evidence' is the expression. Oh no, sir; we haven't reached that stage and I'm sure I hope we never shall. That caution is only given when it has been decided to charge the person concerned. Now I am only making a preliminary enquiry and so there's no need for me to caution you."

Rather a cold-blooded procedure, all this. Eustace was not sure that he liked it ; it was so impersonal. Still, forewarned should be forearmed. He braced himself for the coming interrogation. Chief-Inspector Darnell, however, seemed to be in no hurry. He looked round the room.

" I took the liberty of looking round your bookshelves when I was waiting this morning, sir ", he said. " I'm interested in books myself ; besides, I always think you can learn a lot about a man by the books he reads."

What on earth was the fellow havering like this for ; why didn't he get down to business ?

" I noticed that you'd got a Holt's *Medical Jurisprudence* there ; I've never seen one before, though I've heard of it. We've got our Taylor, of course, down at the Yard, and we've got Smith, but not Holt."

Hell ! Why had he forgotten about that infernal book ? He had forgotten all about it since before he went to Scotland. When changing quarters he had crammed all his books into an old trunk and pushed them into his new bookcase without looking at them particularly ; he had never noticed the Holt. How on earth was he to explain it ?

" Not a new copy, I noticed ", continued the detective blandly ; " been in your possession some time, perhaps ? "

What was he to say ?

" Yes, some time. That is . . ."

But Chief-Inspector Darnell saved him further anxiety.

" No doubt since you were a medical student, Mr. Hendel ? "

Eustace stiffened. So they knew that ! Of course they would—once they began to make serious enquiries. Lucky he had not lied about it. At least this fellow played fair ; he was not trying to trap him.

" That seems a long time to me ", he said, as calmly as he could manage. " I qualified in 1926 and only practised for a year."

" I see, sir. No doubt you'll have kept your old books and instruments ? "

" Not many."

" And drugs ? "

Danger. From the slight change in the tone of Darnell's voice Eustace knew that this was the launching of an attack.

" Oh no. No point in keeping them."

" None at all, sir ? "

Quiet, that question, but deadly insistent. He must make no mistake here. Suddenly Eustace remembered the bottle of morphia tablets. It was in his waistcoat pocket at this very moment, unless Hamilton had removed it. It was all Eustace could do not to feel for it with his fingers. He had meant to get rid of it yesterday, but in the excitement of planning the future with Jill he had forgotten all about it. It was so slight that it must have escaped his notice when emptying his pockets before dinner last night. Now he was wearing the same suit of clothes—his new ones had not yet come. Suppose, after all, that he was arrested now and those tablets found on him !—after he had denied having any ! Besides, the police might already know that he had got them. It had been easy enough to get them, when he was planning David's death ; all he had to do was to write his own order for them ; he was still on the register. The police, if they really were after him, might have traced that. Better to be frank ; it might be that this was a lucky way out of a trap.

These thoughts flashed through Eustace's brain. There was hardly a perceptible pause before he answered.

" Only morphia. I always carry that. One never knows when it may be wanted if there's an accident and a doctor is called for. It may save someone terrible agony."

Eustace spoke quietly. Calmly he put his fingers into his waistcoat pocket. No ; yes ; there it was ; no wonder it had escaped his notice last night. He pulled out the little bottle and handed it to the detective, who took it and examined it carefully.

" Quarter grain tablets, sir. A full bottle. How long would you have had that ? "

" Not very long. I lost my last one ; only about a month ago, I think."

" I see, sir."

Chief-Inspector Darnell handed the bottle back.

" And that's the only drug you keep ? "

" That's all."

The detective nodded and looked at his finger-nails.

" You've had some transactions with money-lenders, I understand, sir ? "

God, what these fellows knew !

" I have. No crime in that, is there ? "

Darnell ignored the sally.

" I have information that you were in debt to a money-lender named Isaacson and that, at the time of your cousin, Mr. Howard Hendel's death, he was pressing you for payment of an overdue instalment. Is that correct, sir ? "

" That is correct ", replied Eustace sullenly.

" My further information is that, a short time after the death of your two cousins in Cornwall, you called on Isaacson and asked for a further loan, on the strength of your improved chances of succeeding to Lord Barradys' estates."

Hell ! That fellow Isaacson had been talking—

the last thing one would expect from a money-lender. Why had he talked ? There was an answer to that question, more sinister than the fact itself. The police had been pressing Isaacson and he had been afraid to get himself implicated in a murder case ! Eustace remembered now that Isaacson had refused to see him when he called after David's death; he had wondered at the time whether the money-lender could possibly have any suspicions. He remembered, too, now that at that interview with Isaacson after Howard's death he (Eustace) had talked indiscreetly about the chances of his succeeding to the estate. That was after he had decided to kill David and it had suddenly struck him what a foolish thing he was doing to talk like that—that Isaacson might remember it if anything happened to David. And he had remembered it ! and had talked to the police.

Eustace became aware that the detective was watching him, waiting, perhaps, for an answer.

" Certainly I did ", he said ; " there's nothing mysterious about that. I was in difficulties and then that accident happened and I played it for what it was worth. I tried to bluff Isaacson and I failed. That's all."

Chief-Inspector Darnell nodded.

" I see, sir. And then again, after Captain David Hendel's death you called once more on Isaacson."

" He didn't see me ", put in Eustace quickly.

" That was with the idea of making a fresh application for a loan on the strength of the still further improvement in your prospects ? "

" It was." No use denying it ; better put on a bold face. " Obviously my prospects were improved—very materially. Any fool would realize that. What was the point of not taking advantage of it ? "

" Quite, sir. And did Mr. Isaacson oblige you ? "

" He did not."

" Why was that, sir ? "

" I don't know. He did not have the courtesy to see me."

" So you went elsewhere, sir ? "

" Why do you say that ? "

Chief-Inspector Darnell shrugged his shoulders.

" Within the next day or two, sir, you had taken this very desirable flat and engaged a man-servant. That represents something more definite than an expectation ; it represents hard cash."

Eustace was shrewd enough to realize that Chief-Inspector Darnell was guessing now. He did not actually know about the £500 advanced by the ' British Loan and Mutual Assistance Society '. Better leave him in ignorance ; Eustace remembered talking rather big to Mr. J. Levy ; better not have the police questioning him too.

" You seem to have got all the facts for yourself,

Inspector ", he said. " I don't think there's any more I can tell you."

The detective looked at him carefully, then shrugged his shoulders.

" I rather thought we were being frank with each other, sir ", he said. " Now, I wonder whether you would care to tell me a little more about your friendship with Mr. Desmond Hendel. That began quite recently, I understand."

" Yes. I knew practically nothing about that branch of the family until I went down to my cousin's funeral in Cornwall. Then they were very kind to me, particularly Mrs. Howard Hendel and Mr. and Mrs. Carr. At Mrs. Howard Hendel's suggestion, I think, I was invited to stay with Captain Hendel in Scotland and I was with him, as you probably know, when he met with his accident. Naturally I was a good deal distressed and I asked Mrs. Howard Hendel, who was there too, about David's son, whom I had not previously met. She told me about him and urged me to go and see him when I got back to London. I did so. That's all."

" You visited him rather frequently in that short time, didn't you, sir ? Was there any reason for that ? "

" I liked him. I thought he was lonely. I thought I could help to keep him amused. Other members of the family did the same, particularly

Bla . . . Mrs. Howard Hendel and Mr. Henry Carr."

" Ah, yes ; so I understand. Did Mr. Desmond express a wish that you should call often ? "

" Not definitely, but I thought he liked talking to me."

" Did you see him alone ? "

" On the first occasion, yes. The second time Mrs. Toumlin stayed with us."

" So you thought you would go again when she was out ? "

Danger again. This was a crucial question. Should he admit it frankly or pretend it was chance ?

" On two occasions when I called Mrs. Toumlin told me that Desmond was too tired to see any more visitors. I thought she was being fussy, so one day I went when I thought she might be out shopping."

" Ah, you admit, then, that you deliberately chose a time when you might hope to be alone."

Eustace flushed angrily.

" That's not at all a fair interpretation of what I said," he protested. " It's not a question of ' admitting ' or of wanting to be alone. I say that it is a fact that I went there when I thought Mrs. Toumlin might be out because I wanted to talk to Desmond ; I thought it was absurd of her to coddle him so much."

" I see, Mr. Hendel," said Darnell smoothly. " And I suppose that, as you had become attached to Mr. Desmond, you took him little presents ? "

" Presents ? "

" Books ? Cigarettes ? Or perhaps chocolates ? "

Chocolates ! Eustace felt himself flushing. Were the police on to that idea too ; the idea that he had so nearly tried ? Instinctively he looked round the room ; that box of Dudeville's ! Ah, he remembered ; he had taken it to Jill only yesterday morning. What a bit of luck. But the single chocolate —the peppermint-cream ? He had thrown it away ; into the waste-paper basket or the grate. Well, there had been a fire last night, and if it had been in the waste-paper basket Hamilton would surely have cleared it away before now. Still, it was not a certainty and this infernal detective had been in the room for half an hour that morning, nosing about.

Eustace felt his confidence oozing away. They knew so much, these police ; they asked such infernally awkward questions. Innocent though he was, he was in a very awkward position.

" I didn't give him any presents at all."

" No presents at all."

Chief-Inspector Darnell stroked his chin, ruminating. After a while he rose to his feet.

" I think that's all I have to ask you at the moment, sir. Unless, that is, you wish to qualify anything that you have said ? "

" Why should I ? "

" Something might have slipped your memory,

sir. For instance, are you quite certain that morphia is the only drug that you have in your possession ? "

" Perfectly certain."

" Or have had ? I must remind you, sir, that it would be a serious matter for you to attempt to mislead the police now. You will realize that it is not impossible for us to find out for ourselves whether you have purchased any other drug."

Eustace shook his head impatiently.

" I tell you I have had nothing except morphia in my possession since I gave up practising."

" Very well, sir ; then we know how we stand. I'll wish you good-afternoon, and I must apologize for taking up so much of your time." He walked to the door, but with his fingers on the handle paused.

" If I may give you a friendly word of advice, sir," he said, " I suggest that you might consider being represented at the adjourned inquest."

CHAPTER XXII

CONSULTATION

AFTER seeing Chief-Inspector Darnell out of the
flat Eustace returned to his sitting-room and helped
himself to a strong whiskey and soda from the
tantalus which he kept in a red lacquer corner
cupboard.

The detective's last words had given him a most
unpleasant shock. They had sounded perfectly
sincere and Eustace knew that the police were never
so dangerous, never so much in earnest, as when
they were being perfectly fair. Not only in earnest,
but also confident. For some reason or other they
believed that he was responsible for Desmond's
death, and though they had not—if Darnell was to
be believed—yet reached a stage at which they
could charge him, they were going to do their utmost
to construct a case against him.

Eustace realized that though there was not—
could not be—any direct evidence against him,
there were circumstances which might reasonably
lead the police to be suspicious. That being so, it
would probably be wise to follow Darnell's advice,
at least to the extent of consulting a solicitor. Who
should he consult ? Eustace had had no professional

dealings with solicitors since the time, nearly ten years ago, when Beryl Fotherwaite had left him all that money. That had been a local firm in the provincial town where he had been in practice, and they would be no use for a job of this kind.

It wasn't going to be easy to explain his position to a solicitor. After all, there was a good deal that he could not tell anyone, and a certain amount more that would be distinctly awkward. For instance, any solicitor whom he consulted would want to know why he had made such frequent attempts to see Desmond in the last fortnight ; the explanation he had given to the police was distinctly thin and the real reason could not be told to anyone. There was a third reason, neither quite true nor quite false, which might convince someone who knew the whole inner history of the case—an inner history which Eustace was reluctant to tell to a stranger.

There was one man to whom he could give this version of the truth and who would understand his thoughts and actions : Henry Carr. And he was a solicitor. Carr already knew all about his hopes and fears. He knew and he sympathized. He would understand if Eustace said : ' I wanted to see Desmond as often as I could—and alone—in order to make a good impression on him, to stop him doing what Lord Barradys advised.' That would be a difficult thing to explain to a strange solicitor, because it would mean admitting that he knew the hoped-for inheritance was on the point of slipping away from him—and that would be half-way to admitting a motive for killing Desmond before he came of age.

It might not be possible to give that explanation in court ; it might be too dangerous. That was a matter for an experienced solicitor to advise, and there was no one's advice he would rather have than Henry Carr's. He was shrewd and he was sympathetic. Eustace believed that Henry liked him, and it was perfectly clear that he did not believe the rumours about David's death which must undoubtedly have reached his ears.

With a sigh of relief Eustace came to his decision, and, true to his one good rule, went straight to the telephone and put a call through to Carr's suburban office. The solicitor had returned, was engaged all the rest of the day, but would be glad to dine with Eustace at his flat that evening.

Eustace spent a good deal of the afternoon in thinking over just how much he should tell Henry Carr. The question of the morphia tablets ; he must know about them ; would he swallow the explanation given to the police ? the fact that they had been bought only a short time after he first heard of the possibility of his succession, and only a short time before David's and Desmond's sudden deaths, was painfully suggestive. He might have difficulty in persuading a jury, and he certainly could not prove that this bottle was only a replacement. The question of the 'Medical Jurisprudence' book; he would not put it beyond the police to discover just when that was bought; taken in conjunction with the morphia tablets, that would be a damning piece of evidence. Should Carr know about it?

Eustace did not go round and see Jill, which he would have liked to do. He was beginning to realize what a serious danger Jill's knowledge of his plans and actions represented. If the police got on to her and questioned her there was no knowing what she might not let out; she was shrewd enough, but women—in Eustace's experience—sometimes spoke before they thought. It would be better to keep right away from her, in the hope that the police would not discover her existence.

Henry Carr turned up in good time and apparently in good spirits. Nothing was said about the subject uppermost in both their minds until dinner was over and port put on the table, when Eustace told Hamilton to take the rest of the evening off; he had no desire that any part of the coming conversation should be heard. Having presently assured himself that Hamilton really had left the flat, Eustace filled up the port glasses and began without preamble.

" The police have been questioning me in connection with Desmond's death," he said. " I should

be glad of your advice, Henry. By the way, you
don't mind my calling you that ? "

" Of course not. I hadn't realized that you
didn't ; I've called you Eustace for some time."
Carr smiled pleasantly as he sipped his port. " I'm
sorry about the police but I'm not really surprised."

This was a bit of a shock, though Eustace tried
not to show it.

" Really ? What made you . . . expect it ? "

" Before I answer that, tell me what sort of advice
you want from me."

" That's easy. The C.I.D. man who was here
to-day advised me to be represented at the adjourned
inquest. I want to ask you to take that on."

Carr nodded.

" I see," he said. " That's good of you, Eustace.
I appreciate that. Now I'll tell you, quite frankly,
why I'm not surprised. In the first place I have
known, ever since David's death, that the Scottish
police were not altogether satisfied that that was an
accident. They thought it happened so conveniently for you and they thought that, though it was
possible, it was such a very unlikely accident to
occur."

" How did you know that ? " asked Eustace,
curiously.

" In the first place from Blanche. She told me
that a girl who was up there with you . . ."

" That Hope-Fording bitch. I thought so."

269

"Yes; that was the name. She tried her best to persuade the Scottish police that you had done it yourself—the knife wound, I mean. She told them you wanted to succeed to the Barradys title and so on, and that you thought that if David was out of the way you were bound to, because Desmond was so ill."

"She wanted to marry David herself," said Eustace bitterly. "That's what made her so wild."

Henry Carr laughed.

"I rather guessed that," he said. "In addition to that I heard something about it from a friend of mine, who's a W.S. in Glasgow."

"W.S.?"

"Writer to the Signet. Scottish equivalent for solicitor. He'd heard about it from a pal in Edinburgh who'd got a friend in the Crown Office—that sort of thing you know; all very improper, but these things do leak out. The Chief Constable of Inverness-shire had been perfectly satisfied but the Procurator Fiscal hadn't. However, they seem to have made up their minds that, whatever suspicions they might have, there was no earthly chance of proving anything against you, so the Lord Advocate marked it ' no proceedings ', and that was the end of that."

"Who's the Lord Advocate?"

"He's the chief officer of the Crown in Scotland—both in civil and criminal matters. He more or less corresponds to our Attorney-General and Director of Public Prosecutions rolled into one. What he says goes, as the Americans say. As a matter of fact it would be one of his deputies who would really go into the details and advise the Lord Advocate—a chap called an Advocate Depute. Anyway, between them they decided on no proceedings, but they did do one thing more—they notified Scotland Yard."

Eustace, who had felt himself growing colder and colder as this story revealed the danger that he had been in, helped himself to a third glass of port with a rather shaky hand. Carr declined, but accepted a glass of brandy.

"Good Lord," said Eustace. "This is a very nasty shock, Henry. I knew they were taking nothing for granted, but I didn't realize it had gone as far as all that. None of the local people, the stalkers and so on, had any doubt at all. Why, how could I . . . good heavens, the idea's fantastic?"

"Well, that's not what we've got to worry about now, anyhow," said Carr. "I've only just heard the last part—that the Scottish authorities had notified Scotland Yard. That was only after a little time and then Scotland Yard sent a man round to talk to Mrs. Toumlin. She was told that it was advisable that you should not have access to Desmond, at any rate not alone. They wouldn't give her any reasons and they helped matters by saying that she mustn't tell anyone else. Naturally, the poor woman lost her head completely and I wonder you didn't realize that something was up. You'll remember that when I met you there I told you that I rather expected you wouldn't be allowed to see Desmond ? Well, I didn't know the reason then, but I had gathered that she'd got something against you and so I thought I'd wait and tell you what I did."

" I see," said Eustace slowly. " But how long have you known about this ? about her being warned, I mean ? "

" Only to-day. After Desmond died the poor woman came out with it all to Blanche, and Blanche told me on the way to the inquest."

" Before you lunched with me ? That was very decent of you, Henry. You might well have wanted to keep clear of a chap suspected of murder."

" My dear fellow." Henry Carr leant forward and patted Eustace on the arm. " Mind if I smoke ? "

" I'm so sorry. What'll you have ? a cigar ? "

" Pipe, if you don't mind."

" Do. Shall we go into the other room ? " asked Eustace with a laugh. Going into the other room consisted of moving into the two large armchairs in front of the fire, Eustace's flat boasting only one reception room, but that a large one.

" Now the question is, what about this inquest ?

Before we go into it, Eustace, I must ask you one formal question : are you in any way responsible for Desmond's death ? ''

" No," declared Eustace whole-heartedly, while thanking his stars that the question had not referred to David.

" Good. I've made it a rule to ask that question in all cases involving criminal procedure, and I've never defended anyone whom I knew to be guilty, except in two very exceptional cases. Of course, this isn't a case of ' defending ' yet, and I don't suppose it ever will be, but I think the principle applies even at the stage of ' representation.' Now tell me all you know, what the police have asked you, what you think they know, and what you think they've got in their minds.''

Eustace was glad that he had spent some time that afternoon in thinking over what he should tell Henry Carr ; without preparation he might have stumbled. He said nothing about Scotland, on the principle that the fewer lies he told the safer. He told of his frequent visits to Desmond, giving the reason that he wished to stand well with the boy and wanted to see him alone. He told of the detectives' questions on this point. He told of his transactions with money-lenders, making no attempt to hide the fact that he had used the deaths, first of Howard and Harold, and then of David, to impress Isaacson and Levy. He revealed the fact that he was a qualified medical practitioner, which Henry Carr declared that he had always known. He told of the bottle of morphia tablets and here for the first time the solicitor looked grave.

" You were right to be frank about that," he said, " but it's an awkward fact. Of course, we don't know yet what they've got in their minds. The P.M. may show—in fact, presumably it will show— that death was due to natural causes . . . or rather that it was due to what Spavage explained and expected. You don't know of anything else ? "

" Nothing, except that Inspector Darnell asked me rather particularly whether I had any other drug besides morphia."

" That probably was only intelligent anticipation. I don't see, Eustace, that there's anything to be worried about at the moment. Presumably the police will show their hand—if they've got a hand— at the adjourned inquest, and we can then decide what line to take. We won't settle anything definitely yet, but it seems to me that you'd better answer any questions you're asked quite frankly. I take it that you've told me everything and not kept anything back ? "

Eustace nodded, with an uncomfortable feeling that his boats were now burned.

" Even about . . . my wanting to see Desmond alone . . . and the reason ? " he asked.

" I think so, though I'll think it over and give

you a considered opinion before the time. It's a bit awkward, but frankness disarms a lot of suspicion. It was a perfectly natural desire on your part; anyone but a hypocrite will see that. If I were you I should try and forget about it now till we know what we're up against; the whole thing may come to nothing."

Eustace nodded.

"Sound advice, but none too easy to follow," he said. "Have a whiskey and soda."

"Thanks, I will."

Eustace rose and took the decanter and syphon and a couple of glasses out of the red lacquer cupboard.

Henry Carr laughed.

"You know how to look after yourself, Eustace," he said. "I don't wonder the C.I.D. man wanted to know where the golden egg came from."

CHAPTER XXIII

ADJOURNED INQUEST

THE adjourned inquest on Desmond Hendel was re-opened on Thursday, 17th October. The Coroner began by stating that the police had expressed their desire to be represented by a solicitor and that he had received a similar request from an interested party.

" It is probably known to everyone," said Mr. Ellinstone, " that the discretion of a Coroner in matters of procedure is very wide, his powers almost unlimited. Those of you familiar with the Coroner's Act will have been struck by the almost complete lack of direction which it displays, so much so that Coroners have to interpret its intentions as best they may, and some of the interpretations may strike the general public as rather strange. There has, for instance, been a tendency of late years on the part of some Coroners to allow their enquiries to develop into a kind of preliminary trial ; persons indicted with no offence have found themselves practically on trial for their lives, examined, cross-examined, re-examined by members of the legal profession other than the Coroner himself, with the result that prejudice has been aroused in the minds of the public which is grossly unfair to the persons concerned.

" I have no intention of allowing this enquiry to develop into anything of that kind. I shall not object to the presence of the solicitors to whom I have referred, and I shall allow them reasonable latitude in asking questions which appear likely to elucidate the matter into which we are here to enquire, but I must remind them that my discretion is absolute and that they must accept any ruling which I make as to what is relevant and permissible and what is not."

Mr. Ellinstone paused and looked round the room. The two solicitors referred to, Mr. Justin representing the police, and Mr. Henry Carr representing Eustace Hendel, bowed slightly in acknowledgment of the Coroner's remarks, and the Coroner bowed even more slightly back.

" Call Sir Hulbert Lemuel," he said.

A tall, clean-shaven man, dressed in a morning coat, moved forward to the witnesses' chair. He explained that he was employed by the Home Office as Public Analyst, that certain organs had been sent to him in sealed jars, certified by two doctors as having been taken *post-mortem* from the body of Mr. Desmond Hendel, that he had examined the organs in the usual way and had isolated various drugs which were present in them in varying quantities.

277

" Before you go into the question of what you found, Sir Hulbert, I must explain to the jury that I have arranged for you to see the depositions of Sir Horace Spavage, the physician in charge of the case, who is unable to be present to-day for reasons which he explained a fortnight ago. You have read those depositions, Sir Hulbert ? "

" I have, sir. I found that the organs contained two drugs, opium and veronal, which were referred to in Sir Horace Spavage's evidence as having been given to his patient by way of medicine ; these two drugs were present in the quantities that I should expect to find under the circumstances described by Sir Horace."

" And that was all ? " asked Mr. Ellinstone.

" No, sir. There was a third drug present. I found traces throughout the viscera, but chiefly in the stomach, from which I recovered roughly three-fifths of a grain. The amount in the liver, kidneys and intestines was negligible. I estimate that at least one grain had been taken by the deceased within a period of eight hours before death."

" And that drug was ? "

" Hyoscine."

Hyoscine ! Eustace started violently. There was a general stir throughout the court. The majority of the general public present realized that here was something of vital importance. Eustace, and others with him, knew that this meant . . . murder !

" Hyoscine ?   That is not a drug you would have expected to find from the history of the case so far as you know it ? "

" No, sir."

" You say that you identified the presence of one grain.   Is that a toxic dose ? "

" Very much so.   Taken even by itself, and by a healthy person, it would have a highly toxic effect and might even prove fatal.   Taken in conjunction with the other drugs which we know that the deceased was taking, it would almost certainly be lethal and that within a comparatively short space of time."

" In your opinion was it the cause of death in this case ? "

" The immediate cause ; yes.   There were pre-disposing causes ; the sarcoma from which the deceased was suffering would of course be one, and the medicinal drugs—the veronal and the opium—would be another."

" Thank you, Sir Hulbert.   Can you suggest any means by which the hyoscine can have been taken by the deceased ?   Any means other than suicidal or homicidal, that is ? "

" It might be given in the form of hydro-bromide as a sedative, but of course not in anything like that quantity."

"In view of the fact that veronal and opium were already being given, do you consider it likely that hyoscine was also being given . . . legitimately?"

"No, sir; I do not."

Mr. Ellinstone was feeling good. It was pleasant to be consistently addressed as 'Sir' by so distinguished a man as Sir Hulbert Lemuel. Moreover, he was pleased with his opening remarks, which had come well off the tongue.

"Perhaps you will be so good as to tell the jury something about hyoscine, Sir Hulbert," he said.

The Home Office Analyst turned towards the jury.

"Hyoscine is one of the atropine group of vegetable poisons," he said. "It is, in fact, the most potent of that group. The pharmacological action of the drug is first to stimulate the higher centres of the brain and later to cause depression and paralysis. The use of hyoscine for homicidal purposes in this country is of fairly recent origin, but it has been used in the east, in varying forms, for many centuries."

"What we want to know is, what's it for and how d'you get hold of it," interpolated the large red-faced juryman who had given tongue on the previous occasion.

Mr. Ellinstone frowned.

"I was about to ask Sir Hulbert that question," he said. "Members of the jury should ask any question they wish to through me, after I have finished my own examination of a witness. Perhaps you will tell us that, Sir Hulbert ? "

The Home Office Analyst thought for a moment.

" That's rather a wide question, sir," he said. " Hyoscine, of course, is a narcotic ; it can be used for insomnia or in conjunction with an anæsthetic. Its most common use is for the control of mania, for which it is especially effective, and also for the inducement of what is sometimes called ' twilight sleep,' in connection with childbirth. I think, perhaps, that is all I can usefully say about the first part of the question.   As to the second part : ' How do you get hold of it ? ', the answer to that is the same as for any other poison scheduled in Part I. of the Pharmacy Acts ; there are stringent regulations governing the sale of such poisons ; for instance, they may only be supplied to someone personally known to the seller, unless vouched for by someone known to him, and every detail of the transaction has to be recorded in the pharmacist's Poison Register."

" Very proper regulations, Sir Hulbert," said the Coroner ; " now will you tell us in what form this drug, hyoscine, is obtainable ; I mean, liquid or powder or what ? "

" It's usual form is hyoscine-hydrobromide, a white crystal ; it is very easily soluble."

" And how is it given—by a doctor, I mean ? "

" Either by the mouth, in liquid form, or, more generally, hypodermically."

" In this particular case, Sir Hulbert—and this is really the vital point—do you consider that this hyoscine can have been administered for a legitimate, medicinal purpose ? "

' No, sir. Not if we assume that Sir Horace Spavage's evidence is correct. He has told us what he prescribed. He did not prescribe hyoscine."

" And hyoscine was the cause of death ? "

" Undoubtedly."

There was a stir round the crowded court. Everyone felt that now the enquiry was really getting down to brass tacks.

Mr. Justin rose to his feet.

" Sir Hulbert has told us," he said, " how this poison may be obtained—by fulfilling the requirements of the law in connection with the sale of poisons. But is it conceivable that any doctor would prescribe this drug in such a way that a layman would have the handling of it ? "

Sir Hulbert smiled.

" I can't answer for the whole medical profession, but it is difficult to imagine any circumstances in which a doctor would so prescribe, and of course it cannot be supplied to a layman without a doctor's prescription."

" So that in fact it would be practically impossible for a layman to get hold of the drug ? "

"Perhaps not impossible, but very difficult."

"But a doctor could get hold of it with the greatest ease?"

"With ease, yes, but not with secrecy."

The jury obviously did not see the point of this question, but Eustace saw it only too well.

Henry Carr rose to his feet.

"Sir Hulbert has told us, sir," he said, "that in this case the drug cannot well have been administered for a legitimate, medicinal purpose. I take it that there is more than one *illegitimate* way it may have been administered. For instance, is there any reason why it should not have been taken deliberately, by way of suicide?"

"There is no medical reason why it should not."

"It would be quite an effective way of committing suicide?"

"Quite, provided you could get hold of it."

Carr sat down. There was no need to elaborate the suicide theory at that stage; it was sufficient that it should be presented.

The Coroner himself seemed still dissatisfied.

"Leaving aside the possibility of suicide for the moment," he said, "and looking at it from the point of view of homicide, it is difficult to see why hyoscine should be used at all. One would have thought that an overdose of the drug which was actually being administered to the patient would be so much safer from a poisoner's point of view. It is the discovery of hyoscine, an unprescribed drug, in the viscera that points so clearly to homicide . . . at least, that removes 'misadventure' from the realm of possibility. 'Misadventure' would, one would have thought, have been the murderer's obvious card."

"He may not have known what drug *was* being used," suggested Mr. Justin.

It was an uncomfortable moment. Eustace felt that several people were trying not to look at him, while he himself had difficulty in not appearing embarrassed.

"I think that is all then, Sir Hulbert. . . . Oh, by the way, can you tell us whether the hyoscine was in fact administered hypodermically or by mouth?"

"By mouth, undoubtedly; the bulk of it was in the stomach."

"And its flavour? Has it a flavour?"

"Yes, it is rather bitter."

"Thank you, Sir Hulbert", said the Coroner. "I think we need not trouble you any more at the moment. Call Mrs. Toumlin."

Mrs. Toumlin, dressed in decent but not demonstrative black and white and looking, Eustace thought, remarkably calm, explained that she had been with the deceased as nurse-companion for two years, with eight years' previous experience in a similar capacity; prior to her marriage she had been a hospital nurse. She had worked under the

direction of Sir Horace Spavage and had administered the drugs as described by him, a mixture,
which she knew to contain a hypnotic drug, at four-
hourly intervals and a sleeping draught at ten
o'clock every night. Mr. Hendel had been wonderfully brave and showed extraordinary powers of
recuperation, but she had thought that for some two
months his constitution had been showing signs of
the strain of his illness.

" And of the hypnotic drugs ? " asked the Coroner.

" Perhaps. I can't say what was the cause, but
he had begun to lose ground."

" Did his death surprise you, Mrs. Toumlin ? "

" No, it did not. I had not expected it to be quite
so sudden, but it always seemed to me that he might
go very quickly."

" Quite so. Now will you tell us, Mrs. Toumlin,
what happened ? "

For the first time Mrs. Toumlin showed some sign
of discomposure.

" Do you mean all day ? " she asked, " or just at
night ? "

" I mean, from whatever period is relative to
your patient's death."

Mrs. Toumlin shot a quick glance towards Chief-
Inspector Darnell, who was sitting near Mr. Justin.
Getting no inspiration from him, she made up her
own mind.

" It was at about nine o'clock on Tuesday night

285

that I first noticed anything . . . unusual. I had been helping the cook wash up the dinner things, as the parlourmaid was out—I often do—and had left the door into the sitting-room, where Mr. Hendel was, ajar, in case he called. I thought I heard him call and went into the sitting-room. He was looking flushed and excited and was talking, apparently to himself, in rather a wild way. I had never heard him do that before. I . . ."

" What was he talking about, Mrs. Toumlin ? "

" Well, I really couldn't make out. Something about Lord Barradys. He said : ' Grandad '—that was what he called him, though he was really his great-grandfather—several times."

" Did he mention any other member of the family ? " asked Mr. Justin.

" Not that I heard." Mrs. Toumlin looked enquiringly at the Coroner, who nodded. " I thought he had had too tiring a day—there had been people to lunch, as well as other visitors—so I got him his sleeping draught at once, hoping it would calm him. I got him into bed and saw that he was comfortable. He had soon quieted down and seemed very sleepy, which was only what I expected. I went in to see him again at ten o'clock and I thought he seemed feverish, so I took his temperature ; it was 101. He was very heavy, practically asleep ; I did not like his appearance. I was worried. I rang up Sir Horace's house but he was out, and it took me some time to find him. He said he would come round at once and he got to the flat at about eleven. By that time Desmond . . . Mr. Hendel was quite comatose and he never recovered consciousness. He died at a little after two. Sir Horace was very kind and stayed with me to the end but there was nothing that could be done."

Mrs. Toumlin spoke calmly, but she was evidently affected by the story she was telling.

" Thank you, Mrs. Toumlin ", said the Coroner ; " that is a very clear account. Now you have heard the last witness say that he discovered traces of hyoscine in the organs submitted to him. Can you account for the presence of that in any way ? "

" Certainly I cannot."

Mr. Ellinstone looked back over his notes.

" You said that there had been visitors during the day ; will you tell us a little more about that ? "

Mrs. Toumlin gave a quick, nervous look round the room. Eustace thought that it rested for a moment on him, but it quickly passed on to the other Hendel relatives sitting beside him.

" Mr. Eustace Hendel came in the morning— about eleven o'clock, I think. I was out shopping at the time and the parlourmaid, Gladys, told Mr. Hendel that she had orders from me that . . . that Mr. Desmond was not to be disturbed."

Henry Carr rose quickly to his feet.

" Why was that ? " he asked sharply.

Eustace drew in his breath sharply. A terribly dangerous question, surely?

"Because . . ." Mrs. Toumlin hesitated. "Because there were people coming to lunch."

"And you didn't think he was up to seeing many people? . . . as he was in the condition that you have described to us?"

"No. I mean, yes; that was the reason."

"Exactly. Thank you, Mrs. Toumlin."

Clever devil, thought Eustace; he had remembered that the police had told Mrs. Toumlin not to tell anyone about their warning; he had gambled on her feeling still bound by that; now she would not be able to say anything different.

"Go on, please, Mrs. Toumlin", said the Coroner, looking coldly at Henry Carr.

"Mr. Eustace Hendel said he particularly wanted to see Desmond, so the maid rang me up and I returned. I explained to Mr. Hendel and of course he went away."

"Without seeing Mr. Desmond Hendel?"

"Yes, without seeing him."

Mr. Justin rose at this point and expressed a wish to ask Mrs. Toumlin one or two questions, to which the Coroner consented.

"You say that Mr. Eustace Hendel did not see your patient, Mrs. Toumlin, but he was in the flat for some time before you returned, was he not?"

288

" Isn't that a leading question, sir ? " asked Carr quickly.

" I think it is. Do not answer that, Mrs. Toumlin."

" I apologize, sir ", said Mr. Justin, blushing. " How long was it between Mr. Eustace Hendel's arrival at the flat and your return to it, Mrs. Toumlin ? "

" I should say about twenty minutes."

" And where was Mr. Eustace Hendel during that time ? "

" In the . . ."

" How can the witness answer that question if she was not there ? " interrupted Carr.

" Oh, Gladys told me and . . ."

" You must not tell us what somebody else told you, Mrs. Toumlin. That is not evidence ", said the Coroner. " Mr. Justin, will you please frame your questions more carefully."

" I must apologize again, sir ", said Mr. Justin crossly. " Where did you find Mr. Hendel when you returned to the flat, madam ? "

" He was in the flat—in the hall."

" *Thank* you. And was anyone with him ? "

" No."

" He was, in fact, alone in the hall."

" Yes, when I arrived."

" What rooms open out of that hall ? "

" Practically all of them ; the dining-room, the sitting-room, both bedrooms—my own and Mr.

Hendel's—the kitchen, the pantry, the best bathroom, and the lavatory."

" And when you returned were any of these open ? "

" No, I don't think so. I can't really remember."

" It would have been possible for anyone in the hall to have gone into one of those rooms without anyone in the flat being aware of it ? "

" Not exactly. Desmond was on the balcony and would almost certainly have seen anyone who went into either the dining-room or the sitting-room, which open on to it. Then there were the maids ; so far as I know, the cook was in the kitchen and the parlourmaid in the pantry."

" Which opens directly onto the hall within a few feet of where Mr. Eustace Hendel was sitting, doesn't it ? " asked Henry Carr.

" Isn't that a leading question, sir ? " asked Mr. Justin in a mincing voice, which caused a titter in the room.

Henry Carr smiled.

" How far is the pantry door from the chair where my client was sitting ? "

" Oh, quite close—just across the hall—perhaps six feet."

" And are you sure that that door was closed ? "

Mrs. Toumlin hesitated.

" Now I come to think of it, I believe I remember Gladys putting her head out of it when I arrived and then shutting it."

" *Thank* you, Mrs. Toumlin."

Henry Carr sat down.

Mr. Ellinstone was looking a little disquieted.

" I am rather afraid that we are drifting in the direction I indicated, gentlemen ", he said. " I don't want to interfere with you more than I can avoid, but I must ask you to help me."

The two solicitors bowed.

" Now, Mrs. Toumlin ; these further visitors.

" Mr. Carr came in for a few minutes in the middle of the day."

" Mr. Carr ? Do you mean . . . ? "

" Yes ", said Mrs. Toumlin, nodding towards Henry.

" And was he also turned away ? "

" Oh, no. Mr. Carr was Desmond's closest friend. That certainly did not apply to him."

" I see ", said Mr. Ellinstone doubtfully.

Eustace had been rather surprised by this news. He did not remember Henry telling him that he had been to see Desmond that day.

Mr. Justin rose to his feet, but Henry Carr was before him.

" And was this Mr. Carr allowed to see your patient alone ? " he enquired.

" Oh, yes ", said Mrs. Toumlin, beaming upon him.

" Dear, dear. Very sinister ", murmured Henry as he sat down.

" Mr. Carr had paid similar visits to your patient over a long period of time ? " queried Mr. Justin.

" Oh, yes ; he was most good. I don't know what Des. . . . Mr. Hendel would have done without him."

" And was that all ? "

" No. Mr. William Hendel and his son came to lunch and stayed for some time."

All eyes were turned upon the wine-merchants, who blushed and looked as guilty as possible.

" And they ? Were they alone with Mr. Hendel at all ? "

" Yes, after lunch. I left them with him for a little, while I went out for a breath of air."

" And they could presumably have had access to any part of the flat as well during that time—had they wanted to ? " queried Carr.

" Yes ; I suppose so."

" This is excellent ", the solicitor whispered to Eustace as he sat down.

" I don't think there is anything more, Mrs. Toumlin—unless any member of the jury . . . ? "

But Mr. Justin was on his feet again.

" There is just one point on which I should like enlightenment, sir . . . if I may ? "

The Coroner nodded.

" Mrs. Toumlin, Sir Hulbert has told us that hyoscine has a bitter taste and one wishes to discover how the deceased can have taken it without being aware of anything unusual. Did Mr. Hendel take anything of a pronouncedly bitter or perhaps pungent flavour ? The medicine, for instance ; what did that taste like ? "

" It had a slightly bitter taste—very slight."

" Anything else ? Any strong spirit ? Any sweetmeat ? "

" He was very fond of *Crême de Menthe*—the liqueur."

" Ah ; and that has a strong flavour ? "

" Yes ; peppermint. Oh, and peppermint choco-lates ; he had a great weakness for them."

" Ah."

Eustace felt a flush of anxiety spreading over him.

" He had a weakness for peppermint chocolates. Any particular sort ? "

" Yes ; he always had a box of Dudeville's by him."

" And did anyone else take them ? "

" No. I do not care for peppermint and I am sure the maids would not touch them. Besides, I always put them away after he went to bed. He may have sometimes offered one to a visitor, but I never saw him do so."

" How often did he take these chocolates ? "

" Generally one after every meal."

" Rather in the way that some men smoke a pipe ? "

" Yes, I suppose so."

" And did he take one that night—the night that he died ? "

" I don't know. I left him immediately after dinner ; he might have taken one after I left."

" Thank you, Mrs. Toumlin. That is all I have to ask, sir."

Henry Carr rose.

" We are hearing a lot about these chocolates, sir ", he said. " If the police are suggesting that that was how the hyoscine was administered, may I ask whether the contents of the box have been analysed ?"

The Coroner glanced towards Chief-Inspector Darnell, who whispered to the uniformed Police-Superintendent beside him. The latter officer rose.

" Yes, sir ; they have ", he said.

" Has there been a report ? "

" Yes, sir ; it was negative."

" That hardly implies that the hyoscine was not administered that way ", said Mr. Justin.

" No, but it leaves the suggestion purely one of conjecture ", replied Carr.

" Please, gentlemen ; we cannot have a discussion ", said Mr. Ellinstone. " Thank you, Mrs. Toumlin ; that will do. We will now adjourn for luncheon till 2.15."

CHAPTER XXIV

TENANT IN TAIL

DURING the luncheon interval Henry Carr was rather silent and Eustace formed the opinion that things were not going quite so well in the solicitor's opinion as in his own. He did not mention the case during luncheon, as other people were present, but walking back to the court they were alone for a time and Eustace asked how things looked.

" Oh, quite all right ; don't you worry, Eustace ", said the solicitor, rousing himself from a reverie.

" Something's worrying you, though."

Carr glanced quickly at his companion.

" Well of course, there is one awkward fact that hasn't been explained yet ", he said.

" Oh ? What's that ? "

" Why, the fact that Desmond was murdered."

" You mean . . . the hyoscine ? "

" Yes. Somebody administered that ; we don't know who or how. Until that is known . . . well, we shan't feel quite comfortable."

" You don't think it was suicide, then ? "

" Not for a minute. How could he have got the stuff ? I shall press the suggestion, of course."

" But, Henry, even if it was murder ; why should it be me ? Nothing has been said so far that inculpates me."

Henry was silent for a moment.

" Nothing has been said yet about possible motive ", he said quietly. " Of course, it may not be, but if that does come up, the inference is . . . rather awkward."

Eustace flushed.

" But that's most unfair ", he said. " I . . . I didn't do it."

Henry Carr patted his shoulder.

" I know, old man. I don't want you to worry ; I'm only having to think over possible dangers."

They finished their walk in silence.

When the court re-opened the Coroner recalled Mrs. Toumlin to ask her where the chocolate peppermints came from. Mrs. Toumlin explained that they were ordered by herself from Dudeville's, a fresh box whenever the supply was falling low. They were never given by anyone else and they were always the same kind.

Gladys Mason, the parlourmaid, was then called and questioned about what happened on the night of Desmond Hendel's death. Her evidence bore out that of Mrs. Toumlin. She had not seen her master take a chocolate after dinner that night, but there was no particular reason why she should. She could not suggest any other way in which the hyoscine might have been given, but then she knew nothing about the stuff.

That was all the Coroner wanted from Gladys Mason, but Mr. Justin wished to ask some questions. On the two occasions on which Mr. Eustace Hendel had visited the flat in the absence of Mrs. Toumlin—that is to say, on Monday, 23rd September, and Tuesday, 1st October—what had Mr. Hendel's attitude been? Had he pressed her to allow him to see his cousin—in spite of Mrs. Toumlin's orders to the contrary?

" Not the first time, sir ", said Gladys, " ——I don't remember the date. The second time—the morning of the day Mr. Desmond died—he did seem rather pressing."

" Can you be a little clearer about that ? " asked Mr. Justin. " In what way did he seem pressing ? "

" Well, sir, he was very nice and . . . and friendly. He smiled and that . . . well, it did seem as he was trying to wheedle me into letting him see Mr. Desmond."

Mr. Justin leaned forward.

" Did he attempt to *bribe* you in any way, Miss Mason ? "

Gladys blushed.

" Well, no, sir ; not exactly. But I thought he might if I gave him any encouragement."

Carr rose quickly to his feet.

" What *does* that mean ? " he asked. " Did Mr. Hendel produce money and offer it to you ? "

" Oh, no, sir."

" Did he go so far as to produce money ? "

" No, sir."

" Then what did he do ? "

" Well, sir ; he had his hand in his pocket and he seemed to rattle some coins."

" Rattle some coins ! " Henry Carr looked at the jury, shrugged his shoulders. " And on that we have to listen to a suggestion of attempted bribery."

He sat down with a flump. Mr. Justin, undeterred, resumed his questioning.

" And your orders were that Mr. Hendel was not to see your master ? "

" Yes, sir."

" Then what happened ? "

" He said he would wait till Mrs. Toumlin came back. I said he'd 'ave to wait in the hall, otherwise Mr. Desmond would know he was there. He said that didn't matter and sat down. Then I telephoned to the Times Book Club to let Mrs. Toumlin know he was waiting and I gave him the paper and went back to me pantry."

" And how long was Mr. Hendel waiting in the hall before Mrs. Toumlin returned ? "

" I'm sure I couldn't exactly say, sir, but it would be about a quarter of an hour."

" And during that time he was alone in the hall."

" Yes, sir."

" Thank you, Miss Mason."

Carr again rose.

" You say he was alone. Where were you ? "

" In me pantry."

" The door of which is within a few feet of where Mr. Hendel was sitting ? "

" Yes, sir."

" And was that door open or shut ? "

Gladys flushed and hesitated.

" I want an answer, please ", said Carr sternly.
" Was it open or shut ? "

" Open, sir."

" Could you see Mr. Hendel through it ? "

" No, sir."

" But you could have heard if he had got up, walked about, opened a door, gone into another room ? "

" I think so, sir."

" And did he do any of these things ? "

" I didn't think he did, sir."

" You *didn't* think so ? Perhaps it has been suggested to you that in fact he did and you have become uncertain ? Now tell me, Miss Mason, on your oath, have you any real doubt in your mind about it ? "

After a pause :

" No, sir ", said Gladys.

" Thank you."

Eustace heaved a sigh of relief at the firmness of this answer, which could not fail, he thought, to have its effect upon the jury. The next moment he heard his own name called. With a shudder of apprehension at the ordeal that was before him he walked to the witness's chair.

" Your full name is . . . ? "

" Eustace Hendel. I am a doctor, but I have not practised since 1926."

There was a rustle of interest, perhaps of excitement through the room. It was on Henry Carr's advice that Eustace had volunteered this information.

" It's bound to come out," he had said. " Better not have it dragged out of you, or have it revealed by the police."

Guided by Mr. Ellinstone, Eustace explained his relationship to the deceased. He said that he had at first been interested in the young man himself and had thought he might help to keep him amused. He acknowledged frankly that he had particularly wanted to see Desmond alone on the morning of 1st October, the reason being that he had recently had an unpleasant interview with Lord Barradys, the head of the family, who—he had heard—had written to Desmond and advised him to exclude Eustace from any will that he might be making in view of his new position as heir-apparent to the title and estates. Eustace declared that he had thought

Lord Barradys most unfair, prejudiced, in fact, by an old family feud with Eustace's father and grandfather. He (Eustace) was not prepared to sit down mildly under such injustice and had determined to talk the matter out with Desmond. As soon as it was made clear to him by the parlourmaid that morning that Mrs. Toumlin really did not wish him to see Desmond, he had said that he would wait till Mrs. Toumlin's return. He had not attempted to bribe the girl, as had been suggested, and he had in fact remained in the hall, reading the paper, during the whole quarter of an hour that elapsed before Mrs. Toumlin arrived.

This frank declaration evidently took the wind out of the sails of the police. Mr. Justin held a long whispered conversation with Chief-Inspector Darnell, and when the Coroner had finished his examination the police solicitor only asked one question :

" You realized then, Mr. Hendel, that your cousin Desmond, *if he lived long enough*, might make a will prejudicial to your interests ? "

It was a damaging question and, after his own story, Eustace could only answer that he had known that Desmond might make such a will, but that the implication ' if he lived long enough ' had not been in his mind. It was not a very convincing answer and both Coroner and jury were quite evidently alive to that fact. But when Mr. Justin sat down Eustace felt that he had much to be thankful for ;

he had not been asked about the morphia, about the
' Medical Jurisprudence ', about his transactions
with the money-lenders ; best of all, no mention had
been made of what had happened in Scotland ; it
was there that he felt his real danger lay, because
there alone had he been guilty.

After Eustace had returned to his place among
the other Hendels, the Coroner spent some time
looking through his notes, while the members of his
jury coughed and whispered among themselves.

" He's stuck," murmured Henry Carr.

" What about ? " asked Eustace.

" The hyoscine, I expect ; they've not traced it
yet."

It was not long before the solicitor's guess was
proved to be right. The Coroner called Chief-
Inspector Darnell.

" You are in charge of the investigations concern-
ing this case ? " asked Mr. Ellinstone.

" I am, sir."

" Have you endeavoured to trace the hyoscine
which has been found in the organs—trace the source
of supply, that is ? "

" I have, sir."

" With any success ? "

" Not yet, sir."

" Do you expect to be able to trace it ? "

Chief-Inspector Darnell allowed himself a slight
smile.

"I am quite sure I shall be able to trace it, sir," he said.

Mr. Ellinstone turned towards the jury.

"I must remind you, members of the jury," he said, "that the purpose of this enquiry is not only to arrive at a conclusion as to the cause of death, but also, if that cause is attributable to the criminal action of some other person, we have to endeavour to discover who that other person may be. This is not, as I have explained, a criminal court and no individual is before us upon trial; it will be open to you, when the time comes and among other possible verdicts, to return one of 'murder by some person or persons unknown.' That always appears to me an easy way out of a difficulty and one which is of little help to anybody. With the information before us at the present moment—that is, in the absence of any direct evidence as to how the hyoscine came to be taken by the deceased—it would clearly be almost impossible for you to give a verdict pointing to one person as being responsible for the young man's death. I think it will be best, therefore, if I adjourn this inquest for another fortnight in order to give the police further time in which to prosecute their enquiries. Does that appear to you a convenient arrangement, Chief-Inspector?"

"Quite, sir," replied the detective politely. It was clearly a matter of indifference to him what the Coroner and his court did. Magistrates and

assizes were the only courts that interested the
C.I.D.

" Well, then . . . oh, there's one other question
I meant to ask you, Mr. Darnell ; it will, I think,
just round off the enquiry up to this point. Have
you formed an opinion as to the vehicle in which
the hyoscine was administered ? "

The detective frowned slightly. He would have
preferred to let things go as they were for the present.

" I've formed an opinion, certainly, sir," he said.
" I can't say I've got definite proof of it."

" And that is ? "

" The peppermint chocolates, sir. Strong enough
flavour to conceal the taste of the hyoscine. Regular
habit of the deceased, known to many people. Easy
to obtain and easy to manipulate ; all the poisoner
would have to do would be to get hold of a similar
chocolate from another source, take out the contents
at his leisure, mix the hyoscine with the peppermint
cream, put it back, seal up the chocolate, and at some
time or other slip it into the box, from which deceased
would in due course take it. It wouldn't necessarily have to be done on the day on which the
death occurred."

The Coroner nodded.

" I see ; yes, that sounds possible. You have
not, I suppose, come across any other source of
supply . . . of these chocolates, I mean ? "

Again Chief-Inspector Darnell frowned. This

time he was seriously annoyed. He had not intended to produce this particular piece of information at this stage. But he could not well conceal it now or it might be difficult for him to produce it later.

" I have come across one such chocolate, sir," he said.

The tired jury sat up and took notice. Eustace held his breath.

" In Mr. Eustace Hendel's flat, sir."

There was a gasp, appearing to come from the whole room at once. Henry Carr looked sharply at Eustace, but as quickly turned away again. Eustace stared straight in front of him.

" Oh ? Will you tell us about this, please, Chief-Inspector ? "

" I visited Mr. Hendel's flat on the Thursday following the Tuesday on which Mr. Desmond Hendel died. Mr. Eustace Hendel was out ; he was in fact attending at this enquiry, sir. In Mr. Hendel's flat I found a peppermint chocolate of the same type as those favoured by Mr. Desmond Hendel . . ."

" How can you tell it was the same type ? "

" It was a Dudeville chocolate, sir. They all have the initial ' D ' under them."

" Where is this chocolate ? "

" I can produce it, sir."

" The jury must see it after the adjournment. Also the chocolates in the box sent for analysis."

The Chief-Inspector bowed.

" Now ; where did you find this chocolate ? "

" In point of fact, it was given to me, sir."

" Given to you ? Who by ? "

Even Coroners are human when it comes to grammar in moments of interest.

" By Mr. Hendel's man, sir."

Hamilton ! Curse the fellow ; a bloody traitor. Eustace found himself shivering with anger and apprehension.

" Why did he give it you ? "

" I asked for it, sir. That is ; I asked if he had seen anything of the kind. He had found it in the waste-paper basket on the Wednesday—the day after . . . "

" Sir, I must protest . . ." Henry Carr had risen quickly to his feet. " This is hearsay evidence. How can Chief-Inspector Darnell say where this chocolate was found or when it was found . . . or even *if* it was found ? "

" You are quite right, Mr. Carr. This man . . . what is his name ? "

" Hamilton, sir."

" Hamilton must be called. In the meantime, Chief-Inspector, your statement is that you received a chocolate from a certain source, purporting to come from a certain place, and you will produce that chocolate when called upon ? "

" That is so, sir."

" Then we will adjourn till this day fortnight."

The foreman of the jury rose to his feet.

" We've been talking this over, sir," he said, " and we think that before we adjourn this time we should like to hear something about this will that's been talked about—about the family estates presumably. It seems to us that that might establish a motive."

" And anyone can go a long way in a fortnight," remarked a female member of the jury, a thin, acidulated woman with a high voice.

" Please, madam, control yourself," said the Coroner.

He looked round the room.

" Mr. Christendome is here," he said. " No doubt he can give us the information which the jury has asked for. The suggestion is, I think, a reasonable one."

Eustace felt Henry Carr stiffen beside him, but he made no comment.

Mr. William Christendome, looking very old and shaken (thought Eustace), took the oath, and explained that he was senior partner of the firm of solicitors in whose hands the affairs of the senior branch of the Hendel family had been for nearly three-quarters of a century. Covering much the same ground as at the reading of Howard's will, Mr. Christendome explained that the Hendel estates had been entailed by the second Lord Barradys upon his son Chandos, the present Lord Barradys, for life, and thereafter upon the heirs of his body.

" That refers only to real estate," explained the solicitor, " which alone at that time was eligible for entail. After the Act of 1926, however, personal estate—that is, money, whether in the form of cash or securities—became equally eligible, and the present Lord Barradys took that fact into consideration when drawing up his will. As Lord Barradys is still alive, however, that is not a matter that can be discussed here."

The Coroner nodded and Mr. Christendome, after gently blowing his nose on a fine linen handkerchief, continued.

" The position for some time remained quite straightforward. Lord Barradys' only son, Albert, died in 1893 and his son Howard thereupon became tenant in tail, Lord Barradys, of course, remaining tenant for life. So matters continued until July of this year, when there came the first of the series of tragedies that have swept away all the direct descendants of Lord Barradys, and created a problem as to the entailed estate, which has been under constant consideration by Lord Barradys and the late Mr. Desmond Hendel right up to the moment of the latter's death."

There was complete silence in the court now ; everyone was listening with intense interest.

" In July of this year," continued Mr. Christendome, " Mr. Howard Hendel, the tenant in tail, and his son, Harold, were accidentally and simultaneously drowned in Cornwall, and the body of Mr. Harold Hendel has never been recovered. Mr. Howard's brother, Captain David Hendel, then became tenant in tail. He, however, met with a fatal accident while deerstalking in Scotland only last month, and the entail thus passed to his only son, Desmond, whose death is the subject of this enquiry."

Again Mr. Christendome gently blew his nose before continuing :

" The position after the death of Captain David Hendel became a very difficult one. Mr. Desmond, as you have heard, sir, was in a very delicate state of health and it was not to be hoped that he could ever marry or produce an heir. After him, where would the entailed estate go ? That of course was easily discovered, but the question arose : was that future disposal of the entailed estate in the best interest of the Hendel family ? and if not, what alteration in its disposal could and should be made ? "

" You mean, should the entail be broken ? " asked the Coroner.

" Exactly, sir. As tenant in tail Mr. Desmond Hendel would, when he came of age, be in a position, with the consent of Lord Barradys, the tenant for life, to bar the entail—either end it altogether or

re-settle it. Now it had, we believed, always been
the intention of the original creator of the entail,
and it has certainly been the desire of the present
tenant, that the Hendel estates should remain in the
Hendel family. If the entail remained unbroken,
that intention and that desire would in fact be
defeated."

" Eh ? how is that ? There is a younger branch,"
said the Coroner, looking across at Eustace, William
and George.

" Not a male member of a younger branch ; not,
that is to say, a male *Hendel*."

Eustace's head was beginning to spin. What was
all this ? No male Hendel ? What about himself ?
and William ? and George ?

" I must remind you, sir, that we are speaking of
the entailed estate, not of the title. There is, of
course, an heir presumptive to the title ; Mr.
Eustace Hendel is the direct descendant of the
third son of the first Lord Barradys, as are Mr.
William and Mr. George Hendel. But we are
dealing with the entailed estate only. That estate,
as I said, was entailed by the *second* Lord Barradys
upon his son Chandos, the present peer, and the
heirs of his—Chandos'—body."

" Ah, I see your point. It was a general entail,
not a tail male ? "

" Exactly, sir. Now, in general entail, as you
are aware, the expression ' heirs of his body ' covers

both sexes and the estate becomes descendable, first to the sons of a first wife, then to the sons of a second or any subsequent wife, and finally, failing such sons, to the daughters, all of whom share equally as co-parceners. In this case, all the male heirs of the body having failed, the estate, should the entail stand, would pass to the female heirs. Chandos, Lord Barradys, had only one daughter, Louisa, who married James Kidd and died in 1912. Through this marriage also there is one female heir, who survives to-day. The daughter of James and Louisa Kidd is Julia, the wife of Henry Carr, and she now becomes tenant in tail of the estate."

CHAPTER XXV

LORD BARRADYS SURVIVES

Eustace's brain reeled under the shock of Mr. Christendome's pronouncement. In a few dry, quiet words the solicitor had destroyed the foundations upon which all the schemes of the last three months had been built. He was not to succeed after all ! After all the trouble, all the anxiety, all the risk ; with one murder on his conscience and another threatening him with danger, an empty title was his sole reward. And the estates—to Julia ! What had happened ? Why had he got it all wrong ? Christendome himself had said . . . Henry Carr had said . . .

Dazed and confused, Eustace hardly heard Mr. Christendome explain the perplexity in which his clients had found themselves. Neither Lord Barradys nor Mr. Desmond Hendel had wished the estates to leave the family, to go to anyone whose heir was not a Hendel. They had contemplated breaking the entail and re-settling upon a male member of the junior branch of the family, the descendants of Augustus, youngest son of the first Lord Barradys. There were three of them alive now, Mr. Christendome explained : Eustace, grandson of Augustus' eldest son, Clarence ; William, son of Augustus' younger son, Hubert ; and William's son, George.   Only within the last few days it had been decided that the re-settlement should be in favour of the latter.   The necessary documents were being prepared and would have been executed as soon as Mr. Desmond came of age, on the fifteenth of November.   Death, however, had intervened and the existing settlement, which he had just explained, would stand.

How had he misunderstood ?   ' The estates pass with the title ' . . . had not Christendome said that ? down at Coombe ? or had it been Henry ? What was clearer than that ?   But, of course, at that time it had been true !   Male heirs of Chandos' body were alive and the estates *were* passing with the title.   Was it his own fault, then ? his own stupidity ?   But, surely, that day in Regent's Park, Henry had told him—or at least led him to believe —that the idea of Desmond barring the entail would cut out him—Eustace ?   Had he again misunderstood ?   It had really been *Julia* who was in danger of being cut out !   Had he misunderstood all along, or had . . . ?

" Come on, for God's sake."

Henry Carr's voice was harsh as he pulled Eustace to his feet.   The court was clearing ; the inquest was adjourned.   Eustace felt a touch on his arm and turning, saw Chief-Inspector Darnell, accompanied by the uniformed Superintendent. The blood drained from his heart ; was this arrest, then ?

" You'll not be leaving town at present, Mr. Hendel ? " asked the detective quietly.

Eustace shook his head, too dazed to speak.

" That's all right, sir. I'd be glad if you'd notify me at the Yard if you have any idea of going away, or Superintendent James here, or any of his officers."

Eustace nodded and Chief-Inspector Darnell stood aside. A minute later Eustace found himself in a taxi with Henry Carr.

" I say, Henry . . . ", he began.

" Shut up, for God's sake," snapped his companion. " I must think."

" Yes, but you told me . . ."

" I told you ? *You* told *me* nothing about this chocolate that's been found in your flat. How the hell are we to explain that ? "

" But it . . . I . . . that isn't what I want to know, Henry. About the entail . . ."

With an effort Carr controlled his rising temper. He put his hand on Eustace's arm.

" Look here, old man, we've got a lot to talk about," he said, " but not in this taxi. We're going to your flat. I want a drink and so do you. Till then, let me think."

Eustace sank back into the corner of the cab and gave himself up to his whirling thoughts. The

drive was not a long one ; very soon they were outside Brandford Mansions. Carr paid the taxi and
followed Eustace into the lift.

That fellow Hamilton ! The thought of him had
just returned to Eustace. The treacherous swine !
Out he should go, that very moment.

His key turned in the lock ; he pushed open the
door of the flat.

" Hamilton ! " he called sharply.

There was no answer.

" Hamilton ! ! "

Eustace strode into the kitchen ; it was empty.
So was every other room in the flat, except the
sitting room, where Henry was already mixing himself a drink. Eustace went out onto the landing
and ran upstairs to the servants' quarters on the top
floor ; Hamilton's room was empty, bare. The
fellow had gone. Slowly Eustace walked down the
stairs. So the rat had left the sinking ship, had he ?
Curse and blast all such men. His ship was not
going to sink. He must have this out with Henry
Carr. Henry had misled him. Deliberately ? By
God, it looked like it. Had he . . . ? Had . . . ?

He strode into the sitting room. Henry thrust
a glass of whisky into his hands. He was drinking
one himself, dark yellow, almost neat.

" Drink that before you talk. We both need it."

Eustace looked at his companion, then at the
whiskey. Yes, he needed a drink ; there was some

straight talking to be done. He drank it off and gave a little shudder ; the whiskey ran like fire through his veins. He was tired, of course . . .

" Damn strong, that . . ."

He saw Henry Carr watching him, a look of intense interest in his eyes.

" What are you looking at me like that for ? " he asked. " Look here, there's something damned fishy about this entail. You told me . . . my God ? "

A sudden shudder had shaken him. A surge of excitement swept over him ; he wanted to talk, to shout. He felt his face flushing ; his throat was dry. His hand jerked forward in little stabs, uncontrolled by any volition of his own will.

" This entail . . . this 'ntail . . . 'ntail . . .", he stammered, seizing Henry Carr's arm and shaking it violently. Dizzy, stammering, barely conscious of what he was saying or even trying to say, Eustace dimly knew that he had something of tremendous importance to convey to this man ; words, jumbled and unintelligible, jostled each other over his flushed lips. Suddenly dropping Carr's arm he tried to walk to the door, but his legs were out of control, he staggered, dropped into a chair ; for a minute or more he sat there, gripping the arms, chattering, his face flushed and almost unrecognizable, wild excitement still driving brain and tongue to their unintelligible task. Then suddenly exhaustion flooded over him ; he sank back, giving way to the surging waves of depression which overwhelmed him. The tumbling words dropped to a whisper—ceased.

Henry Carr heaved a sigh of relief, drained his own glass.

" My God, Eustace, you've given me a fright— you and old Christendome ", he said. " I thought you were going to start talking before I was ready for the last act. Damned awkward, that jury asking for Christendome. However, this'll put them off the line. ' Suicide of suspected cousin ', ' doses himself with the poison used on his victim '. You realize that you've just swallowed a grain of hyoscine, don't you, Eustace ? I was afraid you might taste it, even in that neat dose, but you swallowed it down like a good 'un."

Through the muffled surging of the blood in his ears Eustace heard the voice, though the words meant nothing to him. Through the waves of blackness that clouded his sight he saw a dim face peering at him, but it was impersonal, a mask floating in the shimmering mirage of a dream.

" You've been a wonderfully useful cat's-paw to me, Eustace ; saved me no end of trouble."

Henry Carr lit a cigarette and inhaled deeply.

" I'm sorry you've had to go yourself but it was too dangerous to leave you. Your suicide is just the red herring that'll direct attention from me, even

317

now that they know about the entail. Damned
lucky your Mr. Hamilton taking himself off, though
I could probably have got you to send him out.
Gives me a little time to clear up."

Carr leaned forward and pulled down an eyelid
of the dying man ; the pupil was widely dilated ;
there was no sign of consciousness of being touched.
Rising to his feet, Carr took his tumbler to the
pantry, washed and wiped it ; returning, he put it
back in the red lacquer cupboard. Then he wiped
the outside of the decanter and of Eustace's glass
and, holding them in his handkerchief, folded
Eustace's limp fingers round each in turn.

" Somebody may have seen me come in with you,
but obviously you'll have taken the stuff after I
left. Lucky the C.I.D. man coming out about that
chocolate ; they'll think that's what made you
think the game was up."

A little glass bottle, half full of white crystals, was
put on the table beside the decanter.

" And so, good-night."

Carr took a last look round the room, stirred the
hunched-up figure in the chair. There was no
response. Eustace would sleep on for an hour, two
hours, perhaps three, but from that unfathomable
coma he would never wake.

Going out into the hall, Henry Carr put on his
hat, opened the door into the outer landing, looked
back and said :

" Don't bother to come out, old man. Take things easy and don't worry. See you in the morning."

He slammed the door and walked down the stairs, pleased with the artistry of that little touch. It would probably be wasted, but one never knew—somebody might have heard it.

It was quite dark when he got down into the street ; it was difficult to see whether any police officer was about, though Carr knew that there was quite a possibility that an eye would be kept on Eustace's movements till the next sitting of the Coroner's court. That was a risk he had to take, and in any case, when Eustace's death came to be known, he intended to say that he had gone back to the flat with him, discussed the day's evidence, and left him in low spirits. So that, unless someone found Eustace dead or dying almost immediately, the natural assumption would be that he had taken the hyoscine directly after his solicitor left.

The beauty of the whole thing, of course, lay in the fact that Eustace was a doctor. As Sir Hulbert Lemuel had said, it was an easy matter for a doctor to get hyoscine, an almost impossible one for a layman. In a sense that was true ; he himself had got the stuff from a doctor, but the getting of it had been simplicity itself : a client of his, a doctor, had died ; he (Henry) had had to wind up the dead man's affairs, he had had easy access to his papers and possessions, and had merely extracted a bottle of hyoscine-hydrobromide from the man's medicine cupboard. That had been a year or more ago ; there could be no possibility of tracing the theft to him now.

In the Underground going to Waterloo there was too much bustle and noise to allow of clear thinking, but in his suburban train he was able to find a first-class carriage to himself. It was past the hour of the daily rush return from work, though the third-class carriages were fairly full ; he himself never travelled first-class on ordinary occasions, but this was one on which he thought the luxury was justified.

The train pulled slowly out from the long platform and Henry Carr sank back into his cushioned seat with a sigh of relief. He had a great deal to be thankful for. In the last few months he had been through a period of intense strain ; this very day he had been on the brink of disaster, but he had just managed to pull the game out of the fire ; now it was nearly over and he would soon be able to settle down in peace to enjoy with Julia her hard-won inheritance.

His troubles, of course, had not been of a mere three months' duration—that was only the climax. They had begun soon after the war when he and his partners had done a bit too well, prospered a bit too easily, got careless, and been found out. It was then, Henry prided himself, that he had shown his real metal. Press had shot himself, Orton done a bunk ; he himself had stayed and faced the music. Not only that, but he had actually escaped prosecution ; he had sacrificed all his savings to recoup the clients who had suffered and they had believed in him—believed him an innocent victim of his partners' malpractice. He had been ruined, of course, financially, but his professional honour had survived and he had been able to begin again and, with the indomitable help of Julia, had slowly built up a new business for himself. It had been a terribly difficult and wearing task, and, with the general state of depression in all business, he had been unable to do more than keep himself and his family alive and just respectable. There had been no possibility of putting aside money for his and Julia's old age, and the task of paying for Dick and Helen's education had become increasingly difficult.

So he had faced the situation and decided that honesty was not good enough. Being a solicitor and knowing the family affairs, he had realized that in certain eventualities the settled estates might conceivably come to Julia, or at least that, even if it was decided to re-settle the estates on a male of the younger line, a very handsome provision might be made for Julia by way of recompense. So he had set about the devising of those ' certain eventualities '. Three men at least must be removed from Julia's path—Howard, Harold, and David ; with any luck Desmond, poor fellow, would go of his own accord ; the old peer did not matter because, being only tenant for life, he could not himself disturb the entail. It would take time and intense care ; no risks must be run ; ' accidents ' must happen.

The drowning of Howard and Harold together was to be the master-stroke—and it had taken three years to achieve ! For two years he had taken that house at Coombe—and failed to get Julia's cousins to come and stay. This year, when he was almost in despair, when Desmond—nearly of age and still alive—threatened to become another obstacle in the path, Howard and Harold had come. He had made an excuse to take the house a week before the children's holidays had begun—must get the unpleasant business out of the way before the kids came. Howard and Harold had come and had shown themselves confident swimmers ; he had taken them every morning to bathe in Coombe Cove, which was rather crowded ; he had shown them Davy's Cut, in which no one was mad enough to bathe because of its terrible under-drag, had told them that it was ' supposed to be rather unsafe ' and refused to take the responsibility of allowing them to bathe in it. Then, on the Tuesday morning, when the tide would be at its most dangerous, he had feigned a chill and allowed his visitors to go alone. Being Hendels, full of self-confidence, they had naturally gone to the secluded cove that they had been warned against—and the inevitable had happened.

All that episode had gone perfectly, but Henry had faced the future with considerable apprehension and dislike. One accident in the family, well engineered, could easily be swallowed ; a second would be a thousand times more dangerous. He was actually without a plan for David's death at the time of Howard's funeral down at Coombe, and then, out of the blue, had come Eustace, like Abraham's ram in the thicket, ready to his hand for the slaughter —ready, rather, to become the perfect cat's-paw.

That had not, of course, been obvious all at once ; what did very soon become obvious was that Eustace knew nothing about law ! He had misunderstood Christendome's explanation of the entail ; having the little knowledge which is forever dangerous, he had assumed that because the old man had traced the course of the entail from son to son, *pari passu* with the title, this was a settlement in tail male, whereas in actual fact it was a general entail—as Christendome had explained at the inquest only that day. Eustace had then tried to pump him (Henry) about it and he, seeing Eustace's muddle, had, without saying anything that was untrue, allowed Eustace to deceive himself —to lead himself up the garden path ! It was almost too easy, but it had been astonishingly effective. Almost as if he had spoken, Eustace's

thoughts had declared themselves. He was hard
up, in trouble ; now he saw a golden vista opening
before him—a great prize at its end. Before his
eyes Henry had seen the idea of murdering David
form in Eustace's brain.

After that, for a time, it had almost been a case of
sitting back and waiting for Eustace to do his work
for him. A word to Blanche had been enough to
get her to persuade David to ask Eustace up to
Scotland, and if Eustace really meant business that
would give him his chance ; Eustace, a doctor, with
all the poisons in the pharmacopœia at his disposal.
The actual event had raised Eustace a hundred per
cent. in Henry's respect ; that stalking accident !
Superb !

Then arose the problem of Desmond. As he had
anticipated, there was pow-wow in the family about
the settled estate passing to someone who was no
longer a Hendel. Blanche had told him all about it.
Old Barradys was actually contemplating Eustace
as the object of a re-settlement, to be carried out, of
course, by Desmond on his advice. That would
have ended Julia's chances of succeeding. Well,
Eustace must see about that ; he himself must put
Desmond out of the way before he could bar the
entail.

So had come that conversation in Regent's Park
and the further conversation at his Club. Hardly a
lie was necessary ; Eustace was gently led to deceive

himself. By that time, of course, Barradys had decided that George Hendel should be the heir, but Eustace was left to believe that he himself, not Julia, was to be supplanted. Again Henry had seen murder raising its head in Eustace's expressive eyes.

Unfortunately, the police had warned Mrs. Toumlin about Eustace; she had, in spite of their veto, confided in Blanche, and Blanche, unconvinced, had told Henry. It soon became clear to him that Eustace would be allowed no chance to kill Desmond. Very well, he, Henry, must kill him himself and Eustace must take the blame.

For this occasion palpable murder was preferable to either 'accident' or 'suicide'; murder, with Eustace as the suspected murderer, two birds with one stone. Eustace would be better out of the way, because there was no knowing what he might not say or do when he found out how he had been deceived; he could hardly be able to appreciate that he had only been allowed to deceive himself.

Murder of Desmond, then, ostensibly by Eustace. And then—trial and execution of Eustace? No, too slow, too uncertain, too risky. Suicide of Eustace; that was the way. And so it had come about, that very afternoon. There had been a moment of intense danger, when Christendome had explained the entail to the Coroner's jury and Eustace had begun to realize that he had been deceived. Would he give the show away at once?

Even if he did not do that, was there now any hope that he would give the man who had deceived him a chance to poison him ? His firm handling of that situation appeared to Henry Carr the best thing he had done in the whole complicated scheme. The rapidity and decision with which he had carried the weaker Eustace away from the inquest and up to his flat, refusing to discuss the situation till they got there, had enabled him, not only to keep the fellow quiet but actually to ' force ' a glass of doctored whiskey on a man who was already beginning to suspect him of being a poisoner.

And so Eustace's dead body would be found, to-night or to-morrow. Suicide to escape arrest was the obvious explanation. There would be one more inquest, which would practically clear up all that was left uncertain by the adjourned inquest to-day. Then gradually the excitement would die down and in a short time the whole story would be forgotten. Old Lord Barradys would live on for another year or two, perhaps, in the grim loneliness of his northern kingdom ; then he would die and the great estates would pass to Julia—dear Julia, who had been so brave and patient through all the troubles and privations of their married life.

With a warmth of feeling that only touched him where his wife and family were concerned, Henry Carr left the train at his suburban station. It was easier to bear the hateful smugness and smallness

of this suburb now that one knew it was only for a
short time more. As he walked the half-mile to his
semi-detached villa, Henry's thoughts cast themselves once more back into the recent past, to that
aspect of it which pleased him least—the killing of
poor Desmond. He had been fond of Desmond,
genuinely fond of him—the only human being
besides Julia, Helen and Dick—oh, yes, and perhaps
Blanche—for whom he cared one tinker's curse.

There had been no great difficulty about the
killing. The stuff he had had by him for a year ;
the ' vehicle ' was obvious—the strong flavour of
peppermint was exactly what was wanted to hide
the bitter taste of the hyoscine. He had had the
scheme in his mind long before Eustace came upon
the scene ; his frequent visits to Desmond, over a
long period, had not been without their object ; he
had been studying the boy's habits. It had soon
become clear that they were very precise ; Desmond
ate a chocolate after every meal ; he offered them
to no one else, except to Julia, Blanche and himself.
That was the one risk, that by some appalling mis-
chance the poisoned chocolate should be eaten by
one of those two women. But on the day when he
had planted the chocolate that risk was nil ;
Blanche was away in the west of England and Julia
in bed nursing a cold. Anyone else might take their
outside chance.

The day itself was chosen partly for those reasons

and partly because Eustace, who was to be incrimi-
nated, was just then behaving in a red-hot suspicious
manner that would inevitably attract the attention
of the police, who had already allotted him the bad
name which would take him half-way to the gallows.
It was not till he got to the flat that Tuesday that
he had learnt that Eustace had actually been there
that very morning, doing his utmost to thrust his
neck into the noose ! The news that William and
George were coming to luncheon had been rather
disconcerting, but from what he knew of wine-
merchants Henry had thought that the risk of their
eating peppermint-chocolates was practically nil ;
at any rate, it was a risk that he was prepared to let
them take. Going in to see Desmond he had openly
asked for a chocolate and while taking it had slipped
in the one he had prepared, placing it second from
the end of the half-eaten row. The end one Desmond
would eat after luncheon, the poisoned one after
dinner ; he had selected that time, thinking that the
sleeping draught which would soon follow might
mask for a time the actual cause of death and so
give no chance for drastic treatment to be applied.
So had ended poor Desmond, mercifully, before the
worst agonies of his terrible disease came upon him.
Still, Henry would have been glad if some other
hand could have administered that particular dose
of poison.

Here he was at ' Rosemount '. Julia had wanted

to change the name to something less revolting, but he had said that to see it on his door, night and morning, would act as a spur, goading him on to ever greater effort to fight his way back to a decent sphere of life. So it had been. ' Rosemount ' ! That word had been on the death-warrant of five Hendels : Howard, Harold, David, Eustace, and, alas, poor Desmond too.

Henry Carr let himself in with his latch-key and called to his wife. Her voice sounded from the drawing-room ; good, she was down, her cold was better. He opened the door and saw her snugly curled on the sofa in front of a glowing fire. Delicious homecoming.

" Darling, how late you are ! Have you had a horrible day ? "

Henry kissed her and laughed.

" Not seen an evening paper ? "

" You know I never do unless you bring one."

Oddly enough he had not bought one that evening.

" I'm the newspaper ", he said. " I've got all the news that matters. As a matter of fact I've known it ever since poor Desmond died, but it's been announced officially to-day. Who do you think is heir to the Barradys estates ? "

Julia stared at him.

" Why Eustace, of course. There's no one else now."

Again Henry laughed.

" I thought you'd got that idea in your head ", he said. " Do you remember that morning when we saw Eustace off at the junction, after Howard's funeral ? You said then you hoped he wouldn't succeed."

" I remember. We talked about poor David marrying Joan Hope-Fording. But, Henry, it *is* Eustace, isn't it ? Who else could it be ? "

Henry Carr knelt down and put his arms round his wife.

" Where would you like to live when we leave Rosemount ? "

Julia bent back her head and stared at him.

" How you do jump about. What's that got to do with what you were saying before ? "

" Everything, my darling. When old Barradys dies, his . . ."

The door opened and a small maidservant came in.

" There's someone asking for you, sir, please ", she said breathlessly.

Something in the girl's face caught Henry's attention.

" I'll come ", he said.

He bent down and kissed his wife, pressing her close to him. Then he got up and walked out of the room, shutting the door behind him. In the little hall stood Chief-Inspector Darnell, accompanied by a uniformed police-officer.

THE END

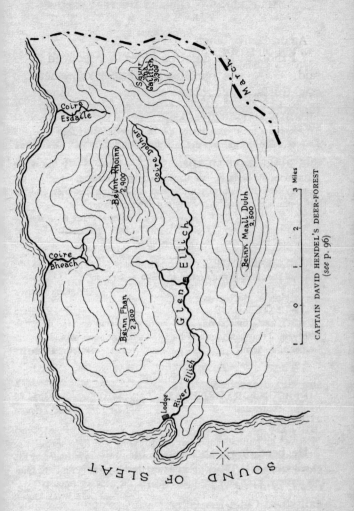

SOUND OF SLEAT

Coire Esdaile

Squrr Gaoith 3,300

Coire Dubhan

Benn Rhonn 2,900

Coire Bheach

Beinn Fhan 2,300

Glen Ellich

Benn Meall Duhh 2,500

March

Lodge

River Ellich

1   0   1   2   3 Miles

CAPTAIN DAVID HENDEL'S DEER-FOREST
(see p. 96)

THE PERENNIAL LIBRARY MYSTERY SERIES

Delano Ames

CORPSE DIPLOMATIQUE   P 637, $2.84
"Sprightly and intelligent."

—*New York Herald Tribune Book Review*

FOR OLD CRIME'S SAKE   P 629, $2.84

MURDER, MAESTRO, PLEASE   P 630, $2.84
"If there is a more engaging couple in modern fiction than Jane and
Dagobert Brown, we have not met them."   —*Scotsman*

SHE SHALL HAVE MURDER   P 638, $2.84
"Combines the merit of both the English and American schools in the
new mystery. It's as breezy as the best of the American ones, and has
the sophistication and wit of any top-notch Britisher."

—*New York Herald Tribune Book Review*

E. C. Bentley

TRENT'S LAST CASE   P 440, $2.50
"One of the three best detective stories ever written."

—Agatha Christie

TRENT'S OWN CASE   P 516, $2.25
"I won't waste time saying that the plot is sound and the detection
satisfying. Trent has not altered a scrap and reappears with all his old
humor and charm."   —Dorothy L. Sayers

Gavin Black

A DRAGON FOR CHRISTMAS   P 473, $1.95
"Potent excitement!"   —*New York Herald Tribune*

THE EYES AROUND ME   P 485, $1.95
"I stayed up until all hours last night reading *The Eyes Around Me,*
which is something I do not do very often, but I was so intrigued by the
ingeniousness of Mr. Black's plotting and the witty way in which he spins
his mystery. I can only say that I enjoyed the book enormously."

—F. van Wyck Mason

YOU WANT TO DIE, JOHNNY?   P 472, $1.95
"Gavin Black doesn't just develop a pressure plot in suspense, he adds
uninfected wit, character, charm, and sharp knowledge of the Far East
to make rereading as keen as the first race-through."   —*Book Week*

Nicholas Blake

THE CORPSE IN THE SNOWMAN   P 427, $1.95
"If there is a distinction between the novel and the detective story (which
we do not admit), then this book deserves a high place in both catego-
ries."   *—The New York Times*

THE DREADFUL HOLLOW   P 493, $1.95
"Pace unhurried, characters excellent, reasoning solid."
          —San Francisco Chronicle

END OF CHAPTER   P 397, $1.95
". . . admirably solid . . . an adroit formal detective puzzle backed up
by firm characterization and a knowing picture of London publishing."
          —The New York Times

HEAD OF A TRAVELER   P 398, $2.25
"Another grade A detective story of the right old jigsaw persuasion."
          —New York Herald Tribune Book Review

MINUTE FOR MURDER   P 419, $1.95
"An outstanding mystery novel. Mr. Blake's writing is a delight in
itself."   *—The New York Times*

THE MORNING AFTER DEATH   P 520, $1.95
"One of Blake's best."   —Rex Warner

A PENKNIFE IN MY HEART   P 521, $2.25
"Style brilliant . . . and suspenseful."   *—San Francisco Chronicle*

THE PRIVATE WOUND   P 531, $2.25
[Blake's] best novel in a dozen years . . . . An intensely penetrating study
of sexual passion. . . . A powerful story of murder and its aftermath."
          —Anthony Boucher, *The New York Times*

A QUESTION OF PROOF   P 494, $1.95
"The characters in this story are unusually well drawn, and the suspense
is well sustained."   *—The New York Times*

THE SAD VARIETY   P 495, $2.25
"It is a stunner. I read it instead of eating, instead of sleeping."
          —Dorothy Salisbury Davis

THERE'S TROUBLE BREWING   P 569, $3.37
"Nigel Strangeways is a puzzling mixture of simplicity and penetration,
but all the more real for that."   *—The Times Literary Supplement*

Nicholas Blake (cont'd)

THOU SHELL OF DEATH   P 428, $1.95
"It has all the virtues of culture, intelligence and sensibility that the most exacting connoisseur could ask of detective fiction."
> —*The Times* [London] *Literary Supplement*

THE WIDOW'S CRUISE   P 399, $2.25
"A stirring suspense. . . . The thrilling tale leaves nothing to be desired."
> —*Springfield Republican*

THE WORM OF DEATH   P 400, $2.25
"It [The Worm of Death] is one of Blake's very best—and his best is better than almost anyone's."   —Louis Untermeyer

John & Emery Bonett

A BANNER FOR PEGASUS   P 554, $2.40
"A gem! Beautifully plotted and set. . . . Not only is the murder adroit and deserved, and the detection competent, but the love story is charming."   —Jacques Barzun and Wendell Hertig Taylor

DEAD LION   P 563, $2.40
"A clever plot, authentic background and interesting characters highly recommended this one."   —*New Republic*

Christianna Brand

GREEN FOR DANGER   P 551, $2.50
"You have to reach for the greatest of Great Names (Christie, Carr, Queen . . .) to find Brand's rivals in the devious subtleties of the trade."
> —Anthony Boucher

TOUR DE FORCE   P 572, $2.40
"Complete with traps for the over-ingenious, a double-reverse surprise ending and a key clue planted so fairly and obviously that you completely overlook it. If that's your idea of perfect entertainment, then seize at once upon *Tour de Force.*"   —Anthony Boucher, *The New York Times*

James Byrom

OR BE HE DEAD   P 585, $2.84
"A very original tale . . . Well written and steadily entertaining."
> —Jacques Barzun & Wendell Hertig Taylor, *A Catalogue of Crime*

Henry Calvin

IT'S DIFFERENT ABROAD   P 640, $2.84

"What is remarkable and delightful, Mr. Calvin imparts a flavor of satire to what he renovates and compels us to take straight."

—Jacques Barzun

Marjorie Carleton

VANISHED   P 559, $2.40

"Exceptional . . . a minor triumph."
—Jacques Barzun and Wendell Hertig Taylor, *A Catalogue of Crime*

George Harmon Coxe

MURDER WITH PICTURES   P 527, $2.25

"[Coxe] has hit the bull's-eye with his first shot."

—The New York Times

Edmund Crispin

BURIED FOR PLEASURE   P 506, $2.50

"Absolute and unalloyed delight."

—Anthony Boucher, *The New York Times*

Lionel Davidson

THE MENORAH MEN   P 592, $2.84

"Of his fellow thriller writers, only John Le Carré shows the same instinct for the viscera."   —*Chicago Tribune*

NIGHT OF WENCESLAS   P 595, $2.84

"A most ingenious thriller, so enriched with style, wit, and a sense of serious comedy that it all but transcends its kind."

—*The New Yorker*

THE ROSE OF TIBET   P 593, $2.84

"I hadn't realized how much I missed the genuine Adventure story . . . until I read *The Rose of Tibet*."   —Graham Greene

D. M. Devine

MY BROTHER'S KILLER   P 558, $2.40

"A most enjoyable crime story which I enjoyed reading down to the last moment."   —Agatha Christie

Kenneth Fearing

THE BIG CLOCK   P 500, $1.95
"It will be some time before chill-hungry clients meet again so rare a compound of irony, satire, and icy-fingered narrative. *The Big Clock* is . . . a psychothriller you won't put down."   —*Weekly Book Review*

Andrew Garve

THE ASHES OF LODA   P 430, $1.50
"Garve . . . embellishes a fine fast adventure story with a more credible picture of the U.S.S.R. than is offered in most thrillers."
                                        —*The New York Times Book Review*

THE CUCKOO LINE AFFAIR   P 451, $1.95
". . . an agreeable and ingenious piece of work."   —*The New Yorker*

A HERO FOR LEANDA   P 429, $1.50
"One can trust Mr. Garve to put a fresh twist to any situation, and the ending is really a lovely surprise."   —*The Manchester Guardian*

MURDER THROUGH THE LOOKING GLASS   P 449, $1.95
". . . refreshingly out-of-the-way and enjoyable . . . highly recommended to all comers."   —*Saturday Review*

NO TEARS FOR HILDA   P 441, $1.95
"It starts fine and finishes finer. I got behind on breathing watching Max get not only his man but his woman, too."   —Rex Stout

THE RIDDLE OF SAMSON   P 450, $1.95
"The story is an excellent one, the people are quite likable, and the writing is superior."   —*Springfield Republican*

Michael Gilbert

BLOOD AND JUDGMENT   P 446, $1.95
"Gilbert readers need scarcely be told that the characters all come alive at first sight, and that his surpassing talent for narration enhances any plot. . . . Don't miss."   —*San Francisco Chronicle*

THE BODY OF A GIRL   P 459, $1.95
"Does what a good mystery should do: open up into all kinds of ramifications, with untold menace behind the action. At the end, there is a bang-up climax, and it is a pleasure to see how skilfully Gilbert wraps everything up."   —*The New York Times Book Review*

Michael Gilbert (cont'd)

THE DANGER WITHIN   P 448, $1.95

"Michael Gilbert has nicely combined some elements of the straight detective story with plenty of action, suspense, and adventure, to produce a superior thriller."   —*Saturday Review*

FEAR TO TREAD   P 458, $1.95

"Merits serious consideration as a work of art."
                                        —*The New York Times*

Joe Gores

HAMMETT   P 631, $2.84

"Joe Gores at his very best. Terse, powerful writing—with the master, Dashiell Hammett, as the protagonist in a novel I think he would have been proud to call his own."   —Robert Ludlum

C. W. Grafton

BEYOND A REASONABLE DOUBT   P 519, $1.95

"A very ingenious tale of murder . . . a brilliant and gripping narrative."
                     —Jacques Barzun and Wendell Hertig Taylor

THE RAT BEGAN TO GNAW THE ROPE   P 639, $2.84

"Fast, humorous story with flashes of brilliance."
                                        —*The New Yorker*

Edward Grierson

THE SECOND MAN   P 528, $2.25

"One of the best trial-testimony books to have come along in quite a while."   —*The New Yorker*

Bruce Hamilton

TOO MUCH OF WATER   P 635, $2.84

"A superb sea mystery. . . . The prose is excellent."
—Jacques Barzun and Wendell Hertig Taylor, *A Catalogue of Crime*

Cyril Hare

DEATH IS NO SPORTSMAN   P 555, $2.40

"You will be thrilled because it succeeds in placing an ingenious story in a new and refreshing setting. . . . The identity of the murderer is really a surprise."   —*Daily Mirror*

Cyril Hare (cont'd)

DEATH WALKS THE WOODS   P 556, $2.40

"Here is a fine formal detective story, with a technically brilliant solution demanding the attention of all connoisseurs of construction."

                    —Anthony Boucher, *The New York Times Book Review*

AN ENGLISH MURDER   P 455, $2.50

"By a long shot, the best crime story I have read for a long time. Everything is traditional, but originality does not suffer. The setting is perfect. Full marks to Mr. Hare."   —*Irish Press*

SUICIDE EXCEPTED   P 636, $2.84

"Adroit in its manipulation . . . and distinguished by a plot-twister which I'll wager Christie wishes she'd thought of."

                    —*The New York Times*

TENANT FOR DEATH   P 570, $2.84

"The way in which an air of probability is combined both with clear, terse narrative and with a good deal of subtle suburban atmosphere, proves the extreme skill of the writer."   —*The Spectator*

TRAGEDY AT LAW   P 522, $2.25

"An extremely urbane and well-written detective story."

                    —*The New York Times*

UNTIMELY DEATH   P 514, $2.25

"The English detective story at its quiet best, meticulously underplayed, rich in perceivings of the droll human animal and ready at the last with a neat surprise which has been there all the while had we but wits to see it."   —*New York Herald Tribune Book Review*

THE WIND BLOWS DEATH   P 589, $2.84

"A plot compounded of musical knowledge, a Dickens allusion, and a subtle point in law is related with delightfully unobtrusive wit, warmth, and style."   —*The New York Times*

WITH A BARE BODKIN   P 523, $2.25

"One of the best detective stories published for a long time."

                    —*The Spectator*

Robert Harling

THE ENORMOUS SHADOW   P 545, $2.50

"In some ways the best spy story of the modern period. . . . The writing is terse and vivid . . . the ending full of action . . . altogether first-rate."

    —Jacques Barzun and Wendell Hertig Taylor, *A Catalogue of Crime*

Matthew Head

THE CABINDA AFFAIR   P 541, $2.25
"An absorbing whodunit and a distinguished novel of atmosphere."
                                    —Anthony Boucher, *The New York Times*

THE CONGO VENUS   P 597, $2.84
"Terrific. The dialogue is just plain wonderful."
                                                      —*The Boston Globe*

MURDER AT THE FLEA CLUB   P 542, $2.50
"The true delight is in Head's style, its limpid ease combined with humor
and an awesome precision of phrase."   —*San Francisco Chronicle*

M. V. Heberden

ENGAGED TO MURDER   P 533, $2.25
"Smooth plotting."   —*The New York Times*

James Hilton

WAS IT MURDER?   P 501, $1.95
"The story is well planned and well written."
                                                —*The New York Times*

P. M. Hubbard

HIGH TIDE   P 571, $2.40
"A smooth elaboration of mounting horror and danger."
                                                      —*Library Journal*

Elspeth Huxley

THE AFRICAN POISON MURDERS   P 540, $2.25
"Obscure venom, manical mutilations, deadly bush fire, thrilling climax
compose major opus.... Top-flight."
                                    —*Saturday Review of Literature*

MURDER ON SAFARI   P 587, $2.84
"Right now we'd call Mrs. Huxley a dangerous rival to Agatha Christie."   —*Books*

Francis Iles

BEFORE THE FACT P 517, $2.50

"Not many 'serious' novelists have produced character studies to compare with Iles's internally terrifying portrait of the murderer in *Before the Fact,* his masterpiece and a work truly deserving the appellation of unique and beyond price." —Howard Haycraft

MALICE AFORETHOUGHT P 532, $1.95

"It is a long time since I have read anything so good as *Malice Aforethought,* with its cynical humour, acute criminology, plausible detail and rapid movement. It makes you hug yourself with pleasure."

—H. C. Harwood, *Saturday Review*

Michael Innes

THE CASE OF THE JOURNEYING BOY P 632, $3.12

"I could see no faults in it. There is no one to compare with him."

—*Illustrated London News*

DEATH BY WATER P 574, $2.40

"The amount of ironic social criticism and deft characterization of scenes and people would serve another author for six books."

—Jacques Barzun and Wendell Hertig Taylor

HARE SITTING UP P 590, $2.84

"There is hardly anyone (in mysteries or mainstream) more exquisitely literate, allusive and Jamesian—and hardly anyone with a firmer sense of melodramatic plot or a more vigorous gift of storytelling."

—Anthony Boucher, *The New York Times*

THE LONG FAREWELL P 575, $2.40

"A model of the deft, classic detective story, told in the most wittily diverting prose." —*The New York Times*

THE MAN FROM THE SEA P 591, $2.84

"The pace is brisk, the adventures exciting and excitingly told, and above all he keeps to the very end the interesting ambiguity of the man from the sea." —*New Statesman*

THE SECRET VANGUARD P 584, $2.84

"Innes . . . has mastered the art of swift, exciting and well-organized narrative." —*The New York Times*

THE WEIGHT OF THE EVIDENCE P 633, $2.84

"First-class puzzle, deftly solved. University background interesting and amusing." —*Saturday Review of Literature*

Mary Kelly

THE SPOILT KILL   P 565, $2.40
"Mary Kelly is a new Dorothy Sayers. . . . [An] exciting new novel."
—*Evening News*

Lange Lewis

THE BIRTHDAY MURDER   P 518, $1.95
"Almost perfect in its playlike purity and delightful prose."
—Jacques Barzun and Wendell Hertig Taylor

Allan MacKinnon

HOUSE OF DARKNESS   P 582, $2.84
"His best . . . a perfect compendium."
—Jacques Barzun & Wendell Hertig Taylor, *A Catalogue of Crime*

Arthur Maling

LUCKY DEVIL   P 482, $1.95
"The plot unravels at a fast clip, the writing is breezy and Maling's approach is as fresh as today's stockmarket quotes."
—*Louisville Courier Journal*

RIPOFF   P 483, $1.95
"A swiftly paced story of today's big business is larded with intrigue as a Ralph Nader-type investigates an insurance scandal and is soon on the run from a hired gun and his brother. . . . Engrossing and credible."
—*Booklist*

SCHROEDER'S GAME   P 484, $1.95
"As the title indicates, this Schroeder is up to something, and the unravelling of his game is a diverting and sufficiently blood-soaked entertainment."
—*The New Yorker*

Austin Ripley

MINUTE MYSTERIES   P 387, $2.50
More than one hundred of the world's shortest detective stories. Only one possible solution to each case!

Thomas Sterling

THE EVIL OF THE DAY   P 529, $2.50
"Prose as witty and subtle as it is sharp and clear...characters unconventionally conceived and richly bodied forth . . . . In short, a novel to be treasured."   —Anthony Boucher, *The New York Times*

Julian Symons

THE BELTING INHERITANCE P 468, $1.95
"A superb whodunit in the best tradition of the detective story."
—August Derleth, *Madison Capital Times*

BLAND BEGINNING P 469, $1.95
"Mr. Symons displays a deft storytelling skill, a quiet and literate wit, a nice feeling for character, and detectival ingenuity of a high order."
—Anthony Boucher, *The New York Times*

BOGUE'S FORTUNE P 481, $1.95
"There's a touch of the old sardonic humour, and more than a touch of style." —*The Spectator*

THE BROKEN PENNY P 480, $1.95
"The most exciting, astonishing and believable spy story to appear in years. —Anthony Boucher, *The New York Times Book Review*

THE COLOR OF MURDER P 461, $1.95
"A singularly unostentatious and memorably brilliant detective story."
—*New York Herald Tribune Book Review*

Dorothy Stockbridge Tillet
(John Stephen Strange)

THE MAN WHO KILLED FORTESCUE P 536, $2.25
"Better than average." —*Saturday Review of Literature*

Simon Troy

THE ROAD TO RHUINE P 583, $2.84
"Unusual and agreeably told." —*San Francisco Chronicle*

SWIFT TO ITS CLOSE P 546, $2.40
"A nicely literate British mystery . . . the atmosphere and the plot are exceptionally well wrought, the dialogue excellent." —*Best Sellers*

Henry Wade

THE DUKE OF YORK'S STEPS P 588, $2.84
"A classic of the golden age."
—Jacques Barzun & Wendell Hertig Taylor, *A Catalogue of Crime*

A DYING FALL P 543, $2.50
"One of those expert British suspense jobs . . . it crackles with undercurrents of blackmail, violent passion and murder. Topnotch in its class."
—*Time*

Henry Wade (cont'd)

THE HANGING CAPTAIN   P 548, $2.50
"This is a detective story for connoisseurs, for those who value clear thinking and good writing above mere ingenuity and easy thrills."
—Times Literary Supplement

Hillary Waugh

LAST SEEN WEARING . . .   P 552, $2.40
"A brilliant tour de force."   —Julian Symons

THE MISSING MAN   P 553, $2.40
"The quiet detailed police work of Chief Fred C. Fellows, Stockford, Conn., is at its best in *The Missing Man* . . . one of the Chief's toughest cases and one of the best handled."
—Anthony Boucher, *The New York Times Book Review*

Henry Kitchell Webster

WHO IS THE NEXT?   P 539, $2.25
"A double murder, private-plane piloting, a neat impersonation, and a delicate courtship are adroitly combined by a writer who knows how to use the language."   —Jacques Barzun and Wendell Hertig Taylor

Anna Mary Wells

MURDERER'S CHOICE   P 534, $2.50
"Good writing, ample action, and excellent character work."
—Saturday Review of Literature

A TALENT FOR MURDER   P 535, $2.25
"The discovery of the villain is a decided shock."   *—Books*

Edward Young

THE FIFTH PASSENGER   P 544, $2.25
"Clever and adroit . . . excellent thriller . . ."   *—Library Journal*

**If you enjoyed this book you'll want to know about
THE PERENNIAL LIBRARY MYSTERY SERIES**
Buy them at your local bookstore or use this coupon for ordering:

Qty	P number	Price
_____	_____	_____
_____	_____	_____
_____	_____	_____
_____	_____	_____
_____	_____	_____
_____	_____	_____
_____	_____	_____
_____	_____	_____
_____	_____	_____
_____	_____	_____
_____	_____	_____
_____	_____	_____
_____	_____	_____
_____	_____	_____
_____	_____	_____

	postage and handling charge	$1.00
	_____ book(s) @ $0.25	_____
	TOTAL	[ ]

Prices contained in this coupon are Harper & Row invoice prices only.
They are subject to change without notice, and in no way reflect the prices at
which these books may be sold by other suppliers.

**HARPER & ROW, Mail Order Dept. #PMS, 10 East 53rd St., New
York, N.Y. 10022.**
Please send me the books I have checked above. I am enclosing $_____
which includes a postage and handling charge of $1.00 for the first book and
25¢ for each additional book. Send check or money order. No cash or
C.O.D.s please

Name_____

Address_____

City_____ State_____ Zip_____
Please allow 4 weeks for delivery. USA only. This offer expires 6/30/85.
Please add applicable sales tax.